CHAPTER ONE

'Julie, come here quickly! I think we've won the lottery!' Malcolm's voice cracked with disbelief, rising in pitch and volume until he sounded as if he were choking. His hands trembled, gripping the ticket like a lifeline.

Julie sighed, shaking her head as she diced carrots at the kitchen counter. 'Come on, love, you say that every week. It's not funny anymore.'

'No, I swear! We've got all five numbers and the two lucky stars! Look!' Malcolm dashed into the kitchen, his face flushed, eyes wide with a mixture of shock and giddy hysteria. He shoved the ticket toward Julie, nearly dropping it in his excitement.

'For heaven's sake, Malcolm–' she started, but his expression stopped her cold. This wasn't one of his pranks. A strange flutter stirred in her stomach as she hurriedly dried her hands and followed him into the lounge.

Malcolm Grainger was half laughing and half crying, his face flushed from excitement as he stared in disbelief at the numbers on the television. Julie snatched the crumpled ticket, her head snapping around to the screen to memorise the numbers before they disappeared. Fumbling with uncooperative reading glasses, she finally caught the winning sequence.

'Seventeen, twenty-one, thirty... Oh, Mal, you're right, we've won the lottery!' With trembling hands, Julie's arms snaked around her husband's ample waist, and he squeezed her until she could hardly breathe. Releasing her, Malcolm flopped onto the sofa and stared in disbelief at his wife. For a moment, neither of them spoke. The world had frozen; the only sound was the rapid thumping of her heartbeat in her ears. Then Malcolm let out a strangled laugh, half joy, half disbelief, and pulled her into a crushing hug.

'We need to call the kids!' Julie squealed, bouncing on her heels.

'No, not yet.' Malcolm pulled back, gulping in air as if he'd just run a marathon. 'We don't even know how much we've won. It is a rollover, isn't it?'

Julie nodded furiously. 'Yes! But maybe we'll have to share?'

'We need to check the official site.' Malcolm lunged for the laptop, yanking it open. The screen flickered to life agonisingly slow. 'Come on, you useless thing!'

Julie grabbed his wrist. 'Move over, you're all fingers and thumbs!' She seized control, navigating to the website with the precision of a woman on a mission.

The jackpot amount flashed in bold, bright red across the screen. £22 million. The world tilted. Malcolm whooped, his feet drumming against the sofa cushions as he jumped up and down like a schoolboy. 'Twenty-two million! And we're the only winners! Julie, we're rich!'

Julie grabbed his face, squeezing his cheeks. 'Malcolm Grainger, we are multi-millionaires!' She returned her gaze to the screen. 'There's the number for the lottery people. Get a pen and write it down!'

Malcolm did so, and the couple gazed at each other, huge grins splitting their faces.

'You ring them, I can't stop shaking.' Julie giggled.

'I need a drink first!' He took a can of beer from the fridge and offered one to Julie, who shook her head.

'Champagne would be more appropriate; pity we don't have any.'

Malcolm tapped in the number while Julie perched on the edge of the sofa, holding her breath and listening to one side of the conversation. A series of stuttering noises was impossible to interpret, but Malcolm was nodding and smiling, which must be positive. He eventually recited their address and telephone number before mumbling a few grunts of thanks and replacing the phone.

'Incredible! We're the only winners, Julie. Twenty-two million pounds and only one winning ticket!' Malcolm's breathing was erratic, and his previously ruddy face suddenly paled.

Julie pulled him onto the sofa. 'Sit down, love, before you fall. So, what happens next?'

'Someone will ring tomorrow and arrange to come here and meet us, probably on Monday. They said something about verifying the ticket, advisers and publicity... I couldn't take it all in, but they'll explain everything tomorrow.'

The hiss of the kettle from the kitchen prompted Julie to her feet and she moved automatically to make a pot of tea, the proper thing to do in all circumstances. Malcolm was sitting in the same spot when she returned with two steaming mugs, his face expressionless. Their little dog, Trixie, was curled on his knee, totally unimpressed by the momentous occasion as Mal mechanically stroked her head.

'I'm going to ring the kids now!' Julie announced, unable to contain the delight bubbling up inside her body any longer and desperately wanting to share their good news.

'No, let's leave it till tomorrow when we know more.'

'What more do we need to know? We've won the lottery, Mal! All our worries are over – and for the kids, too! We can pay off their mortgages and have a family holiday at Disney World like we've always dreamed of. I'm going to ring them now.'

Malcolm shrugged. In need of fresh air to clear his head, he took the dog into the garden while Julie scrolled for her daughter's telephone number.

'Pull the other one, Mum.' Kate Burton groaned at her mother's voice, 'Another tenner, is it?'

'No, it's twenty-two million pounds, actually!' Julie grinned, knowing Kate would assume it was a joke, just as she had with Malcolm.

'Are you serious? If not, and this is a wind-up, I don't think it's particularly funny.'

'I'm serious, girl! Someone's ringing from the lottery tomorrow, but they've confirmed there's only one winning ticket, and we've got it!'

'Wow… really? Mum, you're not winding me up, are you?' Kate eventually accepted that her mother was speaking the truth, incredible though it seemed. They chatted excitedly for only a few more minutes as Julie wanted to ring their son, Danny, which she did as soon as the phone disconnected. Danny expressed similar disbelief, taking even more persuading than his sister that this wasn't a joke. Then his booming laugh echoed down the phone, 'That's brilliant, Mum, congratulations!' Both children promised to visit first thing the next day. If it hadn't been so late and their own families were not in bed, they would have dashed around immediately, but celebrations would have to be postponed until morning.

Julie, flushed with excitement, went to find Malcolm, who

had come in from the garden and gone upstairs. She found him getting ready for bed like a typical Saturday night.

'What are you doing?' She spun her husband around, wanting to dance and sing. 'We can't go to bed now; there's too much to discuss and plan. It's not every day you win millions on the lottery.'

Malcolm extricated himself from Julie's grasp and saved himself from tripping over as he struggled into his pyjama pants. 'I know, love, but I think we're getting a bit carried away with it all. What do you want to do? Go shopping already?'

'I would if the shops were open! Come on, we should be celebrating. This is the best thing that's ever happened to us, and I know I won't be able to sleep tonight.'

Reluctantly, Malcolm followed his wife downstairs. 'I just think we should rein it in a bit, not get too excited.'

Julie would happily climb up on the rooftop and announce their good fortune to the whole world, but now the initial excitement had worn off, warning bells were sounding in his head. Perhaps the win would bring more than simply good things into their lives. After Malcolm's initial euphoria and as reality dawned, he knew that broadcasting this news could potentially bring untold damage to their family. Julie turned to her husband, 'Oh, Mal. This is the best thing that's ever happened to us. Nothing bad is going to come of it.'

But Malcolm remained frozen in place. His gut twisted with unease, a shadow creeping at the edges of his euphoria. Twenty-two million pounds. Enough to change their lives forever. For better... or for worse.

CHAPTER TWO

Julie awoke to the tune of *Joy to the World* as the doorbell chimed its anthem repeatedly until she staggered downstairs to open the door, Trixie barking at her heels. She'd slept surprisingly well, which could have been due to the bottle of wine she'd polished off before eventually turning in, and woken only a few times, aware of her husband's restless night and the number of times he'd left their bed to make a milky drink or to stare into the inky blackness of the night from the bedroom window, his stillness masking an inner turmoil.

Danny took his finger off the doorbell and hurried in, accompanied by a gust of wind. 'Appropriate tune, Mum!' Grinning, he gave his mother a bear hug and lifted her tiny frame right off the ground to swing her around. 'Happy lottery win! It's like Christmas and birthdays have all come together!'

Once he'd put her down, she giggled and straightened her clothes. The reality of the lottery win flooded her sleepy mind once again, and she squealed with delight, brown eyes suddenly wide with excitement.

Danny said, 'Angie's taken the kids to swimming lessons; she'll be round later.' Danny's children, Tom, ten and Becky, eight, had been told of the win. 'Becky's already asking if we can buy a house with a swimming pool!'

Malcolm appeared beside them, bemused by their pleasure, and the three moved automatically into the kitchen. Julie put the kettle on, flopped down at the table, propped an aching head in her hands and grinned at her son. 'Well, what do you think?'

'Amazing, fantastic... what can I say? Tell me again how much you've won. I don't know if I dreamt it.'

'Twenty-two magnificent million pounds and we're the only winners! It hasn't quite sunk in yet!'

'Get away!' Malcolm corrected laughingly. 'You had most of it spent in your head last night. I think you could sort out the country's economy single-handed now. Better buy some shares in M&S, son; their profits are about to take a huge upturn.'

The win couldn't have come at a better time, particularly for Danny, who'd been made redundant from work a month previously and continually worried about the bills he could no longer pay.

'You won't have to downsize now, Dan, and young Tom can still attend that private school you'd set your heart on.'

'Thanks, Dad. It's good of you to say, but we don't have any expectations, you know. This is your win.' Danny spoke from the heart. A windfall would be more than welcome, but he wouldn't assume any entitlement to his parents' winnings.

'You know we'll see you right,' Mal assured him, quietly delighted at his son's attitude. 'There'll be as much pleasure in watching you enjoy the money as in spending it ourselves. Besides, we wouldn't know what to do with such a huge amount.'

Julie rose to make the tea, affectionately squeezing her husband's shoulder in passing. Malcolm was saying all the right things, yet something didn't quite add up – his smile didn't sit right on his face. Perhaps he was still in shock, which would certainly account for it. She could hardly believe it herself, and after all, how should people behave when they'd suddenly become millionaires? When it was all confirmed by the lottery people, it would sink in, and then they could celebrate.

'Now, where's Kate?' Malcolm said. 'It's after eight o'clock. I thought she'd be battering the door down at daybreak.'

Julie filled the teapot. 'She won't want to wake Daisy if she's still sleeping. They've had a few rough nights with teething lately.'

As if Kate had heard her name, the doorbell rang again, and Danny jumped up to let his sister in.

Kate and her husband Geoff entered, and more hugs and squeals ensued. Baby Daisy grinned happily, enjoying the festive mood of the adults while oblivious to what had triggered it. Tea was poured, and the delighted family talked simultaneously.

'We should be having champagne!'

'We'll book a table at The Grange tonight, early enough for the children to come.'

'What time are you expecting the lottery people to ring?'

'Have you told Auntie Susan yet, Mum?'

'We could eat out every night now if we wanted to!'

'Are you going to see your dad and let him know, Mal?'

The noise rose to a crescendo until Malcolm raised his palms, took a deep breath, let it out slowly, then cautioned, 'Let's slow down a bit here, shall we? We haven't got the money yet, so there's no need to broadcast it to all and sundry, right?' He became the voice of reason, silently nursing his fears and hoping to steer his family in a different direction from the one they were blindly heading.

'Don't be a killjoy, Mal. This is the best thing that's ever happened to us. I want to shout it to the world and his wife!' Julie was giddy, on a high with delight.

Kate looked thoughtfully from one parent to the other. 'Perhaps Dad's got a point, Mum. They give you the "no-publicity" option for a reason. Some folk try to take advantage of situations like this. There are con artists who write begging letters and other awful stuff. We should consider such folk, surely?'

'Stuff and nonsense!' Julie replied. 'We know who our real friends are; the rest can go and jump for all I care.'

Malcolm's brow furrowed as he busied himself with the cornflakes. An agreement on this matter was not going to be reached easily.

'Have you thought about what you'll spend it on? Do you think you'll move?' Danny's excitement bubbled over again.

'We haven't had time to think of anything yet, have we, love?'

'No, it's too soon.' Mal's unenthusiastic response didn't go unnoticed by Julie, who was growing increasingly concerned at his lack of enthusiasm.

'Why don't you go to the home and chat with your dad? He'll be thrilled for us, I'm sure.'

'Yes, I thought I'd go later today after we've heard from the lottery people.' His smile provided Julie with only a little reassurance that everything was okay.

CHAPTER THREE

The clouds moved quickly, scudding across the sky, each becoming more ominously grey as they passed overhead. A storm was likely, Malcolm thought, as he tapped in the security number and pushed open the heavy glass doors to Willow Dene Nursing Home.

The wind at his back swirled crisp brown leaves around his feet to land on the doormat as the stuffy heat hit him immediately, in contrast to the cold autumnal gusts outside. The smell of boiled vegetables lingered in the corridor, remnants from the usual Sunday roast lunch. It wasn't a bad place for his father to be; the nursing staff, although always busy, were cheerful and efficient, and Bill Grainger seemed as content as possible in such circumstances. Sunday afternoon was when his son visited alone, and the two spent a couple of hours in each other's company, Malcolm taking the *Telegraph* crossword puzzle for them to tackle together.

It was remarkable how Bill's mind remained alert, considering the little stimulation his present life afforded. A stroke four years previously had robbed him of his active retirement, denying him the simple pleasures of life, such as tending his allotment and visiting family at times to suit himself. Trapped in a body that stubbornly refused to regain its former physical strength, life was lived entirely within his mind and the confines of a twelve-foot square room.

Since his stroke, Bill possessed no mobility in his lower body and could use only a limited number of muscles in his right hand and arm. His face had only half its previous movement, permitting nothing more than lopsided smiles and winks rather than blinks. Malcolm could never decide if it would have been preferable for his father's life to have ended on the day of his stroke, allowing him to be reunited with his beloved wife, who had been dead since Malcolm was eight years old, or if the old man enjoyed this limited existence. Communication was usually restricted to single words, which, with great effort, Bill attempted to verbalise or tap out on the electronic notepad by the bedside, an equally tiring task. A discussion on the topic of quality of life would never happen.

'Hi, Dad!' Malcolm fixed on his usual smile, and the old man responded with his best effort to mirror the expression. Pulling up the chair, Malcolm removed his copy of the *Telegraph* from his jacket pocket and launched straight into the first clue. The silence of their thoughts was broken only for the usual messages from the family to be offered.

'Julie sends her love and will be in on Wednesday evening as usual. We saw the children this morning; they're both well and send their love. Danny will probably pop in later in the week.' Malcolm was sticking to the usual script, procrastinating to avoid what he needed to say.

Bill smiled and, raising his arm, tapped *Mongoose* on the keyboard.

'What? Oh yes, one across, a small flesh-eating mammal, eight letters, Mongoose, very good.' Malcolm filled in the first answer to their puzzle, wondering how to tell his father what was weighing so heavily on his mind. He took a deep breath. 'We've had a bit of a win on the lottery, Dad.' Should he give the watered-down version or be honest?

Bill's right eyebrow arched in a gesture of surprise.

'Well, it's more than a bit of a win; it's twenty-two million. I don't think it's sunk in yet.' Is this how a lottery winner should act, as if it had been no more than a tenner? Malcolm continued, choosing his words carefully.

'The thing is, Julie and the kids are bursting with excitement, ready to share our big news with everyone they know. They want to shout it from the rooftops, eager to tell the world about this new chapter in our lives. But I find myself hesitating. Sure, this news brings the promise of financial security – a huge relief for us all – but I can't shake off the feeling that we should keep things under wraps for a while. There's something about going public which makes me uneasy.' He paused and looked at his father, whose expression was difficult to read. 'It's not only about the joy of the moment; it's about weighing the potential consequences and opting for no publicity, you know? But I think Julie likes the idea of her picture in the papers and everyone envying her.'

Bill slowly nodded. His eyes misted as the gravity of his son's situation settled in. With great effort, he shifted his right arm, heavy and uncooperative after lying still for so long. He reached toward the small table beside the bed, where his keyboard rested. His fingers brushed against its surface, searching for the keys. Finally, he found them and tapped softly, forming a single word, *Remember*.

'Yes, Dad.' Malcolm nodded slowly. 'I remember.' Events from the past, episodes that Malcolm had buried deep in his mind, were coming to the fore. The air was heavy with unspoken, perhaps even unwanted, memories, a bridge connecting their past and present.

CHAPTER FOUR

Julie's head was still in the clouds on Sunday after the children left, and Mal went off to visit his dad. Although she'd had nothing more to drink than tea, she felt giddy, laughing aloud when she thought about their win and even dancing around the kitchen while washing the dishes. If only her parents had been around to share it.

As Julie reflected on her parents, both long gone, a pang of regret pierced her joy. Since their lottery win, she had worn a near-permanent smile, so much so that her jaws ached, but now, thinking of her mother and father, that smile faded. If only they had lived to see this day, to share in this windfall. There was so much she could have done for them.

Julie and her sister, Susan, had been blessed with a close-knit family that found joy in simple pleasures. As children, they had never realised they were poor. Their father worked tirelessly as a railway labourer, while their mother juggled multiple part-time cleaning jobs to make ends meet. Yet despite the financial struggles, their home had been filled with love, laughter, and contentment.

The sisters shared a small but cosy room in their modest

two-up, two-down terraced house furnished with well-worn hand-me-downs. Their few toys were cherished and looked after. To them, this was home – a warm, loving place where life felt good. They never went hungry, always had nourishing meals, and their mother constantly reminded them to be grateful for what they had.

Even the hardships had been woven into their happy memories. Their outdoor toilet, which froze in winter, became an adventure when they wrapped up in layers to brave the cold. And when their father installed a bath under the cramped staircase, they felt like royalty. They were the only kids at school with running water in an actual bathtub, while most of their classmates still used a tin bath in front of the fire on Friday nights.

Material wealth had never mattered to Julie and Susan. They had each other, their family, and a childhood free from worry. And now, with the lottery win, Julie couldn't wait to share her good fortune with her sister. If she couldn't spoil their parents, she would ensure Susan's life was filled with the comfort and happiness she deserved.

Susan had endured more than her share of heartache. Widowed after her husband's tragic work accident, she had been left to grieve while carrying their unborn child. The days following his death had been some of the darkest of her life, overwhelmed by sorrow, uncertainty, and the weight of raising a baby alone.

Julie and Malcolm had done everything they could to support her, offering companionship, comfort, and a shoulder to lean on. Susan, despite her grief, had persevered, raising her son with quiet strength. She lived on a widow's pension, taking work wherever she could, doing her best to provide. Julie had always wished she could do more, but with two children of their own and only one income, love and support had been all they could offer.

Now, at last, she could change that. With this lottery win, things were different. As Julie walked the short distance to her sister's home, she was excited, eager to share the wonderful news, knowing Susan would be delighted for them, and determined to do something special for her sister.

'Is the kettle on?' Julie asked as she opened the front door and stepped into the tiny lounge of a house almost identical to the one where they had grown up.

'Hello, I wasn't expecting you today.' Susan's round face reflected pleasure at having an unexpected visitor.

'Ah, I have news, good news. Let's go to the kitchen and make a cuppa, and I'll tell you all about it. I wasn't disturbing anything, was I?'

'Nothing special. I'm trying to finish knitting this little hooded coat for Luke's birthday. I want to send a parcel off tomorrow.'

'Aw, it's lovely. How's he doing?'

'Oh, he's a poppet! Stephen Facetimed me yesterday, and Luke sat on his knee, grinning away into the screen. He's got two little teeth coming through, and I think he recognises me now, but maybe it's wishful thinking, and I'm kidding myself.'

'No. If he sees you regularly enough, he'll get to know you, even online. The first birthday is always so special. I bet you'd love to be with them?'

'Yes, but that's a dream I'll have to save up for. Or maybe they'll come home for a visit next year.'

Susan's son, Stephen, worked in Calgary, Canada, sent by the company he worked for three years ago. Although initially reluctant to leave his mother, the opportunity was a once-in-a-lifetime chance he couldn't refuse without affecting his career.

A few months into his new job, he met a local girl, and after a whirlwind romance, they decided to marry.

Susan had gone to Calgary for the wedding but hadn't seen her son since. Her grandson was nearing his first birthday, and she hadn't been able to see him or give him the cuddles she longed for. Julie was aware of how much her sister missed her family and was eager to share her news but waited until they were settled back in the lounge with mugs of tea in their hands.

Helping herself to a biscuit, Julie dunked it in her mug and nonchalantly said, 'I think you should go and see Stephen to take Luke's jacket yourself.' She was having great difficulty in remaining serious, wanting to shout out her news and hug her sister.

'Huh! Chance would be a fine thing. You know I've not managed to find another job since the newsagent laid me off. How would I afford to go swanning off to Canada?'

'Maybe now you have a sister who's won the lottery, it might be possible?' Julie grinned over her mug.

'You're joking! Seriously, have you won something?'

'Yes – only twenty-two million pounds, but it's enough to send my favourite sister to Canada.'

'Are you kidding me? And... I'm your only sister.' Susan didn't know if she could believe her, but why would Julie tease her about such a thing?

Julie jumped up from the sofa and hurried to put her arms around Susan, squeezing the breath out of her. 'Of course, I'm not kidding, I wouldn't do that to you! And yes, we have won the lottery – the people are coming tomorrow to get us to sign papers and stuff – we're blooming rich, Susan, and we want you to share our good fortune!' The sisters clasped hands, laughing as tears filled their eyes.

After two hours of excited chatter filled with fantasies and plans, it felt like the years had fallen away and they were children again, engaging in all the magical imaginings of youth – meeting princes, going to balls, and riding ponies. However, this time, their wishes had a more grown-up twist. Everything they desired was now attainable, and they found the idea mind-blowing.

Julie finally decided to leave when she remembered she still had responsibilities to attend to. And Malcolm would be home soon, looking for his tea.

On her way home, she smiled, recalling the surprised look on her sister's face. She and Malcolm had already discussed how they could help Susan and decided to give her a generous amount to secure her future and allow her some of the luxuries she deserved. Yes, winning the lottery brought tremendous benefits and being generous to others was such a blessing. Her head spun with thoughts of all the people for whom they could make life a little easier, and her face ached after having laughed so much.

CHAPTER FIVE

Malcolm Grainger had spent years working as a security guard at Burnbridge Town Hall, a job he genuinely enjoyed. But on Monday morning, he called his supervisor to request the day off for a 'family matter.' It wasn't a lie, he needed to be home when the lottery representative arrived. More than that, he wanted to make sure his family didn't lose their heads with excitement. Danny and Kate were coming over, and from the looks of it, job hunting had all but vanished from his son's priorities.

By 10.30am, the Graingers' small lounge crackled with anticipation. It was rare for the four of them to be together without grandchildren or spouses in tow, and the mood felt like a throwback to years past – laughter ringing through the room as they played Scrabble or Monopoly. Even Julie giggled like a schoolgirl. While Malcolm was thrilled to see them so happy, he couldn't shake the feeling of being on the outside looking in. A cautious voice nagged at him, reminding him that excitement and good fortune didn't always mix well.

Then, the doorbell chimed its familiar off-key tune. Julie shot up from her seat like a racehorse at the starting gate and dashed to the door.

'I hope one of the first things you buy is a new doorbell, Mum. That thing is embarrassing,' Danny called after her.

Laughter dissolved into silence as they listened to Julie greeting their visitor. Moments later, she returned, cheeks flushed, eyes shining. But she hadn't come back alone. She stepped aside, revealing not one but two visitors – a man and a young woman.

The man was shorter than his companion, with a round face and equally round spectacles perched on the bridge of his stubby nose. His body resembled a figure eight, squeezed in at the middle by a rather uncomfortable-looking belt over which his stomach sagged. In contrast, the smartly dressed woman appeared poised and oozed efficiency in a friendly way. After the introduction, 'Please call me John, and this is Bea,' the family studied the pair eagerly, willing them to get down to business. Hugging a bottle of champagne to his chest, John was rather gushing, offering congratulations in several different ways, clearly having had plenty of practice, until Danny could no longer hold the question back.

'When do we get the cheque?' he asked rather bluntly, earning a reproachful look from Julie.

Bea took over the conversation in a quiet, straightforward manner. 'I understand your eagerness.' She smiled. 'Today, we need to see your ticket to confirm its validity, and then there are forms to complete. If everything is in order, which I'm sure it will be, the money will be paid into your bank account by the end of the working week. We don't actually give you a cheque, only one of those huge ones for publicity purposes. Electronic transfer is much safer and quicker all around.' Bea's eyes scanned the faces of the family before her, clearly enjoying the role of benefactor and bearer of good news. 'So, do you have the ticket?'

Julie jumped to her feet to retrieve the precious scrap of

paper from under the mantel clock which acted as a temporary paperweight. It was folded in a crumpled envelope, having spent two nights under her pillow, just in case. She slid it from the envelope and smoothed it lovingly before passing it to Bea. The family stared in silent anticipation as she opened a smart leather briefcase to reveal a neat laptop computer and started typing away on the keyboard.

Malcolm noticed his son eyeing the laptop and knew Danny coveted it and several other items he'd been dreaming of. Malcolm smiled, thinking of everything he could give his children, things they'd never been able to afford until now. He might even treat himself to a new car, a sporty coupe, not too flashy...

John opened his briefcase, extracted a small bundle of forms, and offered them to Malcolm for inspection. After a quick read-through and seeing nothing of concern, Malcolm started to fill them in, digging into his trouser pocket for his chequebook to copy the account details carefully onto the form.

'You mentioned publicity?' he asked casually, handing the forms back to John. 'What's the expectation regarding this?'

'It's entirely up to you, Malcolm. From our perspective, we would be delighted to arrange one or two press conferences. It's a sizeable and newsworthy win. Most winners are only too pleased to do a few publicity shots.' John sounded eager.

'I'm not so sure. My inclination is to keep it quiet. There'll be another millionaire next week, so I think we'll give the publicity option a miss.'

'But, Mal, we haven't decided yet. What's the problem with sharing our good news? People are going to find out sooner or later.' Julie frowned at Malcolm's reluctance.

Bea was quick to offer a compromise. 'You don't have to decide anything now. We appreciate the magnitude of your good fortune probably hasn't fully sunk in yet, and you'll need time to consider all aspects. I'll ring you tomorrow. There'll still be time to arrange something then, and it will give you a chance to discuss it. Naturally, we'd appreciate the publicity. There's nothing like a happy family picture with a huge cheque to sell more lottery tickets, but please, don't feel under any obligation.'

John pushed the bottle of champagne towards Malcolm. 'Congratulations again, Mr Grainger. Shall we, er, leave this with you then?'

Malcolm took the hint and offered their visitors champagne, which was readily accepted.

'Gosh, champagne before lunch, I could get used to this!' Julie chuckled. 'But why no publicity, love? I rather like the idea of our picture in the paper.'

'We'll talk about it later.' Malcolm closed the subject for the moment but knew he had to decide soon. Laughter filled the room as John popped the cork on the champagne and poured it into the glasses Julie brought from the kitchen.

Kate giggled as the champagne bubbles went up her nose. The lottery representatives congratulated them on their good fortune, drained their glasses and left the family alone after John slapped Mal on the back in a rather too-friendly way.

Julie hiccupped. 'Goodness, this is decadent, champagne in the morning! Top me up, please, Mal.'

'Geoff's mum has Daisy for the day, so I thought if you're up for a bit of celebratory shopping, today would be the day!' Kate looked at her mother, knowing what the answer would be.

'Ooh yes, count me in! What about you boys?'

'I could quite fancy checking out that new computer superstore at the retail park. How about it, Dad?'

Malcolm couldn't help but grin at the spark of excitement gleaming in his son's eyes. With a nod of agreement, the four of them quickly made plans to split up and then meet again for lunch before embarking on an adventure to chase their wildest dreams.

'Watch out world! The Graingers are coming!' Danny exclaimed, practically bouncing down the garden path.

CHAPTER SIX

'We headed to Debenhams, and honestly, asking for a personal shopper was the best decision ever – we were treated like royalty!' Kate's eyes sparkled with excitement; her smile was contagious.

Malcolm chuckled, glancing at his wife and daughter, who were practically glowing after their shopping spree. The number of carrier bags piled high was a clear sign that this wasn't just any shopping trip, it was a delightful indulgence for the two of them, an exhilarating treat they could finally afford.

'The personal shopper gave us amazing tips on the latest trends!' Kate beamed at her dad, secretly tucking a few bags under the table. 'I had no idea my old wardrobe was so out of style. I'm definitely going back later this week to snag that stunning blue dress I tried on. Fingers crossed it's still there!'

Dan's purchases included a new laptop with a smart leather case to keep it in and a top-of-the-range phone. Malcolm wouldn't have known how to use it, but Danny seemed delighted with his buys, insisting on listing the merits of each one. He may as well have been reciting the telephone directory as far as the others were concerned.

The family were seated in an upmarket restaurant, a venue they wouldn't normally consider patronising, but it was a celebration. 'Didn't you find anything you wanted, love?' Julie reached for Malcolm's hand and squeezed it.

'Not really, there's nothing I need, but I'm treating myself to the steak here!'

Julie's hand moved to his knee as she leaned in close and whispered, 'I bought some rather sexy new undies!' Malcolm blushed and hid his face in the menu. It was more than apparent how this money could bring happiness to his family. Neither of his children lived beyond their means, so a few extravagances were in order. This was also put into practice when they ordered their meals, as they selected without checking the price on the menu first.

'I did think we could look on the net to see about a holiday, somewhere warm where we can all go together, Florida perhaps?'

Mal's words fetched a squeal of delight from Kate. 'Disney World!' she cried. 'Oh, Dad, I've always wanted to go, it'll be fantastic!' The topic led to more plans and excited chatter. Malcolm decided that for the rest of the day, he would try to enjoy their good fortune without crossing bridges and anticipating events that might never happen.

When Malcolm returned to work at the town hall on Tuesday morning, he was still unsure whether to stay in his job. Common sense told him not to make any hasty decisions; he needed time and space to think things through.

Julie, on the other hand, had already handed in her notice at the school, where she worked part-time as a dinner supervisor. She had agreed to stay on for the rest of the month to give them time to find a replacement. Malcolm just hoped she wouldn't rush in and announce their win to everyone. Her excitement was hard to contain, and he couldn't blame her.

Still, he understood and fully supported her decision to share the news with Susan. The sisters had always been close, and Malcolm was just as thrilled as Julie that they could finally help her financially. He planned to transfer a generous sum into Susan's account during his next visit to the bank.

Julie didn't want to work out the notice period, yet didn't want to let the school down either. Although it wasn't the best job in the world and certainly not the highest paying, she enjoyed it and, over time, had formed firm friendships with her colleagues. The headteacher had sounded genuinely sorry when they spoke on the phone the previous day. Julie explained that she needed time off for personal reasons and wished to tender her resignation. Naturally, she'd miss the children, but there were so many options available to them, courtesy of the lottery win, and the idea of spending more time with their grandchildren was appealing. There were holidays to take, perhaps a new home to look for, and being tied to working hours would restrict their activities.

Hopefully, Malcolm would eventually agree; his reaction to their win was something of an enigma, almost as if he didn't want the money. As Julie pondered their good luck, something she hadn't stopped doing since Saturday, the phone rang, catching her as she struggled into her coat before leaving for work.

'Mrs Grainger?' a female voice enquired.

'Yes?'

'Hi. My name's Penny Jones. I'm a reporter at the *Argos Local*, the free paper for the area.'

'Yes, I know it.'

'I'd like to congratulate you and your family on your recent win. You must be delighted!'

Julie wondered how on earth this young woman knew. It was only Tuesday, and they hadn't told many people about it yet.

'Er, thank you, but how did you find out?'

'Oh, I'm sorry, is it a secret? I'm a friend of your son's wife, Angie. We were at school together, and I saw her out with Danny last night while they were celebrating. Perhaps you would like to share your good news with our readers. Everyone loves a good story – such a change from the constant bad news – and as our paper's only a local readership, I hoped you would let me do a piece on your lottery win?'

Julie was perplexed and didn't know what to say. This girl was undoubtedly good, making it sound like everyone would be so pleased for them, but alarm bells were ringing. Julie had a strong feeling that Malcolm might not like it. 'I'm afraid you've caught me at a bad time, Penny. I'm on my way out to work. Could you ring later, perhaps this evening, when my husband will be home?'

'Certainly, Mrs Grainger, I'd be delighted to! So, you're still going to work, are you? And your husband?'

Julie had visions of the girl making notes of everything she said. 'Erm, nothing's been decided yet. Sorry, I must go…'

'I'll speak to you later then. Goodbye, and thank you so much for talking to me.'

Julie was trembling. The news was out. Angie couldn't have known they didn't want publicity, or Malcolm didn't anyway. She'd let Mal talk to the reporter later and decide for them, although she had an inkling she knew what he'd say.

CHAPTER SEVEN

'Why on earth did Angie have to tell a perfect stranger our business?' Malcolm wasn't pleased to hear about the reporter's phone call.

'She wouldn't mean any harm by it. Danny probably never thought to tell her to keep it quiet. And it was an old school friend, not a stranger, and a nice girl. You can speak to her this evening and decide what to do.'

'I will, and I'm going to call the kids and ask them to keep quiet about it all.' He stomped off to make the calls while Julie went to the kitchen to prepare their evening meal, wondering why he was so determined not to share their good news. Sometimes, she couldn't understand her husband at all.

Malcolm took Penny Jones's phone call later that evening and could see how his wife had been cajoled into speaking to her; the woman was persuasive. Surprising even himself, he agreed to answer a few questions over the phone and to allow a photographer to call around the following evening.

'You can be in the photo, and the kids if they like, but I'll pass.' He told a delighted Julie afterwards. 'Penny already knew the details and was going to run a story, with or without our input, so I thought it better to answer the questions, then at least the facts will be right.' Mal wasn't overjoyed at the prospect of publicity but was appeased by it only being a local rag with a small circulation. Julie kissed his cheek, and he smiled, pleased at her delight. The family had always come first and last for Malcolm Grainger.

The article appeared in the Friday edition of *Argos Local* less than a week after the Grainger's lottery win turned their lives upside down. It wasn't quite front-page news; a factory fire claimed that particular spot, but it featured on page four under the unoriginal headline '£22m lottery win for local family.'

Underneath was a photograph of Julie and the children, looking rather stiff and posed, holding champagne glasses, which were actually filled with apple juice, and grinning unnaturally at the camera.

'Oh goodness, look at my hair. I must make an appointment to get it styled.' Julie grimaced at the photo.

Malcolm was relieved they'd got the facts right and not printed their address, which he'd insisted on. However, he was somewhat disappointed they'd printed the amount of their win. He hoped the matter of publicity would now be dropped, and they could carry on their lives with some degree of normality.

The incredible, almost unbelievable amount of money was currently sitting in their bank account, having been transferred, as promised, earlier in the week. During his lunch break, Malcolm intended to visit the bank to transfer a million pounds into each of their children's accounts and half a million into Susan's account.

As for the bulk of it, the lottery company had scheduled an appointment with a financial adviser the following week. He'd do nothing until then. Julie, who was still in a state of euphoria and considering new ways to spend the money, declared that investing seemed a tad boring.

The lounge was presently cluttered with exotic travel brochures and estate agent leaflets. She claimed these were only pipe dreams, and they didn't have to move unless they agreed. Malcolm, however, could read between the lines, and although remaining quiet on the subject, he wasn't entirely against moving house; he was simply anxious for their lives not to change beyond recognition or too soon. They'd always been happy with things the way they were – uncomplicated, comfortable and certainly not extravagant.

The following Saturday, another celebration meal was planned, this time including friends; they didn't care about the bill and were determined to enjoy themselves. It seemed they'd eaten out every day, and Malcolm longed for a simple meal of pie and chips. On Sunday, he intended to visit his father again, and a wave of sadness washed over him as he reflected that all this newfound money couldn't change his dad's circumstances. Sadly, there were many things money could not buy.

Bill Grainger was still very much aware of current affairs outside his small room. His little portable television was turned on for the news bulletins at least twice a day, and although conversations were very one-sided, he was always keen to hear local news from those who cared for and visited him.

On Friday morning, a member of staff, who'd connected the local newspaper article to his patient, brought in a copy of *Argos Local* and read it aloud to Bill with unconcealed envy. Each word brought a chill to Bill's weakened body as his mind raced with the possible ramifications of his son being in the public eye. By the time Malcolm arrived to visit that afternoon, Bill had mentally lived every possible scenario, none of them good, which could befall his family. His eyes told his son he knew about the article in the paper.

'Ah, you've heard about the publicity then?' Malcolm chewed on his bottom lip.

A slow, one-eyed blink confirmed it, and Malcolm pulled a chair closer to the bedside, speaking in an overly optimistic tone. 'Never mind, Dad. It was so long ago, ancient history, and the *Argos* is just a local paper. It'll never reach Liverpool, and even if it did, who would connect the name to us now? People have moved on, forgotten, so don't worry, will you?'

Bill tried a reassuring smile, but only half his face responded as always. His son took out the *Telegraph*, which was already folded on the crossword page they hadn't finished on Sunday and read the clues to his father, although neither man had the heart to finish the puzzle.

Bill very soon asked about the family. *Julie?* he typed, and Malcolm smiled as he related some of his wife's shopping expeditions, described the new spring in her step and her more outrageous ideas of how they could use the money.

Not all these ideas were selfish, though, and he laughingly told Bill of her plans to donate money to all the local animal shelters, joking about how there would be several cats and dogs better looked after than himself if Julie had her way. Then there were the overseas orphanages she'd been viewing on the internet. Although he was delighted and proud that his wife wished to use the money for such projects, he confessed to a degree of alarm when she suggested visiting some of these places to see the needs first-hand. It was all very altruistic, but Malcolm had never taken to foreign food, and even the heat of a British summer was becoming too much for him these days.

She'll settle down, Bill typed, and his son smiled in agreement.

'I know, Dad, and I know that all this money won't change

my Julie. She's always been one to put others before herself.' As it neared time to say goodbye, Bill grew almost agitated and again typed on his electronic pad, *Never chance to talk.*

'Talk about what, Dad? The past?'

Yes, Mum.

'I know. There's so much I don't remember, but my memories of Mum are good ones, and you always emphasised the positives when I was growing up, which is all I needed to know.'

My boxes, Bill typed.

'The ones in the attic, what about them?'

Journals.

'I haven't opened those boxes since your stroke. I'm keeping them for when you get better.'

Bill gave his lopsided smile to his only child. They both knew this was a fantasy. He typed again, *Read them.*

'Okay, I'll have a look when I get home, but you get some rest. Afternoons are made for dozing and I've kept you talking far too long.' Squeezing his father's hand, Malcolm kissed his forehead and left the room, Bill's eyes following him until he was out of sight.

CHAPTER EIGHT

It took only a few days for Julie to realise how much the lottery win would change their lives. Change could be good, she told herself, especially not having to worry about paying the bills and being able to treat the children. But not everything was better.

Each day, dozens of letters were brought in the post, mostly begging for money – people they didn't know trying to put them on a guilt trip in the hope of a handout. Mal suggested she didn't open them, yet Julie couldn't resist, and there was always the chance some could be genuine, and if they were in a position to help, well...

'We should have gone for the no-publicity option,' Malcolm moaned, not for the first time.

'It'll settle down. We're a novelty at the moment. Can't you just enjoy it instead of looking for the negative side of our good fortune?' Julie felt mean when they disagreed; they'd always had such a close and loving relationship, yet the win appeared to have changed her husband. Malcolm was more introspective than usual and no longer shared his thoughts. It was difficult not to snap at him. Couldn't he be more excited like she and the children were?

Julie tore open another envelope and started reading.

Dear Cousin Julie,

I hope you're doing well! You may not remember me, but I'm your great-uncle's stepdaughter's cousin. I've been meaning to reach out for some time, and I'm so glad I finally found your contact details – it's wonderful to reconnect with family!

I wouldn't be reaching out like this if it weren't truly urgent. I'm facing a serious medical situation that requires a procedure not covered by standard healthcare, and I'm in need of private funding. I know this is a significant request, but any support you could offer, whether financial or simply advice, would mean the world to me.

If there's any possibility you could assist with a contribution of £50,000, it would quite literally change my life. More than anything, I'd love the chance to recover and finally meet in person.

Thank you for taking the time to read this. Family is incredibly important to me, and I feel so grateful to have found you. I'd love to stay in touch, regardless of your decision, and I hope to hear from you soon.

With warmest wishes,
Imogen

Shoving the letters to one side, Julie sighed. 'Well, that's a new angle. Do these people think we're idiots? I'm going into town after I've done my housework. We'll get a Chinese for tea.'

'Can't we have egg and chips? I'm getting fed up with takeaways; we seem to live on them since we won the money.'

Without answering, Julie pressed her lips together to avoid saying something she regretted and went upstairs to get ready.

Malcolm shouted up the stairs as he left for work, and her answer was little more than a grunt.

Housework occupied Julie for a couple of hours, and then she caught the bus into town. Feeling peckish, she decided to treat herself to a toasted sandwich and a caramel latte in Costa. It was a small branch, but then Burnbridge was a small town. Julie collected her order and found a seat in the corner furthest away from the door and the constant draughts. The latte tasted good and she bit hungrily into the sandwich, polishing it off quickly.

Julie's attention was caught by a man weaving past her table, balancing a coffee and a doughnut. He misjudged the space and brushed against her arm. 'Oh, I'm so sorry!' he said, turning quickly. 'It's a bit of a tight squeeze in here...' His eyes darted around searching for an empty table, but every seat was taken.

'Please, sit here,' Julie offered. 'I'm not expecting anyone, and you can't exactly stand and eat your doughnut.' She smiled at his momentary hesitation.

'Are you sure? I don't want to intrude.'

'Not at all. And I promise to keep my latte slurping to a minimum.'

He let out a soft chuckle as he lowered himself into the chair with a sigh. He was around her age, perhaps a little older, with thick grey hair and a strong, defined jaw. When he smiled, his blue eyes crinkled at the corners. 'I'm sure you never slurp,' he said, amusement flickering across his face.

They exchanged grins before he glanced around the café. 'I was just glad to find Costa still open. So many places are closing down these days.'

'Gosh, yes. There are more empty units than open ones in Burnbridge, it's like a ghost town. Are you not local then?'

'No, I'm visiting my mother. I live in Richmond, North Yorkshire, so it's not too far away, just fifty minutes if the roads are good. Mum's not too grand. Dementia, it's an awful disease.' He looked down into his cup, sadness clouding his face.

'How awful for you. Is she in care? Oh, sorry, that's none of my business. I'm just being nosy!'

'No, it's fine. It's good to have someone to talk to about it. Yes, she's recently gone into care and is unhappy about it. I spend as much time as possible with her, but I also have the house to sort out and get on the market. I'm her only child, so it all falls on me, I'm afraid.'

'Oh, how difficult for you.'

'No, I don't mean to complain. I love my mother and I'm sure she'll settle in soon. At least it's reassuring to know she's well looked after. Previously I arranged carers for her at home, but her condition grew worse and safety became an issue.' The man took a bite of his doughnut and sipped his coffee.

'It's a cruel part of getting old, and I'm sure you've done the right thing. It's not an easy decision, but as you say, safety must come first.' Julie thought about Bill. He didn't suffer from dementia, but she had some knowledge of the difficulties of living in a care home.

The man smiled and, wiping sugar from his lips, continued. 'It was getting worrying, with frequent calls from the neighbours about her wandering in the street or the smoke alarm going off because she'd put eggs or something on to boil and forget about them. I could manage the household bills and general running of the house, but the decision was inevitable. Huh, would you believe Mum thinks she's in a boarding school and keeps asking for her dad to come and take her away?' He looked up, a sad frown on his face. 'My apologies, I shouldn't be unburdening to you; you must think I'm awful, and you don't even know me. My name's Sean, by the way, Sean Henderson.' He offered his hand across the table.

Julie put her hand into his warm grasp. 'I'm Julie Grainger, and please don't apologise; we all need to talk sometime, and if it helps, then it's fine by me.'

'You're a very kind lady. Can I get you another coffee?' Sean nodded to her empty cup.

'Thank you, but no, I'll be getting off soon.' Julie blushed, suddenly feeling like a schoolgirl. 'I've some shopping to do before going home. My husband will wonder where I am if I'm late.' How stupid to think she had to mention a husband. This was only a casual meeting of two strangers, but Julie didn't move for another minute or two, reluctant to end their conversation.

'Do you live in Burnbridge?' Sean asked.

'Yes. Born and bred here. I have two children who also live locally, so I count myself lucky.'

'Ah, yes. I have a son who lives in London. I'm divorced, so I don't see him much. He's closer to his mother than me.'

'That's a shame for you. Look, I'll have to be going. Good luck with your mother. I hope she settles well.'

'Thank you, Julie, and thanks for the conversation, I've enjoyed meeting you.' Sean stood when she did and nodded his farewell. 'I tend to come in here most days around this time. If you're in town again and want a coffee, I'd like to buy you one for your kindness.'

'Oh, there's no need, but I occasionally come here, so maybe we'll bump into each other again.' Julie smiled into Sean's blue eyes and felt the colour rise in her cheeks. She left Costa and made her way to the bus stop feeling strangely excited. Julie didn't need any more shopping and decided to go straight home. Perhaps she would cook eggs and chips for tea – she could quite fancy something simple herself.

CHAPTER NINE

Later that evening, as Malcolm reflected on his visit to his dad, he wondered why he would want him to read his old journals. He and Julie had packed them away with various other personal items and stored them in their loft, where they remained as an emblem of hope that one day Bill could pick up the threads of everyday life and would need his belongings again. The reality being that it was never going to happen.

Julie was busy in the kitchen washing up after their egg and chips. 'Like a cup of tea, love?' she asked.

'No thanks, I'm just going into the loft to look for something Dad wants me to read.' Malcolm kissed his wife on the cheek and, working on the premise of no time like the present, went into the hall and, with a firm tug, pulled down the ladders to the loft and then semi-reluctantly climbed into the roof space. The attic was predictably dusty, an untouched time capsule. No one had been up there since after Christmas when the decorations were returned after their annual appearance. Malcolm wasn't one for hoarding. Apart from a few old suitcases that had seen better days, the Christmas tree and assorted ornaments, the attic housed only the boxes containing his father's belongings.

It felt intrusive opening them. They'd been sealed with parcel tape a couple of months after Bill's stroke when it became clear he wouldn't be returning to his little rented house, at least for some time. When they finally cleared the house, most of the furniture was given away, and only personal items like books and photographs were kept, among which were half a dozen leather-bound journals. Malcolm remembered how, as a child, he'd watched his dad writing regularly in these books with his neat script, his preferred writing implement, a fountain pen.

Bill had been Liverpool's town librarian during his working life, a fitting occupation for a man who loved the written word, both to read and to write. The highlight of his job was purchasing new stock, and his wife often remarked that he must have read almost all of the books he purchased on the library's behalf.

Memories sprung to life from the dust as Mal wiped his hand across the first box and opened it. Peering inside, his gaze was met with ancient photographs from his grandparents' day yellowing in an album, barely held together by a crumbling spine. Other images were encased in ornate frames, dated pictures recording his boyhood, pictures that stopped abruptly after his eighth birthday.

His childhood came flooding back to mind, and tears stung Mal's eyes at the inevitable memories. A tinted photograph of his mother, Mary, made him gasp momentarily as she smiled up at him, carefree and beautiful, his favourite image and the one he liked to hold in his mind. Gently placing the photograph inside an album cover to protect it, he moved on to the next box. What he was looking for, yet reluctant to find, was there. Hesitantly, Malcolm lifted the journals from their box and, after wiping away the dust from the cracked leather covers, he settled himself on an ancient armchair and opened the first one.

June 1st 1967

What a sad and strange summer this is turning out to be. I can't believe the doctor's diagnosis is correct. Mary looks like her usual self, a little tired perhaps, yet caring for her mother as well as Malcolm and me must be taking its toll... but cancer, no, surely not, please God, no! I don't want to believe it; I don't want to imagine life without my beloved wife. The day we learned this news was the worst day of my life so far, yet somewhere inside of me, I can acknowledge it as a portent of the inevitable worst day to come.

Cancer. An ugly word synonymous with death. My beloved Mary has ovarian cancer and will not be with us much longer – a hateful, insidious type of cancer which remained undetected until it was too late to treat. Typically, Mary ignored the early symptoms, brushing them away as simply feeling 'under the weather'. My wife has such a beautiful nature and is one of life's givers; she is never a taker and never one to focus on herself. Embracing the role of wife and mother, she has always lavished her love and attention (which, to my shame, I often take for granted) on me and our son.

When her mother took ill, Mary waited on her, too, a caring daughter for whom nothing was too much trouble. Even when Joan became bedridden, Mary insisted on her living with us, attending to her every need with only an hour's help each day from a woman who came in to bathe Joan, a task too difficult for one, especially when the patient could offer no help.

For over a year, we've watched Joan's condition deteriorate. Bed sores and ulcers became a constant source of pain, eventually resulting in the amputation of her left leg, a low point for us all. But Mary remained cheerful, lifting her mother's mood and somehow managing to care for Malcolm and me without either of us feeling in the slightest way neglected. She is the heart and soul of our family, the very lifeblood which keeps us happy and content; her love is a tangible presence filling our home. How will I ever manage without her?

For Mary, the diagnosis typically focused her thoughts on her family rather than herself. She gently prepared us as we talked late into each night about a future I did not want to contemplate, a future that did not include my wife. Mary made plans, and I could see the agony in her eyes as she talked about our son growing up without his mother; he was not yet eight years old and still so much in need of maternal love and support.

'Don't be afraid to hug and kiss him,' she instructed, adding with a smile, 'Just not in front of his friends!' But it's a seemingly impossible task to be both mother and father to our child. It's a daunting one, and I feel so utterly inadequate. And then, when the doctor broke the news that we had only three months left at the most, I nearly crumpled. Mary, however, has continued her planning and instruction. The biggest surprise was her request that after her death, Malcolm and I should move away from Liverpool. I didn't understand why she asked me to do this, even when she tried to explain.

'A fresh start in a smaller town, away from all the memories.' For myself, I don't want to consider any life without her, yet Mary remains so strong, willing her strength into me for Malcolm's sake. So, I write these feeble words, hoping that expressing my feelings on paper will release me from the utter helplessness and overwhelming sadness that are presently my constant companions. Mary's positivity should inspire me, but I lack her strength and selflessness. Each day is one step closer to our parting and brings such agony; is it possible to prepare for such an event?

Malcolm, reading his history from the perspective of his father and, to some degree, his mother, was near to tears. Naturally, he had his memories – sketchy and jumbled, not events Malcolm ever wanted to dwell on. If he continued reading his father's journals, many of those partial memories would be completed, and the missing pieces of the jigsaw puzzle of his life would finally slot into place. Did he want this? If he was honest, it scared him, yet reading the content of these dusty tomes was his father's wish, so perhaps the right thing to do was to trust this man whom he respected and who had never let him down. He turned the page.

June 10th 1967

What a change in such a few days. Mary, my strong and determined wife, is suffering but stubbornly refuses to slow down. She has lost weight, which she could ill afford, and her face is so pale and drawn, but as always, not a word of complaint passes her lips, and all thoughts are of those she loves.

Joan is at a low point, too; knowing your only child will not outlive you must be hard to bear; it's unnatural, so very wrong. I worry about what will happen to the old lady when Mary's strength fails... which is beginning already. As usual, Mary tells me not to worry and that things will work out in the end, but how can they? And I am so weak when I should be the strong one. How pathetic to feel sorry for myself when Mary is so ill yet remains so positive! She speaks confidently as if truly believing we will all survive without her, and even hints at a plan forming in her mind, something she says she must do soon while she has the strength...

The doorbell rang, bringing Malcolm back to the present day. He'd been in the attic far too long and Julie must be wondering what on earth he was doing. Climbing down the ladder and brushing the dust from his clothing, Malcolm found his wife in the kitchen happily chatting with their neighbour, a woman who seemed to desire their company far more frequently than before.

He was, however, reassured that Julie wasn't taken in by this woman's fawning when his wife turned towards him and winked with a rather mischievous look on her face. He grinned and left them to their chatter while he went to catch the news on the television.

CHAPTER TEN

The attic became Malcolm's place of solace, a retreat from a world moving far too quickly for his liking. It was warm and quiet, housing, amongst other things, his father's few remaining possessions, particularly the journals. The attic drew him back repeatedly, scurrying back to those journals as if the past could bring the answers he needed for the future.

Over the years, his grandmother's death often came to mind, and the part his mother played in it, yet it was perhaps only now, through reading the record of those dark days, that Malcolm pieced together the event in its entirety. His memories were vague and patchy, so he turned again to the journal, seeking clarity whilst knowing it would also bring pain.

June 18th 1967

Mary seems but a shadow of her former self. She appears to take up less space in this world every day, and the time she will leave us is approaching too quickly. I feel useless and have no idea how we will cope without her.

June 20th 1967

Why did I not see it coming? I must be blind as well as stupid! Mary had hinted at a 'plan', yet I remained ignorant.

Joan reached out to embrace Malcolm and me last night with tears in her eyes, which I assumed were from the stress of our lives. Now I realise she was saying goodbye!

When had they hatched this plot, for they'd obviously colluded? I found Mary sitting beside Joan early this morning. It appeared Joan had died several hours earlier.

I called the doctor's surgery before persuading Mary to come downstairs. Even then, I didn't suspect the truth and assumed my mother-in-law had passed away naturally. I realised something was not quite right when the doctor arrived and started asking questions. Yes, he told us Joan was elderly, but he was surprised by her death; apparently, her heart was strong, and the pain was under control with medication. As he hadn't seen Joan for several days, he said there would have to be a post-mortem examination. Mary sobbed quietly when the doctor left and I held her close, the only way I knew to comfort her. Malcolm was in school, unaware of his grandmother's death.

Mary then told me everything. When she had been diagnosed with cancer and realised how little time there was left, her thoughts turned to her mother as well as to Malcolm and me. She confided her fears to Joan, fears as to how we would all cope without her, and that was when Joan asked Mary to do one last thing for her. They reduced the number of morphine tablets which Joan took each day, secreting the excess away until the time was right. Mary believed the estimation of three months more for her to live was overly optimistic, so together, they chose the time while there was still strength and resolve within them to carry out their plan. How could I have been so blind as not to have seen what was happening? I don't even know how I feel about it. Horrified? Stunned? Shocked? Yes, perhaps all of these and more. Mary is so quiet, so sad. I can feel her grief. She loved her mother dearly, but was it right to have helped her to take her own life if, indeed, this was what it was? So many questions, so many emotions, I almost envy Joan; she is out of it all now, at peace...

Malcolm laid the journal aside, remembering so well the day his grandmother died. He didn't find out until after school, by which time her body had been removed and his parents were making an effort to carry on as usual.

Mary was in the kitchen making tea and his father took him into the lounge to break the news. Malcolm remembered running upstairs to his grandmother's room, hoping it wasn't true and he might find her there, smiling at him as was always the case, waiting to learn everything about his day at school. But the bed was empty with the sheets and the pretty flowered eiderdown gone too. An open window made the room feel cold, even though it was a hot, balmy day. He remembered his anguish and the hot tears streaming down his face. His much-loved grandmother was gone, and Malcolm felt so alone. Worse still, he was instantly frightened for the future. It was the first time the boy had faced the reality of death, and it brought an uncertainty to life never before experienced. If one constant could depart from his life so suddenly, anything could happen and Malcolm's childhood was changed forever.

...but what about us, Mary, Malcolm, myself? How will we survive if the truth comes out, which it surely must when the post-mortem is done?

Mary's tears seemed to be spent, and she moved about the house like a ghost, attempting to maintain a degree of normality and busying herself in the kitchen. She had shared the facts. Who knows if she would have remained silent if there was not to be an inquest? She may have taken the truth to the grave, but it was not as simple for her or us. And now, I have to break the news to Malcolm. The boy has been so close to Joan, so loving and caring, and I know he will be distressed. I need to be strong for him and Mary but where can I find such strength?

June 27th 1967

It is now a whole week since Joan died, the worst week of my life and indeed of my wife's and son's lives. The police came in the early morning for Mary, three uniformed officers and one detective, four strapping men to take away one tiny woman. They cautioned and arrested her on a charge of unlawful killing. I could hardly believe it when they put handcuffs on her bony wrists.

Were they afraid this shadow of a woman would escape or fight them off? She looked so frail, almost skin and bone now, with unhealthy sallow skin, but she tried to smile as they took her. Malcolm had heard the doorbell and came downstairs, sobbing as he watched his mother being led away. How can you explain such events to a child? But I was all he had left; there was no indication of how long Mary would be gone, and I was utterly ignorant of such matters.

The detective advised me to employ the services of a solicitor, a task which must be done as soon as possible for Mary's sake. Surely, they would let her come home; it was apparent how ill she was. Taking Malcolm with me, I made my way to the only firm of solicitors I knew in Liverpool, Jenkins, Smith and Wilson, who had handled Joan's will. They were very kind and efficient, a receptionist finding a drink and biscuits for Malcolm while I spoke with Mr Jenkins, a thin, wiry man with a long face and pointed chin, who advised me to be truthful, so I related every detail I could recall.

The solicitor sat silent and solemn behind a massive oak desk, elbows spaced on the leather top, hands clasped, and forefingers steepled.

Nodding encouragingly, Mr Jenkins did not interrupt and allowed me to finish my story, after which he stood and walked around to my side of the desk, put his hand on my shoulder and squeezed gently. I saw empathy in his eyes as he returned to be seated again, pulled a notepad towards him and started to ask questions. When these were answered to the best of my ability, I asked some of my own, anxious to know what would happen to Mary, mainly whether the police would allow her home.

The answers were reassuring; he was almost sure Mary would be allowed home on bail due to the circumstances of the charges and her illness, but there was no time to waste. He would go to the police station immediately, advising me to take Malcolm home to await news. It was not quite midday when we set off home, but the day had already seemed endless, with still more hours stretching before me into an unknown destiny.

It was almost an impossible task to console Malcolm. He asked questions I had no answers to, yet I tried to be as truthful as possible, urging patience, which I could barely find within myself.

At four in the afternoon, the doorbell chimed for the second time that day, and my heart leapt. Surely it could only be good news? It was; Mr Jenkins stood with Mary, all but propping her up as he helped her over the doorstep. The relief I felt soon turned to apprehension as I asked about the charges, bail and the dozens of other things swimming through my mind.

Mr Jenkins was patient and informative and talked us through the following process. Mary was bailed to report to the police station daily, with instructions not to leave the city. Having her home was such a relief. We could truthfully tell Malcolm that his mother would not be taken away in such a manner again.

I hoped we could spare our son the details of the 'crime' his mother was accused of, but bad news travels fast. The very next day, he came home from school at midday, face streaked with dirt and tears, trousers ripped at the knee, and several bruises on his arms and legs. Through the sobbing, he told us of the bullying and taunts which had occurred, and we comforted him as best as we could.

Feelings of guilt descended upon me; how could I have been so stupid as to think the news wouldn't have reached our son's school? I decided to keep him at home until things settled down, without actually knowing if the situation would improve at all, but I couldn't let my son suffer at the hands of school bullies. Whatever is to become of us?

Bill Grainger had broken the news of Joan's death as gently as possible but it was still a significant blow to the young boy, a blow Malcolm remembered all too well, even now all these years later.

For a few days, life continued as usual. However, a heavy sadness hung over the house and Malcolm could sense the anxiety of both his parents without fully understanding the complexities of the situation. Today, he could only vaguely remember the police taking away his mother and the trip into the city with his father to see a man in a dusty old office. The first intimation that his grandmother had not died an entirely natural death came cruelly in the school playground at the hands of Phillip Rapier, the school bully. Malcolm remembered the blows, physical and emotional. Rapier repeated over and over that his mother was a murderer, and others blindly joined in with the accusations! Malcolm had run home from school even though it was only lunchtime and had never returned.

The sound of the front door opening jolted Malcolm back to the present. Looking at the clock, he realised it was long past lunchtime. Julie was home and certainly did not expect him to be there.

'Hi, Julie,' he tried to steady his voice as he descended from the attic.

'Whatever are you doing home... and in the attic again?'

He kissed her on the cheek; it was time for some serious talking. 'Let me make you some tea and then I need to tell you something.'

Julie's brow furrowed at this comment; her husband wasn't a great one for talking, and this sounded rather ominous.

'Is everything okay, with the kids, I mean?'

'Yes, everyone's fine. There's something I need to tell you about, something I should have told you years ago.' Malcolm's heavy sigh hinted at the seriousness of what he wanted to say as he led his wife into the lounge to commence his story.

CHAPTER ELEVEN

Julie sat frozen; her face drained of colour. The tea beside her had long gone cold, forgotten, as she stared into Malcolm's eyes, struggling to absorb the story he had just unravelled.

'Your mother was charged with murdering your grandmother?' Her voice came out in a whisper, but the weight of her disbelief hung heavy in the air.

Malcolm gave a slow nod. 'Yes, that's right.'

Julie's breath hitched. 'And you didn't tell me... because?'

He exhaled, rubbing the back of his neck. 'It's not exactly something I'm proud of, Julie. I thought... maybe you wouldn't want to marry me if you knew.'

Her stomach twisted. 'So our marriage started with a lie. And not just a little white one!'

'Don't say that, love...' Malcolm's voice was gentle, almost pleading, but it only fuelled the fire raging inside her.

Julie shot to her feet so suddenly that the teacup toppled, shattering against the floor. The sharp sound barely registered. Snatching up her coat and bag, she stormed to the door, flung it open, and slammed it shut behind her.

From the window, she felt Malcolm's gaze on her as she

marched down the garden path. A small voice in the back of her mind whispered that she should have stayed, that they should have talked this through. But fury drowned out reason. No wonder he had always been so evasive about his past. She had never pressed him, never wanted to open up old wounds, but this? *His mother had killed his grandmother?* It was unthinkable.

The rain lashed against her coat as she wrapped it tighter around herself, hurrying to the bus stop. As if on cue, the bus screeched to a halt, and she stepped aboard, barely registering her surroundings.

Twenty minutes later, she sat curled in the corner of a quiet Costa, her hands wrapped around a steaming coffee. The warmth seeped into her fingers, but inside, she was still cold. Her head bowed, her mind raced. What else hadn't he told her?

'Penny for them!' A voice broke into her reverie, and she looked up to see Sean standing before her.

'Oh, hi. Sorry, I was miles away.'

'D'you mind if I join you, or do you need some space?'

'Please, sit down.' Julie forced a smile. Had she come here hoping to see Sean? Surely not, but it was good to see a friendly face. 'How are things with your mum?'

'Pretty much the same. She says there's a tree growing in the corner of her room and the birds wake her up too early – and then the staff are stealing her clothes and selling them to M&S.' He grinned and Julie laughed, despite her glum mood.

'That's better. You looked as if you had the cares of the world on your shoulders when I first saw you, and I'd pegged you for a glass-half-full person.' His smile was infectious.

'Sorry. I've nothing to grumble about; in fact, life's been rather good to me lately, but then typically, along comes something to take the shine off it all.'

'Life can throw bricks and bubbles in the same day.'

'Yes, what a lovely way to look at it. I think I'll have to try harder to dodge the bricks.'

'If talking about it helps, I've been told I'm a good listener, and you listened to my moans and groans last week. I owe you one.' That smile again. Julie found herself warming to him.

'You wouldn't believe me if I told you.' She grinned.

'Try me.' He took a sip of his coffee and leaned back in the chair.

'Well, I've recently won the lottery.' Julie paused to watch his reaction.

Sean frowned at first, then raised an eyebrow. 'Are you serious?'

'Yes, twenty-two million pounds serious.' Again, she watched his face as a mixture of expressions travelled across it.

He half laughed and shook his head. 'I've never met a millionaire before. Why so sad when you have the world at your feet?'

Julie drew a deep breath. 'Initially, it was a dream come true. You know how everyone talks about what they would do if they won millions? Well, we have, but things have been quite bizarre since, which is probably my fault... You wouldn't believe the begging letters we've had, parents pleading for cash to take their sick children abroad for treatment, men telling us they're dying and their families will be left penniless. Even people who say they run animal shelters and the bailiffs are after them, and they've no money to feed the animals. People are so cunning; I'm afraid I've become rather sceptical of such letters. I almost expect them to be lies but to be fair, the lottery people warned us about this sort of unwanted attention.' Julie paused for a moment, reflecting on recent experiences.

Sean took the opportunity to ask, 'Why do you say it's probably your fault?'

'Well, I agreed to do an interview with the local paper,

which, with hindsight, was maybe a stupid thing to do. Mal, my husband, was against it, but I was so happy, living on a cloud and naively expecting everyone to be pleased for us. Many of them are, but the reaction of others has been a real eye-opener. We've got neighbours who would hardly give us the time of day before suddenly acting like our best friends. I don't think I'm gullible, but you start to wonder. Some of our real friends, though, have gone the other way, almost cutting us off in case we think they're after our money. It's quite surreal and turns your whole world upside down. Then there are the hate letters. They're the worst of all. Strangers who don't know us from Adam say the most appalling things, telling us we don't deserve the money, and they hope it kills us! I can't understand the motive for such behaviour. And I'm amazed at how easily they can find our address.'

'Hmm, I can see how upsetting it could be. Is that what was getting you down today?' Sean's blue eyes stared into hers, and for a moment, Julie thought she might cry.

'Not only that.' She sniffed back her tears. 'My husband's told me something from his past, which is quite upsetting. I could have understood it, but I can't accept him keeping it a secret for so long.'

'Julie, you don't have to tell me any more if it's painful for you.' Sean reached over the table and covered her hand with his. She snatched her hand away, and the hurt look in his eyes made her regret her reaction.

'Sorry. I'll not bore you with the details. It's a problem I have to work out with Malcolm. You must think me a right grouch. I've had the most wonderful win, something most people would kill for, and I'm moaning about a petty argument.'

'No. I think you're a very lovely and sensitive woman. Money doesn't guarantee happiness and isn't the most important thing in life. Having people who love you is far better than great wealth. Your Malcolm is a lucky man.' There was a sadness in his eyes, which Julie hoped she hadn't caused. 'Look, I'm off to see a solicitor about the sale of Mum's house. Let me give you my mobile number, and if you want to talk again, I'll be happy to listen. I'm staying in Burnbridge for at least another week.' Sean scribbled his number on a serviette and passed it to Julie.

'Thank you.' She smiled at him. 'I must get off home too.'

The physical contact with Sean both troubled and excited Julie. On the bus, she found herself fantasising about his touch, wondering what it would be like to kiss him. She'd never kissed anyone since meeting Malcolm and the thought was both thrilling and disturbing.

'Excuse me.' The lady next to her wanted to leave her seat, and as she stood to allow her to pass, her face flushed as if the woman could read her mind. Sitting back down, Julie scolded herself for such foolish daydreams. Sean probably just felt sorry for her, but the look in his eyes had suggested otherwise.

CHAPTER TWELVE

When she returned home, Julie barely spoke to Malcolm, and as he didn't ask where she'd been, the information was not volunteered.

The cool atmosphere prevailed throughout the evening. 'I'm taking Trixie out now. Do you want to come?' Mal asked. Julie shook her head. Often, they took the dog together for her last evening walk; it was an opportunity to talk and catch up with the day's events and they usually slept better for the exercise. Malcolm was disappointed to go alone, but Trixie's excitement made him smile. He put her harness on and scratched behind her ears. 'Come on then, girl, let's go.'

The tension was as thick when Mal returned. At around 9pm, Julie disappeared upstairs, announcing she was having an early night.

The atmosphere was equally strained in the morning. 'Are you going to work?' Julie asked, barely glancing at her husband.

'Yes, perhaps we can talk when I come home? I know this has been a shock, but we need to discuss it. I'm truly sorry I didn't tell you about my mother before. It was wrong of me... Can we move on or at least talk about it? Julie, please. We've always managed to sort out our problems before...' No reply was forthcoming, so Malcolm silently gathered his things for work and left without Julie's customary goodbye kiss.

Julie banged about in the kitchen, cleaning an already spotless oven and sweeping the floor of imaginary crumbs. When there were no more tasks to complete, she slumped at the kitchen table with a mug of tea, rested her head in her hands and sighed. Malcolm's attitude to their win and the resulting publicity was beginning to make sense now.

If only he'd explained, she would never have agreed to speak to the reporter, but Malcolm wasn't one for cosy heart-to-hearts, the strong silent type she'd always joked, but perhaps not so strong now? The lottery win brought excitement and delight; their children's futures looked so much more positive, and there was security for their old age and money to enjoy some of the good things in life. Yet now, it was wholly overshadowed by something as distasteful and ugly as her husband keeping secrets.

Julie was trying hard to come to terms with her disappointment with Malcolm. He'd never been a strong character; even when the children were little and misbehaved, it fell to her to discipline them. Sometimes, she wished he'd be more decisive and not so easily swayed, but then his easy-going nature was a part of his character she'd fallen in love with.

A sudden memory surfaced, catching Julie off guard – one that reminded her of Malcolm's rarely seen softer side. One evening, he had come home looking unusually hesitant, cradling something small in his arms. It was a tiny, shivering puppy. His workmate, who bred dogs as a hobby, had recently welcomed a litter of toy poodles. But one of the pups had been born with a deformed leg. Considered unsellable and not worth the cost of surgery, the breeder had decided to have the pup put to sleep.

It was exactly the kind of story that would tug at Malcolm's heart. Without a second thought, he had offered to take the puppy, bringing her home without so much as considering Julie's reaction.

At first, she had been exasperated. They hadn't discussed getting a dog, let alone one that would need expensive veterinary care. But all her protests dissolved the moment the tiny creature licked her face, her tail wagging frantically as if she somehow knew she had been saved.

They named her Trixie, and before long, she had stolen both their hearts. When the vet confirmed that her leg needed amputation, Julie and Malcolm didn't hesitate. The money they had been saving for a holiday went toward the surgery instead. And they never regretted it. Trixie adapted effortlessly, her three-legged gait a charming mix of a wobble and a skip. She never seemed to notice she was different and became Malcolm's shadow, trailing him everywhere, her bright eyes full of unwavering devotion. Now, as Julie sat reminiscing, she smiled, reaching down to stroke Trixie's soft fur. The little dog looked up at her with that same trusting gaze. She couldn't imagine life without her.

Reaching for one of the holiday brochures from the growing pile on the dresser, Julie flicked through it thoughtfully. Images of ecstatic families enjoying the luxurious resorts filled every page, images she'd assumed could be them in the not-too-distant future. They'd almost agreed on which hotel to stay in, and the family was getting together that evening to finalise their travel plans. But first, they needed to be told of Malcolm's past, and perhaps the knowledge of what their grandfather and father had gone through would help them understand why their dad was reluctant to broadcast their good fortune.

Another pile of letters sat on the dresser, and Julie opened a few before Mal came home. She couldn't help but marvel at the sheer variety of requests – everything from heartbreaking sob stories to outright begging and, in some cases, downright spiteful hate mail. The first letter was immediately torn up after just a few words – one of the nastier ones that was best ignored. The second, however, made her laugh.

To the beautiful lottery winners.

How marvellous it must be to swim in money, with more than you'll ever need! I'm thrilled for you, even though I struggle to put food on the table and keep my house warm. I haven't had a hot meal in weeks, and the electricity company has cut off my supply. But please don't worry about me – I just wanted to take a moment to congratulate you on your good fortune.

If you could spare just a little something, a million pounds would make my life more bearable.

Julie chuckled and moved on to the next batch. One was from a budding singer who claimed to have a voice like Adele and dance moves like Jagger. She wanted the Graingers to sponsor her debut album, promising to pay them back once she became famous. Another letter came from someone who had invented an automatic cheese grater and was looking for a £50,000 business loan. He would happily give them free grated cheese for as long as they wished!

Shaking her head, Julie placed the majority of the letters in the pile to be shredded. Maybe Mal was right – perhaps she shouldn't read them. They made her feel guilty about their good fortune, yet logic told her they couldn't help everyone. Sadly, many of these requests seemed dubious at best, and the more she read, the clearer it became that genuine need was often buried beneath a sea of fake appeals.

CHAPTER THIRTEEN

When Malcolm returned from work, Julie's mood was more conciliatory. With little time to talk before the family was due, they both offered apologies. With her usual practical common sense, Julie declared that what was done couldn't be undone, and they would face the children together. Malcolm's relief almost overwhelmed him. He hugged his wife, who responded by kissing him on the cheek. 'Go and get changed while I get the kettle on.' She smiled. Malcolm climbed the stairs, his mood lighter than it had been all day. He could cope with anything if Julie was by his side.

The sound of activity downstairs warned Malcolm that his family was assembling and it was time to reveal his past secrets. Fleetingly, he wondered if he'd done as good a job of being a father as Bill had done with him. Today could be the day he would discover the answer. Picking up the journals and clasping them gently, almost reverently, Malcolm carried them carefully down the stairs to join the others. Danny and his wife, Angie, had just arrived, beaming faces unable to disguise their happiness. Angie was wearing a new three-quarter-length leather jacket, which Kate was admiring.

Malcolm felt almost traitorous as he walked into the midst of his family, knowing he was about to shatter their buoyant mood. Kate and Geoff had already flicked through the travel brochures, delighted that they could afford to choose whichever package they desired without considering the prices. Julie acted normally and nodded towards her husband as if to tell him to get straight on with the bad news. She was right as always; the sooner they knew, the better.

'Before we get carried away with holiday plans, I've got something to tell you.' Malcolm stood anxiously by the window, clutching the journals to his chest like a shield. Julie caught his eye and smiled before patting the seat next to her, a simple gesture which gave her husband all the confidence he needed. She took his hand as he sat, and Malcolm knew he could take on the world.

Inhaling deeply, he haltingly told his captive audience the circumstances of his mother and grandmother's deaths and the resulting murder charge. Danny and Kate stared at their parents in disbelief.

'Did you know about this, Mum?' Danny was always the first to speak on any occasion.

'Not until the other day.' Julie's voice was laden with emotion. Hearing the account from her husband's lips clearly affected her.

'But why didn't you tell us, Dad? Why didn't you even tell Mum?'

'I can't give you an answer, Danny. There are so many complicated reasons. I suppose initially, I was ashamed of my past and worried it might colour the way your mother saw me. Then, not having told her initially, it became almost impossible later. I've pushed it to the back of my mind for so long that it never seemed appropriate to come out and tell you all. Perhaps now you'll understand why I didn't want our win to be broadcast to all and sundry?'

Danny's anger was mounting. Life had been so good lately, and now his dad was spoiling it all. 'Oh great! So what now, we live in fear of being the centre of attention because our grandmother was a murderer?' The words were harsh, bitter.

'Danny! Don't speak to your father like that, and don't call your grandmother a murderer; you didn't even know her!' Julie's voice was sharp, shocked at how he'd taken the news.

'Come on, Angie, we're going.' Danny stood and took his wife by the hand, leaving before anything else was said. Julie made to go after him.

'No, leave him; he's got to work through it for himself. It's been a shock to him, to you all.' Malcolm looked sheepishly at his daughter. Kate's face was pale, as were her knuckles where she gripped her husband's hand.

'I'm sorry, love. I should have told you all before. I realise that now.'

Kate stood, went over to her father and put her arms around his neck. 'No, Dad. I know you well enough to realise that whatever you did or didn't do, you thought it was for the best. Danny will come around. He's shocked, but he'll see sense eventually. My goodness, now I know why you asked us not to bring the children!'

Malcolm was close to tears. At least Kate wasn't angry with him. Like him, she was always one to think things over before acting or speaking her mind. Danny had his mother's fiery temperament.

Julie picked up the scattered brochures from where they had fallen on the floor. 'I don't suppose anyone wants to look at these now? Another time, perhaps?'

Kate smiled. 'Yes, another time. Geoff and I will go, give you some time to yourselves, and we'll talk later.' Before leaving, Kate hugged both parents, a welcome act of love.

'What are those?' Julie asked after the children left. The journals were still beside Malcolm; he'd been touching them like a talisman as if their proximity offered strength.

'Dad's old journals, which he asked me to read. I thought you might like to read them. I'm sure he wouldn't mind, and they'll probably tell you much more than I can and in a more coherent way.'

Julie's face softened, and a smile reassured Mal. 'Okay,' she said, 'but not today. Maybe another time. I feel positively worn out, don't you?'

Malcolm nodded. The family meeting drained their energy, and they silently agreed to drop the subject. However, they knew that the past would continue to influence their future, at least for the time being.

CHAPTER FOURTEEN

The cogs of the Grainger's life were turning reasonably well again. Maybe things were a little cooler than usual. Mal's revelation remained a considerable shock to Julie, and he'd always found it best to let her mull things over after any altercation. He was confident she would bring the subject up in good time.

So much had happened in the three weeks since the lottery win; they'd both given up their jobs. Julie was delighted to have done so, whereas Malcolm held a few reservations yet eventually was persuaded that the freedom it would bring was worth it. They shared a desire to travel and see more of the world while they were still young enough to enjoy it, and work commitments presented an obstacle to that.

Julie loved cruising, and since many cruise liners stopped at exotic destinations, they agreed it would be a wonderful way to see more of the world at a relaxed pace. Then there was the long-discussed family holiday to Florida, which had been on hold ever since the evening Malcolm revealed his past life in Liverpool. The revelation had cast a shadow over the family. While Kate had been understanding, Danny had distanced himself, refusing to reach out. Malcolm knew Julie had spoken to him on the phone a few times, and he clung to the hope that, like his mother, Danny would eventually come around. If he did, they could finally set their plans for Disney World in motion – a trip even Malcolm found himself looking forward to.

'Want some tea, love?' Julie asked.

'Please.'

The phone rang, and she picked up the kitchen extension. 'Hello?' No reply; she looked at the caller display, *number withheld*. Replacing the receiver, she said to Malcolm, 'That's the fourth one of those calls today, *number withheld*. Someone trying to sell something, I suppose.'

The telephone rang again. Looking puzzled, Julie picked it up and turned to face Malcolm, switching the loudspeaker function on. They were both silent as they listened to the unmistakable sound of a clock ticking. After a few seconds, she replaced the receiver, shaking her head. 'It sounds like an office somewhere, do you think?'

'I don't know, was the number withheld again?'

'Yes, probably another cold caller. They're becoming quite a nuisance.' Julie continued to make tea, only slightly perturbed, but there were no more calls, and after watching a repeat of *Morse,* they made their way to bed.

Malcolm lay awake listening to his wife's gentle breathing. She'd fallen asleep almost as soon as her head hit the pillow while he lay thinking over his dad's journal entries for the period after his mother died, imagining how painful it must have been for Bill. Being widowed so early was terrible enough, but to have his beloved wife's reputation sullied by the press must have been intolerable. The grieving would also have been put on hold as Bill Grainger concentrated on finding a new home in a different area. Malcolm barely remembered the brief period between his mother's death and moving to Burnbridge.

The events must have been close together, as they were undoubtedly linked in his memory.

He hoped Julie would read the journals soon; surely, she couldn't fail to be touched by her father-in-law's words and hopefully understand why Malcolm had never talked about that period of his life. Feeling slightly more optimistic, he draped his arm around his slumbering wife before drifting off to sleep.

The phone sounded louder than usual in the quiet stillness of the night. Malcolm and Julie woke instantly, and Malcolm reached for the receiver. Panic rose within him at the late hour as he anticipated bad news.

'Hello?' There was no reply.

'Who is this?' he asked, but the only response was a clock ticking, which seemed to echo around the bedroom as he passed the receiver to Julie. She listened momentarily before slamming the phone down, annoyance replacing earlier concern.

'It's two o'clock in the morning, is this someone's idea of a joke?'

'It could be anyone, probably kids playing pranks or something.'

'Kids, at this time of night?'

'Well there's nothing we can do about it now. Get some sleep and we'll discuss it tomorrow.' They settled down, but sleep didn't come readily to either of them. An hour later, as they started to doze, it happened again. The phone rang, and the clock ticked – an unsettling event that would probably deprive them of any more sleep that night. Julie went to the kitchen to make cocoa, and Malcolm went to the bathroom before following her downstairs.

'We should go to the police,' Julie said.

'Maybe not. They're only phone calls. The caller will get tired before we do.' Malcolm yawned.

CHAPTER FIFTEEN

Phillip Rapier had travelled to Burnbridge and booked into a cheap B&B almost as soon as he'd seen the social media post taken from the *Argos Local* about the lottery win of a former Liverpool man. Apart from being cheap, the only requirement for his room was to have an internet connection. He was lost without this indispensable link to the wider world.

On his first night, he'd ventured out to look around Burnbridge. It didn't take long as it appeared to be a relatively quiet little town, hardly comparable to Liverpool and presumably why Malcolm Grainger's father had chosen to move here all those years ago. An hour walking the town centre streets was all he needed to get the measure of the place, after which Rapier found a late-night café and ordered an all-day breakfast with a mug of tea. The greasy bacon and eggs were welcome; the tea washed them down nicely, and then he paid the bill and returned to the B&B to plan the way forward on this little mission.

Rapier had been in Burnbridge for nearly two weeks working on his plan and he was growing restless. He calmed himself, knowing his efforts would be amply rewarded if he were patient. It was time to make contact.

Before leaving Liverpool, Rapier had printed off several old newspaper articles from the summer of 1967, although how he would use them was still to be decided. His priority was discovering where Malcolm Grainger lived, which wasn't too challenging; he was bound to be on the electoral roll, and there wouldn't be many men with the same name in such a small town. It had taken only ten minutes to gather all the information he needed. Rapier was amazed at how, in these days of data protection, just a few clicks of the computer mouse could reveal so much about a person.

He discounted Wikipedia, which wanted to lead him on the trail of a Zimbabwean cricketer of the same name. A Google search found two Malcolm Graingers listed in Burnbridge. The age range placed one candidate in the twenty-five to thirty-five age bracket and the second between fifty-five and sixty-five. Bingo, he'd found his man; Grainger was the same age as Rapier, in the second bracket. The site disclosed an address and provided information about court judgements, other residents of the same address, and even the price they'd paid for their property. No court judgements were recorded for Malcolm Grainger – had there been, it would have been the icing on Rapier's cake.

The other occupant at the address was listed as Julie Grainger, confirming this was the right man. Julie Grainger had been featured in the *Argos Local* interview that initiated Rapier's quest, which he now considered his treasure hunt.

With the information to hand and nothing more to do that evening, the immediate temptation was to wander across to the pub opposite and have a drink or two. But Rapier held fast to his hard-won sobriety achieved of late, and besides, he needed to keep a clear head. He was planning on the hoof and would try to get some sleep, then figure out the best way to make contact in the morning.

Sleep didn't come quickly. Counting sheep never worked for Rapier, so he tried his version and eventually nodded into a fitful sleep counting imaginary fifty-pound notes. Yet Phillip Rapier did not sleep well. The mattress was lumpy, with a distinct smell of something he didn't wish to think about, and the room was like an icebox. Added to his discomfort, a multitude of thoughts kept his brain active, resulting in a restless night all around.

Breakfast did nothing to improve his mood; runny eggs and fried bread were the offerings, with weak, barely warm coffee. He was tempted to approach Malcolm Grainger immediately; prolonging this trip to Burnbridge was far from an appealing thought. Yet common sense advised him to proceed with caution.

Thirty minutes later, Rapier was once again sitting opposite the Graingers' house, ostensibly making calls on his mobile phone but, in reality, waiting to see his quarry. The neat semi-detached house was situated in an attractive tree-lined avenue of sturdy red-brick, pre-war dwellings, each with a small forecourt and a more extensive garden at the rear. Two neatly manicured box trees stood on either side of the blue gloss door like sentinels.

It was early, not yet eight o'clock, which Rapier hoped would be early enough to see the Graingers leaving for work, assuming they were still both working, as the article in the paper suggested. The streets were wet from heavy overnight rain, and a grey sky indicated more was coming. Suddenly, the door opened, and Malcolm Grainger stepped outside, followed by a woman he recognised as Julie Grainger. Malcolm kissed his wife and then walked quickly down the road. Rapier grinned and noted the time before settling down to wait and observe Julie's movements.

Over the next few days, Phillip Rapier recorded Malcolm and Julie Grainger's movements. He watched their family visiting and followed them home to learn their addresses. His success would be in finding the right time to make his approach.

CHAPTER SIXTEEN

Having spent several days on surveillance, Rapier concluded that the Graingers had given up work; their movements were irregular. One particular morning, he watched Julie come out of the house earlier than usual, leaving Malcolm Grainger alone. It was a well-deserved stroke of luck, Rapier thought as he smiled for the first time in days. He would approach now, strike while the iron's hot, so to speak. Perhaps he could complete his mission and leave this dull little town sooner than he'd hoped.

Stepping from the car, he pulled his collar closer against the chill wind, a shiver of excitement running through his body. He was so close he could sense success; it was just behind the blue gloss door he was about to enter. Rapier could almost smell the money as the doorbell chimed a ridiculously happy tune, and heavy footsteps clumped down the stairs.

Malcolm opened the door and looked enquiringly at his visitor. Neither man spoke for a moment until Malcolm asked, 'Can I help?'

Rapier smirked as he looked at his old classmate. 'Well, I suppose you've aged pretty well, all things considered.'

'I'm sorry, should I know you?'

'Phillip Rapier, Liverpool Road Infants?' He had the nerve to offer his hand to a somewhat stunned Malcolm. 'Well, aren't you going to ask me in so we can reminisce about old times then?'

Malcolm stepped back as this unexpected visitor almost pushed through the open door. Nausea enveloped him, and a fusion of fear and apprehension brought a sour taste to his mouth. His breathing became heavy as he closed the door quietly before following Rapier into the lounge. Someone from his past resurfacing at this particular time was not good news.

'Nice place. Things must be going well for you, pal?'

'I don't think we were ever pals. Perhaps you could get to the point and tell me why you're here?' Although asking the question, Malcolm was sure he knew the answer. His mind hauled him back in time to see himself cowering in the playground as Rapier, the undisputed class bully, stood over him, demanding his dinner money.

Looking into the face of the man before him, it was easy to recognise the same bully with the same smug expression. The memories fast forwarded to a later incident, probably the last time he saw the boy Phillip Rapier when the intimidation had escalated, and Rapier was kicking Malcolm, showering him with verbal and physical blows, *'Your mother's going to hang, did you know? Hang by the neck until she's dead, and good riddance, too!'* The words, delivered in a childish sing-song voice, were, even now, embedded in the depths of Mal's mind, clawing their way to the fore like a haunting, recurring nightmare refusing to release its icy grip.

Rapier had seated himself on the sofa with his arm stretched along the back tapping his fingers as if he hadn't a care in the world. Malcolm had to admit that the years had been kinder to Phillip than himself. The man was tall with a full head of hair, unlike Mal's balding pate.

'Not even an offer of coffee for an old friend?' Rapier grinned.

'As I said, we were never friends, so get to the point, will you? I'm assuming this isn't simply a social call?'

'You always were the bright one, and yes, you're right. We have a little business to attend to.' His arrogant expression made Malcolm want to punch him, yet instead, he nodded, recognising that the class bully had not changed, only these days, the stakes were much higher than a child's dinner money.

'So, you've advanced to blackmail, have you?' Malcolm asked, sitting down in fear of his trembling legs failing to support him.

'That's such a dirty word, Malcolm, old boy. Shall we call it a financial arrangement; after all, you have more than enough money for your needs, and I don't. Look upon it as sharing your wealth; it sounds much more altruistic, and I assure you I'm a worthy cause!'

'And if I refuse?'

Rapier stood up and deliberately walked to the window where Julie's cherished family photographs were displayed. Picking up a silver framed photo of Danny, Kate and their families, he ran his finger over the image and asked, 'Do they know about your past?'

'Actually, they do.' Malcolm felt his face flush as Rapier laughed out loud.

'I don't believe you. What a happy little family. Your children and grandchildren, I presume? Your daughter is very pretty. Do you think they'll understand the word matricide? Do they know their granny was a murderer? No, they don't know, do they? But even if they did, I'm sure the newspapers would be interested. Human-interest stories are always in demand, and a lottery winner with a secret past is quite a scoop. Nothing like a scandalous past to sell newspapers.'

'That's your version, not mine.'

'Ah, but it's the truth, isn't it? Murder is murder, no matter what fancy name you think up for it. I happen to have the facts right here.' He pulled a crumpled envelope from his raincoat pocket, unfolded it and withdrew copies of the old newspaper cuttings. Malcolm stared in horror. He'd never seen these before. Bill Grainger had been careful to keep any newspapers out of the house.

Malcolm clearly remembered their home being besieged by reporters, and his dad drew all the curtains and refused to answer the door. They stayed inside for three days until the reporters gave up and eventually left. Bill tried to make it into a game, but Malcolm remembered being bored at not being allowed outside. Even footie in the backyard was banned in case some enterprising photographer scaled the back gate. It was a confusing and frightening experience for a seven-year-old boy, but worse was still to come.

Malcolm mentally shook himself back to the present. 'I think you'd better leave!' He stood and turned towards the door.

'So soon? We've hardly had time to catch up on the good old days, well maybe the bad old days in your case. Don't be so hasty, pal, while I explain what will happen. I'm leaving these cuttings with you; you might learn a thing or two yourself, and I'll return in a couple of days at about the same time when you've had a chance to think about your position and what you've got to lose.' Rapier nodded towards the family photographs and gave a low, menacing chuckle.

Malcolm was torn, his mind spinning. The thought of paying a blackmailer was abhorrent, but to let this go public was equally distasteful. He needed time, so he remained silent as he opened the door for Rapier to leave.

'We'll speak soon then?' The unwelcome visitor stepped out of the house and whistled happily as he walked up the garden path into the cold but incongruously bright autumn morning.

Malcolm retreated into the house and slumped onto the sofa. His legs were weak, he felt sick, and his body trembled. Rapier had been inside for less than fifteen minutes, yet it was enough to throw Malcolm's world into complete turmoil. Resting his head on the back of the sofa, he closed his eyes. What would happen to his family if this got into the papers? Would his grandchildren become the victims of bullies as he'd been? And how would it affect his dad? Bill never spoke of their past, and Malcolm had taken his lead. Avoid unpleasantness, avoid confrontation, and don't rock the boat. He was so good at it, yet it appeared the boat was being rocked from outside the family, and he didn't know what to do about it. Mulling over possible repercussions terrified him.

Automatically heading for the kitchen to put the kettle on, Malcolm was grateful he'd given up work as Julie had wanted. Feeling sick to his stomach, he could not think straight, let alone go to work. Pouring boiling water onto his tea bag, he stirred the mug, thinking it was precisely what Julie would do in an emergency: make a cup of tea.

For the first time, Malcolm truly wished they'd not won the lottery. Life before had been uncomplicated, mundane and peaceful. They weren't rich yet, had enough to get by, and were happy; why on earth he'd even bought a ticket escaped him. He should have thought through what winning would mean.

It occurred to Mal that he hadn't even asked Rapier how much he wanted to keep silent, although the money was immaterial. The thought of paying a blackmailer was repugnant, but then so was the alternative.

For a brief moment, Malcolm considered visiting his father but knew in his heart that the old man wasn't strong enough to cope with the shock. Bill Grainger had spent years protecting his son, and now it was Malcolm's turn to step up to the mark and protect his father. For once, he would have to face things himself. There were forty-eight hours in which to make a decision, and he would use the time wisely. Seeking peace and solitude, Malcolm slumped on the sofa with his tea. Trixie was beside him in no time and snuggled into his side as he picked up his father's journal and continued to read.

CHAPTER SEVENTEEN

July 20th 1967

The reporters left us alone after the expected 'three-day wonder' period. Although I expected it, I was devastated when the police officially charged Mary with murder; she never denied helping her mother to take the tablets which they had saved in sufficient quantity to end her life.

The authorities were not interested in the fact that it had been at Joan's request. Initially, there were discussions with Mr Jenkins about a lesser charge of manslaughter or assisted suicide. They soon realised, however, that it was purely academic as it became apparent Mary had not long to go before her own death. Whether out of compassion or the simple futility of the situation, the police decided not to pursue the case, and during our last few weeks together, we were left alone to manage as best as we could.

One night, from the turn of the staircase, I stood in the shadows and listened to Mary talking to our son. I could picture her in my mind, stroking his forehead, kissing his hair and breathing in as much of him as she could, to remember for eternity. Her words were soft and kind, expressing love and regret for having to leave him. There were silences and muffled sobs as our boy tried to be brave. It broke my heart to listen, yet I was frozen to the spot, torn between running in to join my family and giving way to my stifled tears or allowing them time alone together. Malcolm was forced into understanding things no seven-year-old should have to grapple with. His years of innocent childhood had been cruelly snatched from him, and I would be the only one left to love and protect him. I feel so inadequate, so small and weak; if only I could have the same strength Mary has.

July 25th 1967

Mary is at peace. It is barely a month since we buried Joan, a month of agony and despair and now I have lost the love of my life too. I would have crumpled if it were not for Malcolm, but I must go on for his sake. My life feels like it's over, but his life is just beginning, and he must have the opportunity to live it well. During those last few weeks, Mary became so frail in body, but her spirit was strong, a spirit she willed into me, attempting to empower me, instructing and encouraging... but I am slow to learn. Yet now her words come back to me in the dark silent hours, those instructions for our future without her, those wise words I cling to in my despair and sorrow.

August 19th 1967

I decided Malcolm should not return to school after that awful day when he was bullied. I kept him at home and gave up my job at the local library. In the days immediately after Mary's death, I found solace in activity. I spruced up the house with fresh paint, Malcolm being my willing apprentice, and we tidied the neglected garden together before putting the house up for sale. Mary had suggested places where we might move to and there was comfort in knowing we were doing her bidding, so our next task was to seek out a new home.

We settled on Burnbridge, a name at the top of Mary's list. The town was large enough for me to find employment but small enough to provide a friendly atmosphere to raise our son. Mary had always loved the Yorkshire countryside's rugged moors, hills and dales. I knew I would feel close to her there and hoped the peaceful surroundings would be a healing balm for Malcolm and me.

September 5th 1967

Mercifully the house sold quickly and we have found the perfect little home to rent in Burnbridge, a two-up, two-down terraced house with open fields at the back and only a five-minute walk to the local school. Malcolm has been so brave, I sometimes catch him looking at me with the same concerned expression his mother had, and I know I am blessed to have my son despite everything that has happened. It is still not long since we lost Mary and there are times when my heart aches at the almost unbearable pain of loss and grief which attempts to swallow me up, but I look at my boy and see his mother's gentle eyes smiling back at me and I know we will survive.

Malcolm sighed and rubbed his tired eyes. Intruding on his father's privacy was uncomfortable, yet Bill wanted him to see these journals. The words elicited bitter-sweet memories, yet strangely, this written record gave him a much-needed strength. Through the pages, he gained an insight into the remarkable love his parents had shared, and Mal's heart swelled with pride to be the child of two such extraordinary people.

Reading his father's account also caused Malcolm to face, perhaps for the first time, his feelings about his mother's actions. Phillip Rapier assumed Malcolm would be ashamed of the past and his mother, but the more Malcolm thought about it, the more the opposite became true. Although he was against the concept of taking another's life, he would not judge his mother for what she'd done. He even felt pride in her courage to do what she thought was fitting by carrying out her mother's wishes, misguided or not.

In those days, assisted suicide was almost unheard of, although it most probably still happened. The debate was so much more open today, with sympathies from both sides. Would Mary have been called a murderer today, or perhaps a mercy killer? Whatever. Malcolm's memories were of a loving, caring, patient mother who showed strength and courage in her actions; how could he be ashamed of such qualities? How could anyone judge her actions if they had not been there and never walked in his mother's shoes?

CHAPTER EIGHTEEN

Julie arrived at her sister's home early, keen to share Susan's enthusiasm as she prepared for her trip to Canada. Susan had wasted no time telling her son Stephen the exciting news and he promptly booked an open-ended ticket for his mother to Canada. The plan was for her to stay over Christmas, giving her a chance to bond with her grandson and spend quality time with her son. It was only three days until her departure, and she could barely contain her enthusiasm.

'I can't express how grateful I am to you and Mal for your kindness,' Susan said, her eyes welling up with tears. 'Stephen's also indebted to you. He was planning to save up for a ticket for me, but now he has family responsibilities, so it wouldn't have been until next year at the earliest.'

'You don't need to keep thanking us.' Julie smiled. 'You'd have done the same had you been the one to win the lottery.'

The sisters sat at Susan's small kitchen table, coffee in hand, chatting about their upcoming trips. 'It's strange, isn't it? We've never been big on travelling, but look at us now – you're heading to Canada, and we're going to Florida, as long as nothing comes up to stop us. Danny is still upset with his dad, but he'll come around eventually.'

Julie had shared Malcolm's revelations with Susan, who was surprised but understanding. 'The past can't be changed,' she'd said wisely. 'Malcolm wouldn't mean anything by keeping it from you. He was probably protecting you in his way, and you know what it's like – as time passes, telling the truth becomes harder.'

'You're right. I should be more sympathetic. I have to say I'm seeing Bill in a different light, too. We don't know what people suffer, do we?'

Susan poured more coffee. 'Have another biscuit.' She pushed the plate towards her sister.

'No thanks, I'd like to lose some weight before we go away. It's been years since I wore a swimsuit, but it'll be so hot I'll enjoy a swim.'

Susan had no such qualms and helped herself from the plate before her. Changing the subject, she asked, 'Have you had any more of those awful letters?'

'Yes, loads! I thought things would settle down and they'd stop. There aren't as many as at first, but some are awful. It makes me sick how many women have sent disgusting photographs of themselves to Malcolm, offering to make all his dreams come true! It's unbelievable how they throw themselves at him just because he's rich. I'm not letting him open them anymore. To date, he's had four pairs of knickers gifted to him! Can you believe it?'

'You're kidding. Why on earth would they do that?'

'Some people will do anything for money. Mal laughs it off and says they're after his charisma and good looks, not the money. I burn them all now. The sob stories are the worst, especially ones involving sick children. Danny checked a few out and found only a handful of genuine cases. I can't believe the bare-faced lies people tell to get our money. The worst part is that the genuine ones miss out because you become suspicious and don't trust anyone.'

'You should employ a secretary to open your mail,' Susan suggested laughingly.

'It might come to that. Fancy a job?' Julie joined in the laughter, finished the dregs of her coffee, and changed the subject. 'How about we have a last shopping trip before you go away? It'll be lovely to have some new clothes to take with you. I love shopping without having to look at the price tags.'

'You've given me enough, Julie. Spend your money on Kate and Danny and your lovely grandchildren.'

'Susan, the money isn't going to run out and part of my enjoyment is in sharing it. Shall we go now or tomorrow? There are only two shopping days until your flight.'

Susan grinned. 'No time like the present!'

Ten minutes later, arms linked and giggling like schoolgirls, the sisters set off for the town centre to enjoy their good fortune and indulge in some retail therapy.

CHAPTER NINETEEN

Malcolm and Julie's daughter Kate was still recovering from the shock of her father's revelations a few days earlier. It was fair to say that her dad was never one to talk about his past and wasn't a great communicator even under the best of circumstances. She had known he was relatively young when his mother died and had assumed he had very few memories to share; how wrong she had been. It was heartbreaking to realise the depth of the harrowing ordeal that both her dad and granddad had endured.

Kate was furious with her brother for walking out and wasted no time after the event ringing him to tell him so. Typically, Danny shrugged her comments off. He was always a bit of a hothead, yet there was no excuse for treating their father in such a way. Having made her feelings known, she thought it was best to leave Danny to stew over the incident. He usually saw sense in the end.

A few days later, Kate met with Julie, who was visibly upset. Julie confided that she was hurt Malcolm hadn't trusted her enough to share his past. She had always believed there were no secrets between them, and this revelation had shaken her.

Julie's sadness was evident and she admitted she didn't

know what to think. Though she insisted her loyalty to Malcolm hadn't wavered, Kate could tell the truth had unsettled her mother more than she was willing to admit.

The next day, Kate's mind buzzed with all these thoughts as she stopped by the supermarket on her way home. That morning, she had argued with Geoff, and he had left early again – a habit that was becoming far too frequent. Lately, Kate wondered if he was deliberately avoiding her and Daisy. The baby had been up half the night teething, adding to the strain, and home life felt anything but peaceful. The past few weeks had been a whirlwind – first the lottery win, now these unexpected revelations. Where would it all end?

At the checkout, she balanced Daisy on her hip while rummaging in her bag for change to pay for the eggs. As she stepped outside, the first drops of rain began to fall. She pulled up Daisy's hood, smiling at the child's giggles, and hurried toward the car. Lost in thought, Kate didn't notice the tall man nearby, his gaze lingering on her and Daisy a little too long.

Phillip Rapier plugged the phone into his laptop and opened the photographs he'd taken that morning. They looked pretty good, and he'd gotten reasonably close without being spotted. But then, no one took notice of people holding mobile phones anymore; everyone seemed to be obsessed with them and devoted more attention to their phones than their companions. A bit of cropping on one would make it perfect. The other was an absolute dream, with the baby looking directly at him and smiling as if she knew her picture was being taken. He hit the print button and watched the photos slowly come out of the ancient printer he'd borrowed from the lady who ran the B&B, two copies of each.

Rapier wasn't particularly pleased to still be in Burnbridge, but recent unemployment had become his lot and an alternative form of income needed to be secured.

Reading about his old nemesis, Malcolm Grainger, and his good fortune, it had seemed fitting to make this his new venture. Rapier didn't think of it as blackmail, simply a redistribution of wealth that Grainger could afford. It was amazing how he could justify almost anything – Rapier chuckled at his entrepreneurship and gazed again at the photographs. Yes, they were good; the woman was indeed a looker, with a nice body, petite like her mother and a pretty face. Grainger was a lucky man. A family *and* money; some people had it all.

He carefully placed the photographs at the bottom of his case and shoved them back under the bed until he decided what to do with them. Rapier opened another can from the six-pack, his third one so far, and downed it in one go. Having the photographs brought a smile to his face, and as he'd previously followed the young woman home from her parents, he knew her address and that of her brother. If Grainger refused to play ball, Rapier would be ready with other options.

Malcolm's attitude had surprised him a little. His quarry was frightened, that was clear, but he didn't roll over and agree to hand over the money. It wouldn't be as simple as taking the weedy boy's dinner money in the playground. Perhaps Grainger needed more persuasion, and what better way than to exploit his family?

Rapier was confident he would succeed. He just needed a little patience and imagination. But it was time to make another telephone call.

CHAPTER TWENTY

Malcolm frowned as a headache started to develop and tension filled his body. While he was relieved that his wife seemed to have moved past their recent issues, he now had the bigger problem of Phillip Rapier. He was sure the man would return and thought it prudent to tell Julie about him. The nuisance caller could very well be Rapier, and if the calls continued, Julie would eventually find out. It would be better to tell her first.

After breakfast, Malcolm carried two cups of coffee into the lounge and asked his wife to join him. Julie shot him a suspicious glance but sat beside him on the sofa as he indicated, accepting the coffee despite having had enough with her breakfast.

'I had a visitor yesterday.' Mal blew on his coffee while his wife waited in silence. 'A man called Phillip Rapier; he was at school with me in Liverpool and has heard about our win.'

Julie tutted and frowned. 'Not another scrounger. What sob story did he spin? I hope you didn't fall for it.'

'No, I didn't. But he did want money, plenty of it, and he's threatened to go to the papers with the story of my mother unless I give it to him.'

'What! You mean he's blackmailing us?'

Malcolm noted her use of the plural and dared to hope it meant they were still a team and Julie would stand beside him. 'Yes, blackmail. He always was a horrid child, the school bully, and it appears he hasn't changed.'

'We'll go to the police.' She sounded decisive.

'No, let's think it through first. I'm worried about how this will affect everyone. Dad's not strong enough to have it all dragged up again, and the kids...'

'But the police can be quite sensitive in situations like this. You know the man's name so they can arrest him before he goes to the papers.'

'I'm not so sure. It would only be his word against mine – would it be enough for them to get involved? Rapier could say he was looking up an old friend, hoping to touch him up for a few quid. There's nothing illegal in that.'

'Great! Are you saying we have to wait until he does something else before we involve the police?'

'Maybe we could give him something to keep him quiet?' Mal was thinking aloud.

'No way! We are not going to give him a penny. He'll only come back for more and there is no way I will reward a blackmailer!'

If the situation hadn't been so severe, Mal would have smiled. This was his Julie, feisty and righteous and he loved the bones of her. 'I wondered if he could have been the one making those calls last night.'

'Yes, I bet you're right. We'll have to think of a way to get rid of him.'

'We can't risk him going to the papers. Dad would be devastated. I remember what it was like being the centre of such negative publicity, and I don't want him to go through it again, or you and the kids.' Mal placed his half-empty cup on the coffee table. 'He's coming back tomorrow, Julie.'

'Good. I'll be here to give him a piece of my mind.'

'No. I don't want you here – he could turn nasty and if I can't get rid of him, who knows what he might do. He was arrogant as if he had a right to money from us. And we'd better warn the kids. It's unsafe for them to come round until this is sorted.'

'Malcolm, you're scaring me! Surely he wouldn't turn violent. You know his name. He'd be daft to do something physical. When he comes, tell him we've discussed it, and we're not giving him anything. Call his bluff. If he thinks we're not worried about him going to the press it might be enough for him to go away. Tell him to go ahead and do his worst. I'll be happy to be with you. Let him see we're presenting a united front.'

Malcolm thought about his wife's words. Calling his bluff was worth a try. Rapier was coming the following day, but the last thing Mal wanted was for the man to see Julie. 'No, love. I'll tell him. I don't want him to meet you or the kids; we don't know what he'll do when he knows he's not getting anything. Get off into town or to Kate's, and I'll ring you when he's gone.'

'Are you going to tell the kids?'

'I think we should. They need to be vigilant in case he turns nasty. I'll tell Kate to keep away for a few days until things settle down. Danny's still angry with me, so maybe you should ring him and explain the situation.'

Julie stood to do so straight away. Malcolm could tell she wasn't happy leaving him to face Rapier alone, but he wouldn't relent. His family were too precious to put them in harm's way. He'd face the man alone.

CHAPTER TWENTY-ONE

Phillip Rapier parked in the same spot as two days before and drummed his fingers against the steering wheel. The feeling of déjà vu curled his lips into a satisfied smirk. Anticipation buzzed in his veins – the payoff was imminent. He was in touching distance of all he felt he deserved. It was a heady feeling. At first, he'd considered demanding a cool million pounds – just a fraction of the winnings and such a satisfyingly round figure. But after careful thought, he revised his plan. Seven hundred and fifty thousand. A sum just shy of a million seemed more palatable, more likely to make Grainger cave without too much resistance. The thought sent a thrill through him.

Right on cue, Julie Grainger stepped out of the house. Same time as before. A creature of habit. Rapier sank lower in his seat, watching as she disappeared around the corner. The moment she was out of sight, he sprang from the car, striding toward number thirty-four Acacia Avenue. This was it – his big payday! He forced himself to suppress his grin, instead arranging his features into something darker, more menacing. He wanted Grainger afraid.

When Malcolm finally answered the door, the anguish was plain on his face. Rapier, unmoved, shoved past him and was seated in the living room within seconds. The game was on.

'Hmm, you look done in; not been getting your eight hours, pal?' He thought this was funny. 'Well, you've had time to reflect on my proposition. Let's get down to business.' Rapier allowed himself a smug smile. 'I thought seven hundred and fifty thousand would be a fair price for my silence, and I don't take cheques.'

'You're despicable, Rapier. A low life who hasn't changed a bit since school days. Well, I have. I'm no longer the scared little boy you used to bully, so you can get out of my home before I call the police.'

'Oh, playing the big man now, are we? You won't feel so big when your family find out about your shameful past.'

'I told you before, they already know.'

'I don't think I believe you, Malcolm, old pal. But what about your friends and neighbours? How will they feel about you being a murderer's son?'

'I think many of them will be quite understanding. You know as well as I do that it wasn't murder. They call it a mercy killing these days, and many people would like to make it legal.'

Malcolm's words disappointed Rapier. Having expected the same weakling he'd known in childhood, this man was unfamiliar, and Rapier needed to instil fear in him to regain the upper hand.

'It appears you've forgotten what I said; if you don't pay me, the national papers will. Quite a story it'll be, lottery winner – the son of a murderer. Do you think your children and grandchildren will enjoy reading about it in the papers? It'll make quite a juicy human-interest story – exactly what the tabloids want!'

Malcolm remained silent, his face impassive.

Swallowing his anger, Rapier let out a forced, ugly laugh. 'Okay then, this is your last chance. Twenty-five thousand cash, and I'll disappear forever; if not, I'll sell the story to the nationals.' Silence ensued, broken only by the clock ticking on the mantelpiece. Rapier no longer felt in control of the situation.

Malcolm walked calmly to the front door and opened it. 'You're not getting a penny out of us. I'd rather burn the money than let you get your hands on it!' Mal's sharp words threw Rapier momentarily, yet he quickly recovered his composure.

'Fine, have it your way, but I promise you'll regret this!' Phillip Rapier retreated, this time minus the smug smile.

Rapier was seething. The plan had been perfect in its simplicity, foolproof, he'd thought, a certainty he'd come away with something for his efforts. He'd even lowered the figure, which he thought was a generous concession. Now he was out of pocket with a crumby B&B to pay for, not to mention the petrol. The last thing he wanted was to go home empty-handed. He'd hoped to have enough cash to forget about finding a poxy job and retire in comfort. The last thing he'd expected was to be sent away with a flea in his ear. No, this wouldn't be the end of it; he would make Grainger wish he'd paid.

Climbing into the car, Rapier thumped the dashboard in frustration, resulting in bruised knuckles rather than easing his dark mood. Perhaps a cold beer would calm his nerves – just one – and then he'd work out what to do next. The Graingers weren't going to get off the hook quite so easily. Letting go of such a golden opportunity wasn't an option; he'd make Malcolm Grainger regret sending him away.

Rapier pulled up outside the B&B, then walked over the road to the grimy pub which was opening up for business.

Returning to his temporary home, half drunk, he pulled out the images of Grainger's daughter and granddaughter. His anger abated as he worked and ten minutes later, Rapier sat back in the chair to admire his handiwork. 'Not bad at all, old boy, especially for someone who flunked art O-level,' he told himself. Sliding the finished results into two envelopes, he addressed the first to Malcolm Grainger at 34 Acacia Avenue, and the second to Kate Grainger – he didn't know her married surname – at 40 Drakes Lane. He couldn't be bothered to find either postcode but had every confidence the good old Royal Mail would deliver them to the correct recipients.

Rapier laughed softly to himself as he imagined the reaction of the Graingers and their daughter when the post arrived. This little campaign was proving quite diverting, and he'd surprised himself at how inventive his imagination could be. If the photographs didn't produce the desired effect, he would enjoy thinking up new ideas to unsettle the family and maybe implement plan B. Rapier checked the clock, the only adornment on the bland walls of the pokey room he presently occupied. If he went out to post his letters now, he'd easily catch the last post. Perhaps he'd even splash out and use first-class stamps.

The letters should arrive the following day, and then he would contact Grainger to see if he felt more generous towards his old school friend.

After posting the letters, Rapier walked the 200 yards back to the local pub. He'd earned another drink or two, and he could stop drinking again whenever he wanted to; he'd done it before, hadn't he? But for now, a couple of drinks would help him sleep, and he had quite a thirst.

CHAPTER TWENTY-TWO

Malcolm rang Julie as soon as Rapier left. She was in town and said she'd be home in an hour, so he briefly recounted what had happened. His wife didn't comment, suggesting they discussed it when she was home.

'Have we done the right thing?' Malcolm looked searchingly at Julie when she finally arrived.

'We'll soon know if we haven't, but I think he's bluffing and won't go to the papers. Surely, they've got bigger stories to report on than the history of a lottery winner. He'll get laughed out of their offices if he ever gets that far. The papers are only interested in which celebrities are sleeping with whom.'

'Thanks for supporting me, love, you've been great. At least he knows where we stand.'

'We'll have to see, and I did it as much for the kids as for you. I can't pretend I'm not disappointed in you, Mal. I didn't think we had any secrets, and even after you told me about your mother, it took you a while to tell me about this blackmailer.'

Malcolm was suitably chastened. He knew he deserved her disapproval but hoped this wouldn't have a lasting impact on their marriage. They had always been close, and he would hate to lose that intimacy.

Julie didn't tell her husband where she'd been while he was facing their blackmailer and didn't intend to, either.

Feeling surprisingly upbeat, considering what was happening that morning, Julie decided to ring Danny and ask if they could meet for coffee. Perhaps time alone with her son would prove fruitful in reconciling him and his father. Danny agreed despite guessing her ulterior motive, so she walked to town. It would be invigorating, good exercise to offset some of the weight she'd been gaining from eating out so much.

Pride filled Julie's heart as she watched Danny enter the café and search the customers for his mother. He was well over six feet tall, broad-shouldered, and handsome, and Julie loved him to bits, as she did all her family. However, it was a rare treat to have Danny all to herself. Naturally, the first question was an enquiry about Angie, Tom, and Becky. Danny was happy to report that all was well with his wife and children.

'I know they've been looking forward to Disney World. Are you still keen to go?' She knew where this topic would lead, and Danny grinned.

'You're so transparent, Mum. Is the holiday to become a carrot on a stick for me to make up with Dad?'

'No of course not, but we'd almost settled all the details that night when you got all huffy and left.'

'It was a shock! How did you take it when he told you?'

'Pretty much the same, I suppose,' she admitted. 'But I'm doing my best to get over it.'

'And so am I. I'll come round later to apologise. I don't like these atmospheres any more than you do. Will that make you happy?'

'You know it will. Thanks, love. Dad's not having an easy time at the moment and I'm only just beginning to understand how all this has affected him. Like a typical man, he's tried to ignore what happened all those years ago. It's been dragged up again by that nasty Rapier man or whatever his name is, and it must be upsetting to be forced to re-live it all.' Julie went on to tell him about the mysterious phone calls. Danny suggested they go ex-directory or get rid of the landline altogether.

'A mobile number's much harder for people to find, and you can get a new iPhone now; you can certainly afford it.'

'Sounds sensible, but I don't want anything too complicated, and you'll have to show me how to work it. You know what I'm like.'

'Yeah, I will, but if there are any more phone calls or anything else, you will go to the police, won't you?'

'I'd have to persuade your dad first. He still thinks involving the police will bring the past out into the open again and he's worried about the effect on your granddad as well as on us.'

'Does he honestly think anyone would be interested these days? There are loads of people who favour assisted suicide, and I could easily be included among them.'

'Danny, surely not!'

'Well, why not? If I were in a vegetative state, I'd want someone to pull the plug for me. They wouldn't be doing me any favours by keeping me going with no quality of life.'

Julie was shocked to hear her son's opinions; she'd never considered the subject seriously before but had always believed that only God has the right to take life.

'Yes, I can understand all that, but getting someone else involved is different. They'd be breaking the law and would be held accountable, which I suppose is what happened with your grandmother Mary.'

'But if you were in a position where you needed someone to physically help you to die, what would you do then?'

'Oh, Dan, do we have to talk about this? It's so depressing.'

'Yeah, it is, yet it probably happens more often than we know. Even doctors can't agree on the issue, but I bet lots of people help terminally ill patients to end their suffering. One day it'll be legal, I'm sure.'

'That would be terrible. What about when the patient can't communicate? Will the doctor or the family decide for them? Playing God is a dangerous game.'

'Perhaps you're right, Mum. Let's change the subject. This one's always going to be contentious. It wasn't actually what Grandma Mary did that upset me, and saying she was a murderer was a poor choice of words; it was Dad keeping it from us all this time, which I find hard to accept.'

'I know, love, that's how I felt, and I'm trying to be more understanding. Thanks for agreeing to come and see Dad. He needs our support at the moment.'

'I'll pop round tonight and bring Angie and the kids. Perhaps we can sort this holiday out then.' Danny grinned at his mother, who was smiling once again.

CHAPTER TWENTY-THREE

While Malcolm waited for his wife to return home, he made a cup of tea and took the opportunity to retrieve his father's journals from the drawer in the sideboard, which had become their new home. As he settled down on the sofa, Trixie jumped beside him, her tail wagging frantically, until he allowed her to curl beside him, where she fell soundly asleep, her soft snores a comforting backdrop to the words he was about to immerse himself in.

There were very few pages of the journals left to read. It seemed Bill had needed to write down his thoughts during that dark period, but after that, the need abated, and the entries became, at best, spasmodic. Malcolm lifted the last journal his dad had written and started to read.

September 20th 1967

Malcolm loves his new school which is such a relief. His enthusiasm increases almost daily; although he is only in his third week, the difference in him is amazing. The first day was understandably tricky, a new school in a new town and having recently lost his mother, but he put on a brave face and even smiled to reassure me! While he lives, Mary will always be with me and I thank God for him.

But I can take no credit. Mary prepared him well and her strength endures in his young life. She would be as proud as I am; he is the one ray of hope in my life at present, the one reason to keep going.

Our new home is taking shape, too. It's nothing like it would have been had Mary been here, but we're comfortable, and I'm learning to cook, if it can be called such. I have an interview at the library tomorrow and hope to get a position soon. Malcolm will be able to come there after school and do his homework while he waits for me. I do hope things work out. Surely it's time for our fortunes to change.

This entry was almost the last, and the following week, another entry confirmed that Bill had successfully secured the post of senior librarian. The journal entries ceased, having served their purpose in getting Bill Grainger through the most dreadful period of his life.

Malcolm could vaguely remember those early days in Burnbridge. Going to the library each evening after school, walking home with his dad when work was over, and talking over their respective days were simple pleasures. He continued the habit throughout his education, and it became an invaluable opportunity to study with all the books he needed close at hand. Malcolm remembered his pride in being the librarian's son and spending time with his dad each day.

Other memories of those early years were patchy, yet in

hindsight, he did recall his father's conversation being centred very much on the present and the future. There were days when Bill talked about Mary, but they were infrequent and Malcolm never knew whether it was for fear of upsetting himself or his son.

And so, Mary Grainger became a beautiful if distant memory to her only child, who remembered her selfless love and care, the smell of lavender soap and the gentle touch of soft hands. Malcolm dearly wished he could have known her better; she had been taken too soon. It didn't matter what she'd done, only who she was: an extraordinary woman who loved her family passionately and did her best for each of them.

Arriving home after meeting with Danny, Julie's mood was much more buoyant. The family were her world and even the slightest division or hint of animosity between them was unwelcome. Danny had promised to call around to see his dad, hopefully returning things to normal. She would bake a chocolate cake. Tom and Becky loved cake and they could sit with her in the kitchen while Dan spoke to Malcolm. So, almost everything in the garden was lovely.

The only problem was that awful man, Rapier, but Mal assured her he'd got the message that they would never pay out to a blackmailer. Hopefully, he would have returned to Liverpool with his tail between his legs. He should be ashamed of himself for putting them through such misery when they should be enjoying their good fortune.

Julie busied herself in the kitchen, stirring the cake while Malcolm watched from the kitchen table, having told her all about his encounter with Phillip Rapier.

She changed the subject. 'Danny and the family are coming round tonight.'

'I might have known the chocolate cake wasn't for me.' Malcolm smiled. 'I finished reading Dad's journals this afternoon and left them out for you.'

'Thanks. Are you okay, love? It must have been upsetting to read about such a grim time.'

'It was, but I'm okay. I want Danny and Kate to read them too when you've finished. They need to know the truth about my early years and their grandmother. I'm only sorry for not telling you all before, but hiding it had almost become a habit, and there never seemed to be a good time to bring the subject up.'

'It's all right, Malcolm. I'm sorry, too, for making such a big issue about it. I understand your reasons; it was just a shock. I'll read the journals and pass them on to the children, and then we'll put it all behind us, shall we? Hopefully, Rapier won't trouble us again, and we can start enjoying ourselves as planned.'

Malcolm crossed the kitchen floor to put his arms around his wife, grateful she'd forgiven him. The money would mean nothing if he didn't have Julie.

With the cake out of the oven, Julie sat quietly in the lounge for almost two hours reading through her father-in-law's journal, finding it very emotive, her tears spilling onto the yellowing pages several times. The words were clearly from the heart and profoundly moving – a side of Bill Grainger Julie had never seen before. Yes, they'd always had a good relationship, but now, reading what he'd suffered highlighted a completely different aspect of the man she thought to be a pleasant, quiet soul. The depth of his love for Mary shone through on every page, equalled only by his love for Malcolm. Previously, Julie had assumed raising a son alone would have been tough for Bill, but reading what he'd gone through was quite harrowing, and only Malcolm had kept his father going. How he managed to live through such a nightmare was incomprehensible: Mary's diagnosis of cancer, Joan's death, the arrest, the publicity, Mary's death... however did the poor man survive? And yet, he'd come through those dark days to build a new life for himself and Malcolm.

Julie understood why Bill had never remarried. It would have been nearly impossible for any woman to take Mary's place, and Bill remained devoted to Mary even after her death. The journals affected Julie deeply, stirring her desire to cherish and love her husband in an inadequate attempt to make up for those arduous, formative years when Malcolm had needed a mother's love. And as for Bill, Julie knew without a doubt that she'd underestimated the depth of character of her father-in-law. He'd been a good man, parent and grandparent, yet there was so much more to him than any of them had ever imagined. Julie would view him with different eyes from now on, with more respect, love, and gratitude for what he had done for Malcolm.

'Dan will be here soon, love.' Malcolm's gentle voice interrupted her thoughts. Laying the journals aside, she stood and ran into her husband's arms, holding him as if she would never let go again. Eventually, pulling away.

'Thank you for letting me read these.' Julie picked up the journals, and Malcolm nodded solemnly. 'Come on, we'd better get ready.'

Danny, Angie, and the children arrived as planned, their chaotic presence and welcoming laughter filling the house. Danny made straight for his father and hugged him, a simple gesture sufficient for them both and making words superfluous. Julie witnessed the exchange with a sudden rush of love, thinking things were bound to work out for them now. Tom and Becky had already pulled out the travel brochures and eagerly flicked through them.

'The pages marked with red pen are the ones we thought looked the best. Take a look and see which hotel you like,' Julie suggested to the children, who needed no further encouragement. While they were busy, Mal told Danny about Rapier's attempt at blackmail.

'There have been some strange phone calls too – just silence or the sound of a ticking clock, and they've come at all hours of the day and night,' Malcolm explained.

'Yes, Mum mentioned them. Do you think it could be the same person?' Danny asked.

'If it is Rapier, he'll likely get bored soon and move on to bothering someone else. But the calls might not have come from him; it could just be kids messing around,' Mal replied.

The conversation then shifted to a more enjoyable topic: holidays. The children eagerly showed the adults the hotels they were interested in. Julie smiled; a holiday was exactly the distraction they needed to take their minds off recent events.

CHAPTER TWENTY-FOUR

Kate Burton picked up the morning's post and smiled at seeing the name 'Kate Grainger' on the envelope. It had been a long time since she'd been called Grainger. Opening the envelope and wondering who could have sent it, her smile disappeared as two photographs fell from the inside, one of herself and the other of Daisy. Someone had drawn a red jagged line from the cheekbone to the chin on her image. The one of Daisy was untouched, but the sight of her little daughter looking at whoever took the photo and smiling, almost reaching out to them, sent an icy shiver throughout Kate's body.

The red line was raised and appeared sticky, probably painted on with nail varnish, giving the effect and appearance of congealed blood. Kate touched her face and felt suddenly nauseous at the thoughts it conjured up in her mind. Was this some idea of a joke? The background was easily recognisable as the mini-market where they'd called for some eggs a couple of days ago. She hadn't noticed anyone taking pictures, but juggling Daisy and the shopping demanded her full attention. What did it mean? Was it some kind of threat?

Geoff had already left for work, so she called his mobile,

her hands trembling while tapping the numbers. The phone rang out, and Kate left a message asking him to ring immediately. Daisy, who by then had finished breakfast, was demanding a playmate, oblivious to her mother's mood after receiving such a shock. Kate tipped a box of toys onto the carpet for Daisy to rummage through and then called her brother's number. With no job to go to, Danny would almost certainly be around, and Kate needed to talk to someone she loved and trusted.

'I'm coming straight over!' Danny's decision brought instant comfort, and true to his word, he was with his sister in less than twenty minutes.

'We should ring Mum and Dad. I think this might be connected to that blackmailer.' Danny was appalled by the photographs and agreed they constituted a threat or, at the very least, an attempt to frighten Kate. Her parents had told her about Phillip Rapier but played the seriousness down, giving Kate the impression that the man had been sent packing. Turning to her brother, her voice trembled. 'Should we call the police?'

'Not until we've talked to Mum and Dad – but don't worry, I'll stay with you until you get hold of Geoff.' Deciding it would be better to go straight to their parents' home rather than talk on the telephone, Danny drove while Kate desperately hoped they'd be home. Her relief upon finding them in was palpable, and soon, the four of them were discussing this latest development.

'We received the same photographs this morning,' Malcolm admitted. 'I never dreamt Rapier would send them to you as well, which, assuming it's him, means he knows your address.'

'Which also means he's been following Kate!' Danny was fired up. 'We need to go to the police, Dad. This madman's gone too far now.'

Julie looked expectantly at Malcolm; she'd said the same thing when they received the photographs.

'Yes, you're right. Do we go to the police station or ring them?'

'Perhaps we should ring to explain the situation and let them decide what's best?' Julie spoke quietly, pleased Malcolm was finally going to do something. The photos made her feel physically sick, and she was still in shock. It was clear to her that they were from Rapier, and now she was sure he'd been making the strange phone calls, too. Over the last few days, there'd been more calls at various times of the day and night.

Malcolm was finally persuaded that this had gone far enough and picked up the telephone to ring the police station, his family anxiously listening to the outcome. After some explaining and a transfer to a detective, it was arranged for a police officer to visit them as soon as one was available.

'It's probably better if they come to the house. We can all be here then and present a united front.' Danny was relieved that the police were to be involved. Looking again at the photos on the kitchen table, he shook his head. 'The man's a lunatic. Does he think he can threaten and scare us into giving him money?'

'Well, he's got me frightened, that's for sure,' Julie admitted. 'He knows our address, telephone number and even Kate's address.'

'And I don't like the idea he's been following me. It's beyond creepy!' Kate added.

'Well, it's up to the police now; they can handle it. I'm sorry for all the trouble it's caused. Perhaps I should have called them at the beginning.' Malcolm was saddened that his family had been put through such an ordeal.

Kate moved over to hug him. 'It's not your fault, Dad; we don't blame you, none of us expected this to happen. Let's hope the police can put a stop to it.'

Within an hour, the doorbell rang, and Malcolm opened it to admit the two police officers who stood with their ID badges visible for inspection. Kate's husband, Geoff, had joined them a few minutes earlier, and they made space for the officers to sit down. An atmosphere of nervous tension filled the room. Having never had cause to seek help from the police, the family were anxious and unsure of the protocol.

DS Tim Matthews introduced himself and his colleague, DC Claire Whittaker. He then asked if they could explain the events that led to their call to the station. While Claire took notes, Tim listened intently, occasionally asking questions for clarification.

Malcolm spoke for the family, with Danny stepping in whenever he felt his father was overlooking important details. By the end of their account, Malcolm seemed almost apologetic for his past and for winning the lottery, which had triggered the entire situation.

'You don't need to apologise, Mr Grainger; you're not in the wrong here. Do you have the photographs?'

Malcolm passed the images to Tim, who studied them before passing them on to his constable.

'I can see how these would be distressing. This man's trying to make a point here, a veiled threat. Can we confirm his name again?' He looked to his DC, who repeated the name, Phillip Rapier, to check it was correct. They asked Malcolm if he knew anything else about him which might be helpful.

'Not really. I assume he's still living in Liverpool, but it might not be the case. He was in my year group at school, so I know he was born in 1959 or thereabouts.'

'That's fine, Mr Grainger. It should be fairly straightforward to track him down, especially with an approximate date of birth. Now, you say he's been here twice? Do you think he might come back?'

'Well, his parting shot was that we hadn't heard the last from him, and assuming these photographs and phone calls are from him, I think he'll likely be in touch sometime soon.'

'I agree. Rapier seems intent on getting something out of you and it's likely he'll contact you again. We should be able to trace him from the information you've given, but if he contacts any of you again, I'd like you to ring me immediately.' Tim proffered a card. 'This has the office number and my mobile number. You can ring anytime, but if there's a problem, or he approaches you when you're out and about, don't hesitate to ring 999.'

'What will happen when you find him?' Julie was curious.

'We'll see what he has to say, and in the meantime, we'll pull a case together. I want to take these photos for evidence and to test for fingerprints, but presumably, you've handled them, so we'll need your prints for elimination. We also require you all to visit the station as soon as possible to provide fingerprints and formal statements. Could you please ring DC Whittaker to arrange a convenient time? Rapier's already made several mistakes in trying to blackmail you, which shows he's not a professional. On the other hand, being an amateur makes him unpredictable and I would advise caution. I'll keep you informed as to any progress we make. If I can ring you, Mr Grainger, as a point of contact, would you update your family?'

Malcolm agreed and thanked the sergeant for coming.

When the police left, a solemn mood hung over the family. Geoff spoke first, addressing his wife. 'I don't think you should go out alone until this man's locked up. I'd take time off to be with you but we're presently snowed under with work.' Geoff worked for a firm of solicitors, managing their conveyancing department.

Danny rolled his eyes which earned him a stern look from his mother. 'And I need to speak to Angie to warn her to be on her guard and keep the children close by.' Danny went off to phone his wife.

Julie and Kate sat quietly, pondering the last hour. Malcolm felt the need to offer reassurance. 'It will probably end pretty quickly. Once the police find Rapier, we won't have to worry about him anymore. We'll be able to put this behind us.' Even as he spoke, the words sounded hollow. They knew that if the police found a Liverpool address, Rapier would likely not be there; he was probably still somewhere in Burnbridge planning his next move.

All Kate could think about was the ugly red line painted onto the photograph and the image of Daisy smiling trustingly at a stranger.

CHAPTER TWENTY-FIVE

While his dad and granddad were reporting recent incidents to the police, Tom was coming to the end of another day at Beaconsfield Junior School, unaware of the problems within his family.

'Did you see the look on the goalie's face when you kicked the ball right between his legs? It was ace!' Tom kicked his foot as if scoring a goal. 'He looked like he'd swallowed a wasp.'

Adam, his best friend, burst out laughing. He was happy to share the credit for his goal. 'Great assist, Tom. He froze. I thought he was going to cry when the ball went in. I reckon we're a good team on the pitch.'

'Best duo in Year Six,' Tom agreed. 'Premier scouts are probably watching us already!'

Josh caught up with them as they left the school grounds. 'Hey, I heard you banging on about your goal. Some of us were actually defending, you know.'

'Yeah, we'll remember you when we're famous.' Tom laughed.

Walking home from school alone was still a novelty to Tom and was in preparation for moving to senior school in

September. The boys crossed the main road with the lollipop man. 'Thanks, Mr Patel!' Tom shouted.

'So, when are you off to Disney?' Adam asked, shrugging his backpack further onto his shoulder.

Tom hesitated, remembering his dad's warning – don't mention the lottery win – keep it low-key. But it was hard to keep his excitement bottled up.

'A week on Saturday. Florida, Disney World! Can you believe it?' His eyes sparkled.

Adam gave a dramatic sigh. 'Not fair. I've never even been on a plane. Swop places with me?'

'Nah, but I'll bring you something back. Mickey Mouse ears?' Tom laughed as his friend pulled a face.

Josh, who lived in the opposite direction, waved goodbye to Tom and Adam, who continued on together. Neither boy noticed the man who had fallen into step a few yards behind them, quietly following along as they chatted happily, unaware of his presence. The shadowy figure kept close to the wall, his collar up and a cap pulled low over his head.

Adam pushed Tom's shoulder playfully and halted at the corner. 'Right, I'll be off. See you tomorrow.' The boys high-fived before Adam turned the corner onto his street while Tom continued his route home.

Suddenly, the man was beside him, too close. Tom barely had time to react before the stranger overtook him, stepping directly into his path. The boy skidded to a stop as his heart pounded against his ribs. The man's long black coat billowed slightly in the breeze, and his cap cast a shadow that obscured most of his face, appearing eerie to Tom.

'Aren't you Malcolm Grainger's grandson?' the tall man asked, his voice smooth but laced with something that sent a shiver down Tom's spine.

Tom hesitated. His parents had always warned him about

strangers, and his school had drilled into him the dangers of talking to people he didn't know. But this man knew his granddad. How? Tom swallowed hard and slightly nodded, his palms suddenly damp with sweat. The man smiled, but it wasn't a warm, friendly smile – it was the kind that didn't quite reach his eyes. 'I'm an old friend of Malcolm's. We went to school together when we were your age, maybe a bit younger.'

Something about the way he spoke made Tom's stomach churn. The man did seem about his granddad's age, but there was something off, something that made the boy instinctively want to take a step back. So he did.

The man moved forward immediately, blocking his way. His coat shifted, and for the briefest moment, Tom thought he saw something gleam beneath the heavy fabric. A flash of metal? A knife? His pulse kicked up another notch.

'Can you give your granddad a message for me?' the man asked, his tone casual, his stance anything but. Tom nodded again, his voice caught in his throat.

'Tell him I'll see him soon.'

A grin stretched across the man's face; slow, deliberate. Then, before Tom could react, the man's hand shot out, reaching for his shoulder.

Terror exploded inside him. Tom's instincts screamed at him to run, and before the stranger's fingers could brush his jacket, he moved. Ducking low, he twisted to the side, adrenaline pumping hot and fast through his veins. Then he bolted.

The world blurred as his feet pounded against the pavement, his legs burning with the effort. His breath came in ragged gasps, the cold air slicing into his lungs. Behind him, he thought he heard the scuff of hurried footsteps; was the man following him? He didn't dare look back. The stories his parents had told him, the warnings from school, the news reports about missing children – all of it crashed into him like a tidal wave. He wasn't going to be one of those kids.

Tears streaked his face as he pushed himself harder, his house looming ahead like a beacon of safety. His vision tunnelled. Just a few more steps.

Tom reached the front door, nearly tripping as he flung himself inside, slamming it shut behind him. His breath came in frantic gasps, his chest heaving. For a moment, he stood there, frozen, ears straining for any sound outside. Nothing. But that didn't mean the man was gone.

Swallowing the lump in his throat, he locked the door with shaking hands. Then, without wasting another second, he screamed for his parents.

Danny arrived home while Tom was still shaking from the experience and trying to explain to his mother what had happened. Angie became tearful and hugged her confused son. 'I didn't want to be rude as he said he was a friend of Granddad's, but then he reached out to grab me, and I was scared, I thought I saw a knife...' Tom looked from his mother to his father, still trembling and unsure if he was in trouble.

'I'm not angry with you, son. You did the right thing by running home. If you see this man again, promise me you won't let him get anywhere near you.' Danny knelt to look his son in the eyes. Tom nodded, and his dad ruffled his hair. Not wanting to alarm his son even more, Danny took his phone into his study to make a couple of phone calls while Angie fussed over Tom, offering him snacks and a drink.

Tom didn't completely understand what was happening, but he had felt scared of the man and was relieved that he'd run away, even if the man was a friend of his grandfather. He hoped the stranger wouldn't tell Granddad that he'd been rude. Sometimes, it was hard to know what grown-ups expected him to do.

Danny rang DS Matthews, his hands shaking as he tapped in the numbers and related everything Tom had told him. The detective listened carefully, then explained that the incident added weight to the case against Rapier. 'But it's probably too late to send a squad car to the school. He'll be long gone by now. Maybe you should accompany your son to school until this is sorted out and let his teachers know so they can be vigilant, too.'

'Don't worry, we'll not let the children out of sight. He might have kidnapped Tom! He's dangerous! Tom thought he saw a knife. He must have been following him like he did with Kate.' Danny ranted for a few more minutes, getting everything off his chest. He was appeased that DS Matthews took the incident seriously and the detective assured him they were doing everything possible to locate Phillip Rapier. Danny thanked him and promised to be at the station early the following day to give his fingerprints and make a statement, which now included the intimidation of his son.

Immediately afterwards, Danny called his dad, a fifteen-minute call that he found utterly frustrating. Malcolm was shocked but didn't seem to take the incident as seriously as Dan did. Tom was unhurt, and assuming it was Rapier, Mal appeared to think the incident was engineered to intimidate and the man wouldn't have harmed a child.

'Dad, are you crazy?' Danny bellowed. 'We don't know what his intention was. We know he wants money; he might have kidnapped Tom! DS Matthews agrees and suggests we tell the school so they can keep an eye on the children until Rapier's caught.'

'I'm not saying this wasn't serious, but Tom's okay, isn't he? We'll have to take extra precautions, but I'm sure it will all blow over.'

Danny muttered something about his dad always being eager to see the good in people and how naïve his attitude was, and then ended the call and returned to his son. The incident rattled Dan; his wife and children were the most precious thing in the world. He'd kill Rapier if he approached any of them again.

CHAPTER TWENTY-SIX

It was a grey, foggy morning, and a heavy drizzle began as Julie made her way to Burnbridge Police Station. The station was located behind the market square, in a Victorian building with a sixties-era annexe that seemed hastily constructed without consideration for aesthetics or comfort. This annexe was the main entrance to the entire building, its steel-framed windows bleeding rust down the concrete exterior. An oblong hall housed a reception desk, where a full-length plexiglass screen protected the personnel on duty. Plastic bucket seats lined one wall, most discoloured with stains that were probably best left unidentified.

Julie had never been inside the building before and felt slightly nervous. She was directed to a chair while waiting for DS Matthews to collect her and felt the damp draught from the window behind her as the rain trickled down outside. The only other occupant in the reception area was a heavily tattooed young man, his face obscured by several piercings and a shock of greasy blue-black hair. Julie perched on the opposite end of the row of chairs, feeling like a criminal waiting to give her statement and have her fingerprints taken. Kate and Danny had been to do the same thing earlier that morning, and Malcolm, who was visiting Bill, would provide his evidence later in the day.

DS Matthews arrived and guided Julie to a room prepared for them. He instructed her to ignore the camera as he switched it on. She then described the events involving Phillip Rapier, fully aware that her account was vague and based on second-hand information. Ultimately, it was Malcolm's testimony that mattered most; he had encountered Rapier personally and had even been threatened by him.

An hour later, on leaving the station, Julie furtively looked around hoping no one she knew had seen her, and then scolded herself for being silly. When Malcolm came home, they planned to go out to eat, something which used to be a treat but was becoming a regular feature in their lives. She'd have to be careful; all this dining out was piling on the weight. Perhaps after the Florida trip, she would go on a diet, join one of those slimming clubs or something before it got out of hand.

Julie enjoyed dressing up to go out; her wardrobe was bulging, much like her waistline, and she felt good in the new clothes bought with their lottery winnings. Her idea of designer wear had always been M&S or Debenhams; now, she could spoil herself without waiting for the sales or worrying about the figures on the price tags. Hearing the front door open and closing, she called, 'Is that you, Mal?'

'Who else are you expecting?' he replied. Julie rushed downstairs, anxious to ask how he'd got on at the police station and to compare notes about their experiences. Mal was in the kitchen, his face already buried in the local paper, Trixie dancing around on her three legs, attempting to gain his attention.

'Well, how did it go?' she asked.

'I didn't do the statement.' Malcolm kept his face hidden by the paper, avoiding eye contact.

'Why? Wasn't DS Matthews there?'

'He was, but I decided not to press charges.'

'No! I don't believe you. Why on earth would you do that?' Julie was horrified.

'Because it's true, I don't want to press charges.' He put the paper down and turned towards his wife, who sat beside him, shaking her head.

'Look, Julie, we've got such a lot going for us: a wonderful family, money, and each other. And what has Rapier got? Nothing. Okay, I know he did wrong and had us all worried for a while, but will it make us any happier to see him suffer the indignity of a trial?'

'Yes, it'll certainly make me feel better! He needs to pay for what he's done, Mal. How could you do this without talking to me about it first?'

'Sorry, love, perhaps I should have spoken to you, but I was at the police station feeling unsure about what we were doing, and I made the decision there and then. I'm sure when you think rationally about it, you'll agree. You're not a vindictive person. For all we know, Rapier hasn't had a decent break his whole life.' Mal took hold of Julie's hand and explained, 'I remember his family. They were notorious for violence, even among each other. Phillip didn't have much of a home life, and if either of us had had the same upbringing, we might have turned out like him or bitter in other ways. And I couldn't tell you because I only decided when I got to the police station.'

'Malcolm Grainger,' Julie sighed, 'I don't think I'll ever understand you. This man bullied you at school, tried to blackmail you and scared your family half to death, and you don't want to press charges? You'll happily see him let off? I don't know what Danny will say, especially now Rapier's approached Tom, but I hope I won't be around to hear it!'

'Well, it might not be dropped. DS Matthews said they were continuing the investigation, and as it's the CPS who decide whether to bring charges, they may still proceed. I got the polite lecture about how extortion is a very serious crime and, in the public interest, Rapier needs to be held accountable.'

'Good, at least someone's got some sense. What happens now?'

'If they decide to bring the case to court, I'll have to give evidence, and you will too. I think DS Matthews was disappointed, and I do feel bad after he's put in so much work, but I honestly think sending Rapier to jail will serve no purpose. He'll be living at the taxpayer's expense, and a trial would be costly. Being in jail might even make him a hardened criminal, so what's the point?'

'The point is he put us through hell! Why shouldn't the man be prosecuted?' Julie felt a mixture of emotions, understandably angry with Malcolm but, in another way, proud of his forgiving nature. Shaking her head sadly, she took hold of his hand. Thinking it a game, Trixie placed her front paw on their hands and wagged her tail.

'You never cease to amaze me. Will I ever know the real Malcolm Grainger?' Her tone was softer now, gentler, and Malcolm knew her anger was abating.

'DS Matthews said he'd keep us informed on any progress, but as we already knew, it could take a few months.

'You'd better let me tell Danny and Kate. We don't want any more rifts in the family caused by that awful man. I know you feel sorry for him; he is a pathetic figure, but he's done wrong, and I for one will be happy if the police continue with the case. Anyway, I'm changed and ready to go out, so let's forget about Phillip Rapier and enjoy our evening together, shall we?'

CHAPTER TWENTY-SEVEN

As soon as DS Tim Matthews returned to the station after interviewing the Grainger family, he wasted no time. A few swift clicks on the computer revealed Phillip Rapier's Liverpool address. The man lived alone – an advantage. Tim immediately contacted Merseyside Police, requesting Rapier's arrest for attempted blackmail. Once they had him in custody, Tim would head to Liverpool to interrogate him himself.

Everything seemed to be falling into place until the following morning when Malcolm Grainger threw a wrench in the works. Julie Grainger had made her statement but when her husband arrived some time later, without warning, he changed his mind, refusing to press charges. Annoyance flared in Tim. He didn't take kindly to people wasting his time, and he made sure Malcolm knew it. Regardless of the sudden reversal, Tim informed him the case wouldn't just disappear. He would hand it over to the CPS and let them decide. As far as he was concerned, Rapier was a dangerous man who needed to be stopped.

Tim wasn't the least bit surprised when his colleagues in Liverpool reported that Rapier was nowhere to be found. A neighbour recalled seeing him leave with a suitcase a couple of weeks ago. Just as Tim suspected. The blackmailer wasn't holed up in Liverpool – he was here, in Burnbridge, lurking nearby, waiting for the right moment to cash in on his scheme. If he resurfaced, it would be to make contact with his targets. And that moment came sooner than expected.

Just before lunchtime, Tim's phone buzzed with an urgent call from Malcolm Grainger. His voice was tense, laced with panic. 'He's here. Rapier's at the door. I'm alone.'

Adrenaline surged through Tim. 'Stay calm,' he ordered. 'Let him in. Play along. Stall him – I'm on my way.' Without hesitation, he abandoned his half-eaten sandwich, grabbed his keys, and bolted for the car. He barked a call for backup, his pulse hammering as he sped toward the Grainger house. The trap was set. Now, it was a matter of getting there in time.

Phillip Rapier was very drunk. His ancient Triumph Dolomite, complete with silver duct tape, which appeared to be holding most of it together, was parked awkwardly on the grass verge outside the Graingers' home. He rang the bell three times before banging on the door with both fists.

Malcolm, after calling the police, stalled for time, only answering when the noise rose to ear-splitting levels. Rapier was leaning heavily on the doorjamb, looking more than a little dishevelled and smelling of whisky. Malcolm made an instant assessment and decided that Rapier's inebriated state would at least give him an advantage if things became physical, which he hoped they would not.

Rapier tripped over the doorstep. Malcolm steadied him, and together, they stumbled into the lounge, where Rapier dropped heavily onto the sofa, looking as if he might fall asleep.

'We got the photographs,' Malcolm said quietly.

'What photographs?' Rapier was suddenly alert and attempted to laugh, but it came out as more of a hiss through his teeth. Clearly thinking he was clever, he appeared to be enjoying his little game.

'We know they were from you!' Malcolm's eyes flashed angrily. 'And you approached my grandson on his way home from school. I want you to keep away from my family.'

'Ah, but have you got something for me, old pal?' The words were slurred and sounded almost comical. This version of Rapier elicited something akin to pity from Malcolm, even through his anger.

'Twenty-five thousand, eh?' Rapier's eyebrows arched in an exaggerated expression of hope.

Malcolm knew he needed to play for time, so sitting opposite the drunkard attempting to blackmail him, he began to open a dialogue. 'How did you get to this state, Rapier?' His tone was soft, and the question posed like he genuinely wanted an answer. Rapier tucked his chin into his chest and his brow furrowed as he tried to focus while Mal continued. 'And why do you dislike me so much? Is it something I did at school? If it is, I have no recollection of it. What have I ever done to make you hate me so much?'

Rapier's eyes were misty, and his demeanour changed, almost as if he was seriously considering the question. Before there was time to respond, a police car pulled up outside the house, and Malcolm raced towards the door to open it. Rapier looked out the window and saw DS Matthews and a uniformed officer hurrying down the path. Suddenly, he was wild again, eyes flashing with anger.

'You bastard,' he spat the words, 'I said no police! You'll regret this, Grainger, and that's a promise. You and your perfect little family will regret it!' Rapier was in no state to run. He could barely stand, and Malcolm wondered how on earth he'd managed to drive and still be in one piece. While the uniformed PC cuffed Rapier, DS Matthews cautioned him, and then he was half led, half carried to the police car and expertly assisted into the back seat.

DS Tim Matthews considered it futile to interview Rapier while he was so drunk, so he took him to an interview room and asked a PC to ply him with black coffee for the next couple of hours before attempting to question him.

After the coffee and dry biscuits produced the desired effect, Tim commenced the interview and asked Rapier about his recent activities concerning the Grainger family. His questions received only the briefest of answers. Rapier did not, however, deny approaching them for money, nor did he request the presence of a legal representative, as was his entitlement. It appeared Rapier had decided the game was up, although he was not prepared to concede every point. As his brain cleared slightly, he attempted to twist the events in his favour, even suggesting it was a light-hearted prank played on an old school friend. Tim pushed the photographs under his nose.

'If my wife and child received these in the post, I would consider them more than a prank. They're sick and menacing, and there's no doubt in my mind they were intended to intimidate. As was your "message" to Grainger's grandson. Coupled with the fact that you've approached the family for money, it seems clear this has been an attempt to blackmail.'

'Oh come on, that's a bit strong! Maybe I went a bit too far, but it was all intended to be a joke. I thought he could take it, but it seems old Malcolm has lost his sense of humour.' Rapier attempted to trivialise the events, yet Tim wasn't about to release him without letting the man know how seriously they were taking the whole affair and that they intended to proceed with charges.

Tim left Rapier stewing in the interview room for another two hours before releasing him, by which time he'd sobered up completely and was growing increasingly angry. He was finally released on the condition he was not to approach any member of the Grainger family or go within a hundred yards of their homes and was to report each day to his local police station in Liverpool, until further notice. When Phillip Rapier finally left the station, Tim rang Malcolm Grainger to update him on the afternoon's events.

CHAPTER TWENTY-EIGHT

'Well, what a relief!' Julie sighed as Malcolm relayed his conversation with DS Matthews. 'So presumably, if he comes here again, we'll ring the police?'

'Yes, and I mentioned his car. They know it's here and will send someone to tow it away.'

'Thank goodness. Hopefully, we won't see anything more of Phillip Rapier.' Julie took hold of Malcolm's hand. He'd spent the last hour filling her in on how Rapier's visit had played out and they were both finally able to relax. Perhaps they could now make plans without this hanging over their heads.

During their discussions, they agreed Rapier was an idiot for ever thinking he could make money from threats to expose Malcolm's past. It was so long ago, and the papers were far more interested in drug-taking celebrities or which politician had been fiddling his expenses to be in the slightest way interested in what had happened to an ordinary family nearly half a century ago.

'Let's go out to eat tonight,' Julie suggested. 'Just the two of us, to that nice little Italian place you like?'

Malcolm smiled in agreement. It would be good to enjoy an

evening without fear of what might happen the next day, and according to DS Matthews, if the CPS decided to prosecute, it would be several months before Rapier's case would come to court.

Julie was singing to herself as she went upstairs to have a shower. Malcolm smiled until a sudden, urgent banging on the front door startled him. Trixie offered a token bark and then retreated to her basket. To Malcolm's surprise and dismay, a more sober Phillip Rapier was again on the doorstep.

'What do you want, Rapier?' Malcolm asked rather wearily. He had no fear of this man now but was curious to learn why he'd returned. Rapier's eyes grew even darker as he moved closer, but Malcolm didn't flinch.

'To finish our conversation,' he snarled. 'Are you alone?'

Malcolm nodded, confident he could get rid of Rapier before Julie came downstairs again and stepped aside to allow him to enter.

Rapier sat without being invited and launched into an angry diatribe. 'You wanted to know why I hated you so much? Well, I'll tell you! You were always the golden boy at school, good at this, good at that, the teacher's little pet, the first one chosen for the football team. And as if that wasn't enough, you had the perfect home life, too! I watched your mother walk you to school and pick you up each day, smiling and holding your hand. She would kiss you goodbye and smooth your hair. You always had clean clothes and a full lunch box... and there was Daddy, too, cheering you on at sports day, lifting you onto his shoulders, laughing, chasing you! And what did I have? Nothing, that's what! Absolutely, nothing, unless you count a mother who was a slut, a drunk for a father, a filthy home and never any food in the house. I got beatings instead of kisses; the old man didn't care who he took it out on, his wife or his kids.' Spittle was running down Rapier's chin, and his face had turned crimson.

Malcolm feared the man might have a heart attack, so intense was his mood as he continued. 'Oh yes, it might have been years ago but look at today, Grainger. Here you are in your smart little semi with a good-looking wife, two children, and grandchildren.'

He waved at the array of family photographs displayed in the room. 'You've even won the lottery! Is it fair, I ask you? And what have I got? A wife who left me for someone I thought was a mate, kids who won't speak to me, no job, and no money. Where's the justice in that? Go on, tell me?' Tears of anger ran down his face, and he trembled after pouring out so much venom. Rapier's warped and twisted logic blamed Malcolm for everything wrong in his life.

'I can't answer you, Phillip, because I don't know. Admittedly, you haven't had it easy, but maybe how you deal with life's knocks makes the difference. Yes, I've been fortunate, although not in everything. If you remember, I lost my loving mother when I most needed her. Now, if you've said all you wanted to say, I think you'd better go. If you leave now, you can take your car before the police tow it away. I won't report you being here this time, but if you ever come back, be sure I will.'

Rapier was silent. With a last hateful glare, he turned to leave without another word, a lonely, pathetic figure, a man who'd made a mess of any chances he'd ever had in life. Malcolm watched with a heavy heart, then turned to go back inside. Julie was still in the shower, and he deliberated whether or not to tell her about their unexpected visitor.

Twenty minutes later, when Julie came out of the shower, he decided honesty was the best policy; keeping things from his wife only got him into trouble. While she dressed, Malcolm told her what had transpired between him and Rapier. After getting over the initial shock of the man being in their home again, Julie's mood softened and she sat on the bed beside her husband. Mal put his arm around her shoulder. 'So, this whole debacle has been about nothing more than jealousy? What a sad man, but he's right about many things, isn't he? I might have had a difficult start in life, but it's certainly been made up for by what I've got today.'

'Malcolm Grainger, you never cease to amaze me. You have a soft side which often surprises me, and I love you for it. And, of course, I particularly agree with what Rapier said about you having a good-looking wife!'

CHAPTER TWENTY-NINE

Without exception, the Grainger family were growing increasingly excited as their trip to Florida drew nearer. Tom and Becky could talk of nothing else, and although Mal and Julie's youngest grandchild, Daisy, didn't understand, she seemed aware of the excitement and squealed with delight each time she visited her grandparents.

Julie had purchased a whole new wardrobe of summer clothes, yet there always seemed to be something else she needed to pop into town for. Malcolm teased her whenever she left on another shopping trip, but in a good-hearted way. Julie knew he would deny her nothing.

A sense of eagerness invigorated Julie as she turned into the High Street and headed for Costa Coffee. She knew Sean would be waiting for her. Their meetings had become regular occasions and something she anticipated with pleasure. Maybe she should have told Mal, after all, it was just a friendship, nothing more – two people enjoying each other's company and finding they could confide in one another – there was no harm in the relationship, even though Julie did find him attractive.

Sean stood to greet her as she approached their usual table.

His smile lit up his face; he'd confided how much these meetings meant to him as the situation with his mother deteriorated rapidly. Taking her seat, Julie returned his smile and asked what kind of week he'd had.

'Terrible. I thought I had a buyer for Mum's house, but they've dropped out, so I'm back to square one. And she's causing trouble at the home; a proper little magpie she's become, taking anything shiny which catches her eye.' Julie laughed at the comical face he pulled. 'It's not funny. If they put her out it won't be easy to find a new place which takes kleptomaniac dementia patients!'

They both laughed. 'Anyway, I don't want to spend our time together moaning about my problems. How are you? Are things any easier at home?'

Julie sometimes wondered if she'd confided too much about her situation and if she'd been disloyal to Malcolm, but Sean was so easy to talk to. He didn't judge; he just listened and then found some way to make her feel better or even to make her laugh at herself.

'Yes, I suppose they are. Our family holiday is looming and the grandchildren are wild with excitement. I worry it might not live up to their expectations although everyone I talk to who's been to Disney World says it's amazing.'

'They're lucky kids. And what about you? Will you enjoy it?'

'Oh, undoubtedly. As long as the family are happy and I have a couple of weeks off cooking, I'll be okay.'

'You're a very special lady, Julie.' Sean smiled, making Julie blush, embarrassed as much by how he looked at her as his words.

'Behave, Sean! I'm a boring housewife just trying to hold things together.'

'Don't put yourself down; you're so much more. Sorry, you've finished your coffee. Can I get you another?'

'Thanks, I'd like that. Then you can tell me more about your mum.'

While Sean went to the counter for their drinks, Julie engaged in some serious thinking. She was aware that Sean wanted more from this relationship than she was prepared to give, and denying it wasn't fooling anyone, least of all herself. It was time to tell him she couldn't meet him again. A friendship was one thing, but some of his comments made her uncomfortable. She'd miss their little chats, yet it was the right thing to do.

Sean returned with the coffee and grinned at her. 'You know I'd much rather talk about you than my mother.'

'I know, Sean, and that's becoming a problem.'

'What do you mean?' His face took on a hurt little boy expression, and Julie felt terrible.

'Maybe I've given you the wrong impression about our meetings. I enjoy chatting with you, but I think perhaps you're expecting more than friendship?'

'Ah.' Sean paused before answering and sipped his coffee. 'My feelings have given me away. You're right, Julie. I would like more than friendship. Are you trying to tell me you don't feel the same?'

'I'm afraid I don't. I love my husband, Sean, and I'm sorry if I've given you cause to think there could be anything between us. Perhaps it's best if we don't meet again. You've been a good friend and a great listener, but it's time to leave it there.'

Sean sighed heavily. 'I understand, but can I request one more meeting? The truth is I think I've fallen in love with you. Will you meet me after your holiday?'

'I won't have changed my mind.'

'Okay, you say that now, but I'll miss you, Julie. Maybe some time apart – a bit of space they call it, don't they, will give us both a chance to think about how we feel, and if you're still of the same mind, we'll make it our last meeting. Deal?'

'Deal.' Julie hated hurting this gentle, kind man, but her heart lay with Malcolm. The least she could do was agree to one final meeting, and then they would say goodbye.

CHAPTER THIRTY

A week later, Bill Grainger was reading a book on his bedside computer when his son appeared in the doorway. Malcolm joked that his father must hold the world record for the highest number of books ever read. It had been his passion throughout life and he always considered himself fortunate to have worked in a library – a fitting place for a bibliophile. Books were now his solace and his faithful companions. The only way Bill could escape the room he inhabited was through their pages when he was transported to far more exotic locations than Willow Dene Nursing Home. Reading electronically wasn't quite the same as a good old paper copy. Still, in Bill's situation, eBooks allowed him to continue his passion when physically turning a page was almost impossible. He switched the reading app off to give his full attention to Malcolm.

'Ready?' he mouthed.

'Yes, we've packed everything bar the proverbial kitchen sink and I think Julie would take that too if she could.' He smiled. 'Will you be all right, Dad?' Malcolm was concerned about the whole family being away together. Usually, when they took holidays, Danny or Kate would be around to pop in and see Bill more regularly, but this time, they were all going to Florida.

'Fine... enjoy,' Bill managed to say, and Malcolm knew he meant it; his father was the most selfless person he'd ever known, with the exception perhaps of his mother, whom he'd not had a chance to know for long enough.

'It's only two weeks and I don't think we'll be making a habit of it. It's been a nightmare arranging things to suit six adults and three children. I think we'll opt for quieter, less hectic holidays in the future.' Malcolm took hold of his dad's hand and the older man smiled.

'I've been thinking, Dad. When we come home, Julie's set on looking for a new house. We said we wouldn't move, but we've changed our minds. It'll be nothing flashy, just a nice modern place, a bungalow perhaps, with more space. We wondered if you'd like to come and live with us?'

Bill squeezed his son's hand and shook his head.

'Hear me out first, please. We could find somewhere with enough space to build an extension, something specially designed to suit your needs, and we could have private care for you. Money's no object now, Dad. It would be best if you don't answer yet, but think about it while we're away, and we'll talk some more when I come home. And I don't want you to think we're doing it just for you. It's what we want, too. Seeing your things in the attic, waiting for you to come home, has given me the idea, but I'd love for you to be out of this place. Don't wrinkle your nose like that.' He laughed at his father's comical, lopsided expression. 'I know it's been a good place, and the staff are great, but it's not home, is it? Just think about it, Dad, that's all I ask.'

Bill nodded, eyes glistening with tears and pride. Father and son settled down to tackle their usual crossword together, and the time slipped swiftly by.

'I suppose I'd better go home and check Julie hasn't sneaked anything else into the case. She started packing a week ago.' Malcolm kissed his father's forehead and left the old man to his beloved reading.

'What did he say?' This was Julie's first question when Malcolm came through the door.

'At first he said no. I'm sure he thinks he'll be a burden to us, but I discussed it with him and asked him to consider it while we're away. I hope he'll go with the idea.'

'Me too. I feel I know your dad so much better now than when he was active and we saw more of him. That journal was certainly an eye-opener. Still waters do run deep in Bill's case. There's a depth to him I never understood before, yet I didn't know the full story, did I?' A pained expression crossed Mal's face. 'Oh, love, I'm not getting at you. You did what you thought was best, and knowing what you and Bill went through in those years has helped me better understand him and you. I'm over that you never told me. You and Bill are like two peas in a pod in keeping your thoughts to yourselves, but I'm glad I know now.' She hugged Malcolm briefly and then pulled back, remembering something else.

'Oh, I almost forgot, DS Matthews rang while you were out. It looks like the CPS has decided not to bring charges against Rapier. I know you'll be happy, but I'm not so sure and I know Danny won't like it.'

'Danny will have to live with it. Yes, I'm pleased. Rapier is more to be pitied than punished, and he's not gotten away with it completely.'

'Well, DS Matthews was going to ring Kate. If she wants to continue, there's a possibility they can get him on a charge of stalking. She probably won't go for it, having inherited your soft centre, so he'll get away with it all, won't he?' They'd agreed to differ on the issue, each knowing the other would never change their mind.

'Hmm, I wonder if we should pack some extra towels. I could squeeze them into the cases. What do you think?'

'I think we've got everything we need. If not, you'll surely find a shop to buy them; we don't have to penny pinch anymore.' Malcolm grinned at Julie. Life was good. He was looking forward to their holiday, even if he was a bit old for Disney World.

'Come on, we need an early night. The flight's at an unearthly hour, so we'll have to be up before the larks.'

CHAPTER THIRTY-ONE

Florida was a huge success. It helped relieve some of the family's recent stress, with little to worry about other than where they should eat their next meal. The days were packed with excitement for the children as they embraced the delights of the theme park. Although Daisy was too young to appreciate much of it, she enjoyed the happy atmosphere. She loved seeing the colourful Disney characters, chuckling as she was pushed around in her stroller.

Tom and Becky threw themselves into the holiday spirit, swept up in the charm of the Magic Kingdom. Every morning, despite late nights filled with fireworks and parades, they sprang out of bed with boundless energy, eager to race through the crowded gates and into another day of adventure. The scent of freshly baked 'Mickey' pretzels greeted them, mingling with the sugary aroma of cotton candy and the buttery warmth of popcorn. Even after a huge breakfast, they couldn't resist grabbing one, laughing as they took big, doughy bites while planning their first ride.

Every corner of the park held a new delight, sending their excitement soaring higher with each discovery. Becky had declared The Seven Dwarfs Mine Train her absolute favourite and would dart ahead, challenging Tom to beat her to the queue. Far from being bored by the wait, they found even the lines thrilling – spinning barrels, sparkling gems, and looping videos of the Seven Dwarfs kept them engaged, their laughter ringing through the air. The thrill of the ride itself, the rush of wind against their faces as they sped through the twists and turns, only fuelled their joy.

By the end of each day, they were exhausted but exhilarated, already buzzing with plans for the next morning. Tom, grinning from ear to ear, summed it up perfectly, 'This is the best time of my life!'

Family unity was mostly restored, although Danny didn't hold back in expressing his feelings about his father's decision to drop the charges against Rapier. Julie could tell that part of their son admired Malcolm's forgiving nature, and she was relieved once Danny had voiced his opinions and moved on from the matter. Kate decided to take her father's lead and not pursue stalking charges. It seemed to them all that Rapier was just a sad man and probably not dangerous. He wasn't a successful man either, having bungled his attempts to blackmail and intimidate the family and leaving a trail of evidence to incriminate himself.

Another factor which helped restore harmony within the family was Bill Grainger's journals. All the adults had now read them. The story within and the emotion scribed on each page were heart-wrenching. Bill's suffering shocked them all, eliciting a new respect for the man when they considered the difficulties he had faced and overcome.

With their financial worries over, and as they enjoyed the luxury the money brought them, they also discussed how the same money could be used to help others, conversations prompted by Julie. As charity began at home, they unanimously supported the plan to bring Bill home to live; he was now the family hero. Naturally, the decision lay with the man himself, but they hoped he would agree to go along with their plans. Julie's imagination had already been active and she had mentally designed a suite to suit his every need.

One afternoon, as they gathered with drinks in the hotel bar and the children were having a much-needed nap, they intended to have a serious discussion or at least an exchange of ideas, Geoff's phone rang before the conversation began. He looked at the caller ID, made an excuse about it being work, and left the room to take it. Kate's eyes followed her husband, and she sighed.

'Why does he have to take work calls on holiday?' Danny rolled his eyes. 'The place won't fall to pieces without him!'

Kate was quick to snap back at her brother. 'And why do you always have to criticise? Can't you stop having a go at him for once?' Despite her angry words there were tears in her eyes.

'I just think you deserve better.' He shrugged.

'Isn't that up to me to decide?'

'You're right.' Danny winked at Kate to lighten the mood. 'I suppose no one will ever be good enough for my little sister.'

Geoff returned to the room, and the conversation resumed, the awkward moment forgotten. The general consensus was to use the money to help those going through difficult times, and the idea of forming a charitable trust was mooted, with Danny to oversee the administration rather than seek another job. Even though it was only an idea, the list of options increased each time they discussed it. Julie's passion for helping children overseas prompted her desire to direct money abroad for better living conditions, healthcare and education. Danny's wife, Angie, was a cat lover and identified several cat shelters needing finance.

When the children woke and joined them, Tom and Becky chipped in with grand ideas of opening a donkey sanctuary.

Julie persuaded them this would take time and research; Danny would have his work cut out in trying to suit everyone.

The family's selflessness moved Julie, and her pride in them grew. Winning the lottery had brought unexpected sorrow, which she hoped was now behind them so they could enjoy the benefits of financial security and use the money wisely. Her resolve to end her meetings with Sean was also strengthened. She would meet him as agreed one last time to tell him her decision, and then contact would finish. It was for the best.

As their holiday drew to an end, the children elicited from their parents promises of a return to Florida – there was still so much to see and do.

Although it had been a wonderful experience, Julie would be happy to get home. She was keen to commence her search for a new home for herself, Malcolm, and hopefully Bill. And there was her final meeting with Sean to face.

CHAPTER THIRTY-TWO

'I can't believe we had so much excess baggage to pay for.' Malcolm sighed as they carried the suitcases from the taxi into the hall.

'It was a once-in-a-lifetime holiday, Mal. We were supposed to enjoy ourselves, and we can afford it.' Julie smiled at her husband's exasperated expression. 'You'd better put the cases in the spare bedroom until I can sort them out. I'll put the kettle on. I'm dying for a cuppa!'

'Are you sure we haven't got the kids' luggage here as well as ours? I don't recognise two of these cases.'

'Mal. You know they're the new ones I bought while we were away. There were so many things I wanted to buy, things I've never seen for sale here.'

'Yes, and now I know why you want a bigger house.' Malcolm picked up two of the cases and heaved them up the stairs.

By the time the tea was made, all the cases were upstairs, and the couple sat down to enjoy the familiar tranquillity of their home. 'It's been lovely to have the family around but exhausting, too. I don't know where Tom and Becky find their energy, and Daisy keeps up remarkably well. With any luck, they'll sleep off the jet lag and let their parents get some rest.' Julie looked at Malcolm, who was already half asleep beside her. Smiling, she took his cup from his hand, placing it on the coffee table with hers. Snuggling into his shoulder, she closed her eyes and sighed. A nap would do them both good and nothing was spoiling.

An hour later, Julie woke up and extricated herself from Malcolm's arm, which lay across her shoulders. Moving silently from the room, she crept upstairs to start the unpacking. Most of the clothes would go straight in the wash, although there was no hurry to get them clean again. The weather had turned quite autumnal while they'd been away with temperatures they were unused to. By the time Julie had finished her chores, Malcolm was up and about, asking what was for tea.

'What do you fancy?' she asked.

'Boiled eggs with bread and butter.' Malcolm would never be a caviar man, but she preferred plain food, too.

The following morning, Malcolm's priority was to visit Bill. He'd missed his dad, and although the staff assured him he was well each day when he rang, Mal was keen to see for himself. Julie declined to go, saying she was going to make a start on the ironing before going into town to buy some fresh food at the market. 'Tell Bill I'll pop in to see him tomorrow.' She kissed her husband as he left.

Julie wrestled with her conscience for only telling Mal half the truth. Before shopping, she intended to meet Sean Henderson but salved her conscience with the knowledge it was to be their last meeting. After Malcolm left, she'd found the number Sean had given her and rang him to say they were home from holiday. He sounded pleased to hear from her and quite animated as he asked how she was.

'Fine, thanks. I'm coming into town and wondered if you're free to meet?'

'Yes, I'd love to.'

'Okay. Is about 10.30 okay for you?'

'I can't wait.'

Julie grimaced at the note of excitement in his voice, knowing she was about to disappoint him. He was a lovely man, but there was no way they could continue to see each other, even just as friends. It wasn't fair to Sean – or Malcolm.

The autumn wind seemed more penetrating than usual after the Florida sunshine Julie had grown accustomed to. With her head down and collar turned up, she hurried to the bus stop and arrived as the bus pulled up. It stopped within a few yards of Costa, and she entered the coffee shop within twenty minutes of leaving home.

Sean was already there, seated at their usual corner table. He stood when he saw her arrive, a huge smile lighting up his face as he raised his hand in greeting. 'Julie! How good to see you. Sit down, and I'll get your caramel latte.'

'Hi, Sean. Let me get the drinks. It must be my turn.' She turned towards the counter to place her order before he could protest, needing the extra few moments to gather her courage. It seemed strange that Sean knew her preferred drink – Malcolm wouldn't have a clue.

'Here you are.' Julie placed the coffee on the table and sat opposite Sean, who nodded his thanks and then busied himself with adding sugar.

'How are things with your mother?' Julie filled the awkward silence.

'I don't want to talk about my mother. You know what I'm hoping, Julie. Have you given it any thought?'

So, there was to be no small talk. Julie sipped her latte, avoiding meeting his eyes. 'Of course I've thought about it.' She raised her head to look at him. 'I'm sorry, Sean, I haven't changed my mind. Your friendship has meant a lot to me, but I still think we shouldn't meet again.' Her heart ached for him, hating herself for disappointing him when he struggled with many problems.

Sean remained silent for a moment, then smiled sadly and nodded. 'I understand, it's what I expected and I respect you even more for your decision. Malcolm is a very fortunate man.'

Julie felt terrible and could barely look at him. 'I think I should go now. There's no point in dragging this out and making us both miserable. It's been good to meet you, Sean, and I'll never forget your kindness.' She gathered her bag and stood up to leave.

'Don't go just yet. I need this to sink in, Julie. I feel quite devastated.'

Julie hesitated, feeling awful for letting him down. A few more minutes might help calm him, allowing them to part on friendly terms. Noticing that his coffee cup was empty, she spoke softly, 'Let me get you another coffee so we can discuss this a little more.'

'Thank you,' Sean replied with a sad smile. Julie walked to the counter to place the order. While she was away from the table, Sean pulled her half-empty coffee towards him, sprinkled a white powder into it, and stirred it quickly before returning it to her side of the table.

Julie returned with a smile and placed the latte in front of him. 'Here you are. Drink it while it's hot.' They both drank their coffee, Julie unsure of what she could say to ease his disappointment.

'Are you staying much longer in Burnbridge?' It was a feeble question but she hoped to take his mind off their relationship, or non-relationship, before they parted.

'Once I've sorted my mother's house, there'll be no reason to stay.' Guilt washed over Julie at his pitiful look.

'Well, I hope you manage to sell it soon. How's she settling in the home?' Speaking suddenly felt like hard work. Julie struggled to find the words she wanted, so she listened as Sean answered her question, having difficulty taking in what he said.

'Actually, I'm not feeling so good so I think I'll have to go now, Sean.' Pushing her half-finished latte away, Julie stood to leave. Before she knew what was happening, she had tripped over Sean's foot and landed on her hands and knees.

'Julie, are you all right?' Sean's arms were around her, gently lifting her to see if she was hurt. One or two other customers gathered in a huddle to help, embarrassing Julie even more.

'I'll be fine. I'll sit down again for a minute or two.' With Sean taking her weight, she struggled back onto the chair, a sharp pain shooting through her knee.

'Oh!' Julie rubbed her knee.

'Have you damaged your leg? Shall I run you to A&E?'

'No, please, I don't want a fuss. If I rest it for a minute, it'll be all right.' *Well*, Julie thought. *This hasn't worked out as I planned. It didn't happen like this in* Brief Encounter.

'Did you come on the bus or drive?' Sean asked.

'What? Oh, the bus, but the stop's not far. I'll be okay.' Julie felt anything but okay and wanted to be away from the coffee shop and safely back home. Her head was throbbing, and the pain in her knee made her feel nauseous.

'There's no way I'm letting you go home on the bus. My car's in the car park across the road. I'll go and get it and give you a lift.' Sean stood and Julie tried to protest. 'No, I insist. It's the least I can do, seeing as it was my big feet you tripped over. I'm so sorry, Julie.'

He looked quite miserable, and her knee was painful. She smiled and thanked him for the offer, knowing she'd probably not get as far as the bus stop. 'I'll park outside and come back in to help you out. Don't try to walk. I'll be five minutes, tops.' Sean turned and hurried out of Costa.

Julie wondered if she'd bumped her head: she felt pretty confused. An image of Malcolm came to mind and she hoped he wouldn't be home when she returned. How on earth would she explain being driven home by a strange man?

CHAPTER THIRTY-THREE

Immediately after Sean left, the coffee shop manager hurried over to Julie. 'I'm terribly sorry, are you okay?' The cynical side of Julie assumed the man was worried about culpability. Would she claim negligence on the side of Costa?

'I'm fine, thank you. I tripped over my friend's foot; it had nothing to do with your café. He's gone to get his car to take me home.' She smiled to reassure him when she only wanted to put her head on the table and sleep.

'Okay. If you need any help, please shout.' The manager's features relaxed in relief, almost making Julie sorry she'd let him off the hook quite so easily.

True to his word, Sean walked through the door in five minutes and headed towards her. 'How's the knee? Are you sure we shouldn't get it checked out at A&E?'

'Positive. If you can take me home, an hour with a bag of frozen peas should do the trick.' Julie smiled and allowed him to help her up. It felt strange to have another man's arms around her but she needed the support. Putting weight on her leg was painful, yet she did not want to appear a complainer, so hobbled from the shop without saying a word. Sean's car was directly outside, and he opened the passenger side door while holding Julie's elbow to steady her. Easing into the seat, she grimaced, hoping there was no severe damage. Simultaneously, she wondered how to explain the situation to Malcolm.

Sean was swiftly beside her, helping her with the seatbelt. 'Comfortable?' he asked.

'Yes thank you, Sean. Would you mind if I tell Malcolm you were a customer in Costa who offered to bring me home when I fell?' Julie bit her lip, hating asking him to lie but explaining him to Malcolm wouldn't be easy.

'Don't worry about Malcolm.' Sean's expression was somewhat enigmatic as he turned the key and engaged the gears, moving slowly into the traffic.

Julie wondered what he meant and was gripped by a strange unease as they turned off the High Street and entered the roundabout towards the bypass.

'This isn't the way, Sean. You don't need to go on the bypass. I live on the west side of town...' Sean made no effort to alter direction, nor did he answer her. Julie felt dizzy. Was she imagining this? Was she concussed?

'Sean!' A knot of dread tightened in her stomach as she registered the unfamiliar glint in his eyes, the way he gripped the steering wheel a little too tightly. The easy banter they generally shared now felt hollow, replaced by a chilling silence broken only by her shallow breaths. Doubt, cold and sharp, pierced through the fog of her initial trust. The realisation hit Julie like a physical blow – she was in trouble.

'Sean. Stop the car, now! I want to get out!' It was an effort to speak, never mind attempting to leave the car. Her protest fell on deaf ears. They were on the bypass and their speed was fifty miles an hour and rising, Julie grabbed the door handle and pulled. It was locked. Her heart hammered against her ribs, a frantic drumbeat urging her to react. Every instinct told her to do something, to scream – anything but sit passively beside this man she had thought she knew. Yet a paralysing fear froze her in place. Her mind raced, desperately searching for an escape route as the car picked up speed, carrying her further away from safety and deeper into the terrifying unknown.

Mentally shaking herself to rid herself of lethargy and stir some of her usually feisty spirit, Julie turned to Sean and grabbed his arm. He shook free of her grasp with surprising strength and violence, and she flopped back in her seat.

'Don't even think about it!' he snarled.

Julie shivered. She had never been so afraid. Turning towards the window, she banged on the glass and waved her arms in alarm, hoping to catch the attention of other drivers. Sean seized her by the hair and pulled her down until she was on her knees in the footwell. Pain exploded in her leg. His fist thumped into the side of her head, and she screamed as pain shot through her face and blood trickled from her mouth.

Gasping, Julie put her head in her hands and sobbed. Where was he taking her, and why? *No.* She wasn't going to travel down that road. *Think only of the moment, of how to escape.*

Julie dragged herself back onto the seat, pulled a tissue from her pocket and wiped her face, attempting to compose herself and think rationally. 'What do you want, Sean? Is it money? Have you been playing me along all this time?' Her words were slurred, she was losing all sense of reality.

Sean sniggered. 'Did you actually think I was in love with you? Eh?'

Julie was shocked. How gullible had she been? Her head swam, and everything felt unreal, perhaps a dream.

'Had you fooled, didn't I?' He laughed.

Julie had no words to reply. How stupid she'd been to think Sean, if that was his name, was interested in her. Tears of embarrassment and shame stung her eyes as she turned her face to the window.

By the time Sean pulled off the bypass and onto a series of quiet minor roads, Julie was sinking into unconsciousness. She was only vaguely aware of the narrow lane they took with hardly any other traffic. Julie had never felt so low, and barely registered the car pulling up in front of a pretty cottage. She briefly wondered what would become of her, then her eyes closed, and she slipped into oblivion.

CHAPTER THIRTY-FOUR

'I'm home, love! Is the kettle on?' Malcolm closed the front door behind him and shrugged off his coat. 'Julie?' Silence greeted him. His wife was still out; he'd have to make his own tea. Malcolm was pleased with how his visit to his dad had gone, and taking his tea into the lounge, he reflected on their conversation.

Initially, Bill was leaning towards refusing their offer of living with him and Julie, so Malcolm had another shot at persuading him otherwise.

'I don't know what to say, Dad, to make you realise how much we want you to come and live with us. We wouldn't have asked if it wasn't what we wanted. I don't want you to refuse because you think we're simply being kind – honestly, it's what we want.'

Bill reached up and tapped the keys on his bedside computer. *Too much work for you*. It took several minutes to write.

'No, not at all! We'll get help from a professional team of carers. I'm not daft enough to think there's not a lot of work involved in caring for you, but it's no problem. We've already been looking at houses on the internet, and Dan's researching specialised equipment which we can have installed. You'll have a much bigger room than this, and one with a view, which is top of our wish list. You can see the kids when they come round and be part of the family again.' Malcolm stared at the old man, who looked tired and worried. 'Dad, will you answer two questions for me and answer them honestly?'

Bill looked apprehensive but nodded his agreement.

'Is it because you're so happy here and you don't want to leave this place?'

Bill smiled lopsidedly and shook his head as best as he could.

'Would you like to see more of Julie, me, and the children?'

Another smile. Bill appeared to know he was defeated and attempted a nod.

'Okay then, I don't see the problem, so here's one more question... honesty, remember. Do you want to come and live with us?'

The nod continued, and Bill's smile grew wider than Malcolm had seen it for years. He hugged his father.

'That's settled then. As soon as we find a place and make the necessary alterations, you'll come home to us!'

On his way home from his visit to Bill, Malcolm went to the kennels where Trixie had been boarded. The welcome he received was nothing short of rapturous. The little dog scrambled at his legs to be picked up and then wouldn't stop licking his face.

As the manager gathered Trixie's belongings, she said, 'Trixie's such a pleasure to have. All the staff love her, and I'm afraid she gets spoiled!'

'Thank you. I know she's happy here, and thanks for the pictures you sent of her playing in the field. It's reassuring to know she's not pining.'

'No, it's like a holiday for Trixie, too. She's such a brave little sweetie.' The manager rubbed the dog's ears and said goodbye. Man and dog headed home, delighted at being together again, with Malcolm anxious to tell Julie the good news about his dad, knowing she'd be pleased.

Alone in the house with just his dog, Malcolm glanced at the clock and realised it was 12.30pm. Nothing was prepared for lunch in the kitchen, and the ironing Julie was going to do was still sitting in the laundry basket. Where could she be? Malcolm tried calling her mobile phone, but it went straight to the answer phone, so he left a message. 'Hi, Julie, I've got some great news – I can't wait to tell you. Where are you? Ring me back when you get this. Love you!'

All he could do was wait until she arrived home or rang. To fill time, Malcolm fired up his laptop and started trawling through the listings of houses. It wasn't much fun without Julie's perceptive comments on each one, but some new ones on the market might be worth a look. He'd show them to Julie when she came home.

An hour later, Malcolm was growing concerned. He rang Kate to ask if she'd heard from her mother that morning. A negative answer did nothing to allay his fears. He'd tried Julie's phone several times but it still went to her answerphone.

Danny had heard nothing from his mother either. 'She's probably got carried away shopping or met someone for coffee and forgotten the time.' He tried to reassure his dad, but Malcolm knew his wife would have rung to let him know; Julie was always mindful of how much he worried.

To fill the time, Mal rummaged in the freezer and found a tea cake, which he toasted and then made another mug of tea. There wasn't much else in the house to eat until Julie came home with the shopping. Where was she? He should have gone with her and visited his dad later. Huh, hindsight.

By 3pm, Malcolm was seriously worried. There was still no

answer on her phone, which wasn't at all like Julie. He considered calling the police, but they'd probably laugh at him – what woman doesn't lose track of time when shopping? He didn't want to worry the children again, but what else could he do?

Deciding to give it another half hour before ringing Danny and Kate, Mal prowled restlessly around the house. He'd just come downstairs to call the children again when the phone rang. He grabbed at it and almost shouted, *Julie?* But the voice which answered wasn't his wife's.

CHAPTER THIRTY-FIVE

Danny and Kate were with their father within half an hour of his emotional phone call. Both were horrified at his words, 'Your mother's been abducted,' and left their homes immediately to be with him. Kate left Daisy with a neighbour, claiming a family emergency and Danny's wife remained at home as it was time for the children to return from school.

After exchanging hugs, the three of them sat in the lounge, feeling more shocked and worried than they had ever thought possible. Kate had never seen her father cry and was taken aback by how distraught he appeared.

'What did he say, Dad? Tell me his exact words.' Danny wasted no time in getting to the point.

Malcolm sniffed and blew his nose. 'He said he had Julie and she would be returned safely when he received a million pounds in cash...'

'And are you sure it was genuine, not another crank call?'

'Absolutely! He used something to make his voice sound sort of robotic, it was terrifying!'

'You can get an app to do that. What did he say?'

'He said there was to be no police involvement. He wouldn't

let me speak to Julie – said she was asleep. Hell, Danny, do you think he's hurt her?' Malcolm's eyes filled with tears again, and Kate gasped at his words.

'No! Don't go down that road, Dad. Whoever it is wouldn't risk hurting Mum. She's too valuable to him. Did he say when and where he wanted to collect the money?'

'He'll give us forty-eight hours to get the cash and ring again with details. I told him I'd need to speak to Julie first, and he just laughed. That's when he put the phone down.'

'We'll have to call the police, Dad.' Kate was shivering even though it wasn't cold in the house.

'But he might... hurt her...' Malcolm looked from one to the other of his children, hoping for inspiration.

'I don't think we should go to the police. He specifically said not to, and if he thinks they're involved, he might panic and do something stupid.' Danny was thinking more rationally than his father and sister. 'The safest thing to do is to go along with him, do exactly what he says and get Mum back. Then we can go to the police – and if they track him down and recover the money, all's well. Even if they don't get the money back, having Mum safely home will be worth it!'

Malcolm and Kate nodded in agreement as he outlined what seemed to be a simple transaction. 'First thing in the morning, we must go to the bank to withdraw the money.' Danny was taking charge and Malcolm was relieved. 'I think we should each withdraw a third of the money, Dad – if you go into your bank and ask for £1m, they'll be suspicious. They may even have a legal responsibility to call the police.'

'What if we can't get a third of it? Don't they have daily limits on cash withdrawals?' Kate's eyes were wide with fear as she looked to her brother for an answer.

'We'll think of something. I know my bank manager was tripping over himself to be of service when Dad deposited a million into my account. I'm sure he'll agree to help if we come up with a plausible story.'

'I hope you're right, Dan. But what can we do now? The banks are closed. We can't just carry on as if nothing's happened.' Kate sniffed.

'I'm going to stay here with Dad tonight. I'll ring Angie and let her know. Maybe we'll not get much sleep, but we can jot down any ideas that come to us. For starters, we need to work out our approach to the bank. You'll be better off going home to Daisy. We can keep in touch by phone if there are any developments. Discuss it with Geoff and see if he has any ideas, particularly for getting the money.'

Kate pulled a face. 'Can't I stay too?'

Malcolm shook his head. 'No, love. Danny's right, you should be with Daisy and Geoff. We'll keep in regular contact and meet again early in the morning to decide our next move.' Malcolm kissed his daughter on her forehead and steered her towards the door. 'Let us know if Geoff has any ideas.'

When Kate left and Danny had phoned his wife, he asked his dad more questions. 'Have you told me everything about your conversation with this man? You weren't holding anything back to avoid upsetting Kate, were you?'

'No, son, I told you everything. I wish he'd have let me talk to Julie then I'd know she was safe.'

'And did you check the caller ID after he rang?'

'Of course, I did. I'm not stupid. The number was withheld.'

'Okay, Dad. I'm sorry I asked. Now, let's see if we can find something to eat, and then we'll start our brainstorming session.'

CHAPTER THIRTY-SIX

Julie woke up in an unfamiliar place that was dark and draughty. Her head throbbed painfully, and a thick fog clouded her thoughts. Her tongue was stuck to the roof of her mouth, and when she managed to free it, she discovered her lip was swollen and sore from when Sean hit her.

Panic surged hot and immediate as her eyes flickered open. Where was she? How did she get here? Julie's emotions were in turmoil, and her heart raced as disjointed memories flitted through the haze, and the image of a man – Sean Henderson – came to mind. Dizziness overtook her as she tried to sit up, but fear, cold and sharp, gripped her when she realised her hands and feet were tied. She flopped back down again, internally urging herself to think. She remembered being driven down an isolated lane and catching sight of a cottage at the end. Was she inside it? And where was Sean Henderson?

Afraid to shout out, she decided that being alone was preferable to attracting the attention of that hateful man. Lying still, she tried to ignore the pain from her knee and organise her thoughts. With no street lights outside, the darkness was thick and solid; Julie couldn't make out any shapes to give her a clue to her surroundings. A scratchy rug was beneath her, and her foot touched a wall as she stretched her legs.

Suddenly, she felt nauseous and turned to the side to vomit. Remembering the wooziness in the coffee shop, she wondered if Sean had drugged her. This man had planned his actions. Julie didn't know where she was, but felt certain the drive hadn't been too long so it wasn't far from Burnbridge, although it was an area unfamiliar to her.

As she rolled onto her right side, away from the smell of her vomit, tears leaked from Julie's eyes. Not usually one to feel sorry for herself, she indulged in a few moments of pity – for her stupidity of falling for 'Sean' and his fake attentions. What a fool she'd been. He'd played her along, and she'd been taken in by his sob story – the man probably never had a mother – if he had, she'd certainly not be proud of him!

A noise abruptly ended Julie's pity party. Sniffing and blinking back her tears, she prepared to come face to face with Sean. A door opened and light flooded into what appeared to be a hallway, momentarily blinding Julie as she squinted against the glare.

'Enjoyed your sleep?' Sean's mocking voice sounded gruff, unfamiliar. How had she ever thought she'd known this man – found him attractive even? Shame washed over her. How could she have thought of him in such a way?

Sean hauled her to her feet, ignoring Julie's cry as pain ripped through her knee. Terror drowned out the pain as she saw a blade glinting in the light. For a moment, she thought he would kill her, but mercifully, he reached down and slit the rope binding her ankles together. Sean gripped her arm tightly and half dragged her into the room he'd come from, roughly throwing her onto a small sofa. Julie's protective instinct was to curl into a foetal position, but she was determined not to show her terror. She sat straight, lifted her head, and looked him in the eye. The man laughed, moved silently toward the kitchen, and returned with two mugs of steaming liquid, one of which he placed on the coffee table in front of Julie. She raised her bound hands to indicate that she couldn't drink, but he laughed and said, 'I'm not falling for that. If you want the drink, you'll find a way to manage.'

Julie leaned forward, grasped the mug, and took a welcome sip of the hot tea. With no idea of the time or how long she had been unconscious, all she knew was that she needed a drink because her mouth was dry. She scanned the room, taking in her surroundings and searching for a potential escape route. The cottage was comfortably furnished, possibly a holiday let, which she would have been enthusiastic about at any other time. It was small but warm and clean.

'Do you like our little holiday home?'

Sean's words shocked her. What sort of game did he think this was? 'I'll be missed at home. Malcolm will probably have called the police by now.'

'No, he won't. Malcolm's had his instructions and knows not to be so foolish as to call the police – that is if he wants you back.'

'I'm assuming you want money?' Julie was sickened by the man she'd thought was a friend.

'Unless there's anything else on offer...' He grinned as she turned away, unable to look at him. 'And we were getting on so well, Julie. I thought you would willingly walk into my arms, but you had to spoil it, didn't you? Deciding you couldn't be unfaithful to poor old Malcolm, and your duty lay at home. How saintly of you!'

Julie wanted to spit at the man, but resisting, she asked, 'Did you plan this from the start or after I told you we'd won the lottery?'

'Oh, it was all planned out before we met. The article in the local paper went viral online, telling me all I needed to know. When I saw your smiling face, I knew you were ripe for the picking.'

Julie despised herself for being so incredibly foolish, her naivety a bitter pill to swallow, and now she was dealing with the consequences. They'd freed themselves from that terrible man, Rapier, but now a new predator had taken his place. How many more people would attempt to con them out of their money? Julie had been stupidly optimistic in assuming folk would be happy for them, and it seemed greed was a powerful motive for acts of evil. The joy of their lottery win felt like a distant memory. Julie sincerely regretted their windfall.

CHAPTER THIRTY-SEVEN

Sean untied Julie's hands only to allow her to visit the bathroom and to then clean up the mess in the hallway where she'd vomited, and an unpleasant smell lingered.

He then bound her wrists with the same type of rough cord he had used before. Julie winced at the pain, bringing a smile to Sean's face. 'If I could trust you to be nice to me, we could forget about the binding.' He leered at her – his face too close. When Julie turned her head away, he shoved her roughly on the sofa.

She had no idea of the time, but her growling stomach and the darkness outside hinted at the lateness of the hour. She was back on the sofa from where she watched Sean in the kitchen area of the open-plan space. He opened a fridge and removed two wrapped sandwiches. From what Julie could see there wasn't much else in the fridge – a loaf of bread and a few brown paper packets, possibly from a bakery. She wondered if the lack of provisions was a good sign and perhaps their stay would only be for a short time. He threw one of the sandwiches at her and opened the other for himself.

After struggling to open the wrapper, Julie wolfed down the sandwich, grateful her ordeal was apparently not to include starvation. It was hardly enough to fill her, but when Sean finished his, he made a cup of coffee, which Julie drank gratefully.

'How long are you going to keep me here?' She braved the question which troubled her greatly, along with several others.

'That all rather depends on dear old Malcolm. If he can get the money for your release, he can have you back as soon as he pays me. If not... hmm, maybe we'd best not go there!' He laughed as Julie's face paled and she thought better of asking more questions.

It was probably late evening when Sean grabbed her arm and steered her up a flight of stairs to the bedroom. Julie's heart raced as she stumbled into the room, followed by relief as he pushed her inside and left, closing the door behind him.

Struggling to stand, pain shot through her knee, and her wrists stung beneath the taut binding. It was no longer pitch black as a small lamp burned on a bedside cabinet, casting shadows over the room. Sean must have switched on the light earlier, and she offered a prayer of thanks for small mercies. Was it also a sign that he wasn't going to hurt her? Hopefully, his only interest in her was as a bargaining tool. Julie sat on the edge of the bed and attempted some serious thinking.

Was escape possible? With no idea of how long Sean had given Malcolm to get the money together, yet assuming it wasn't long, she doubted he would leave her alone in the cottage until he went to collect it. Sean would want this over almost as much as she did. He'd clearly made plans... finding an isolated cottage and the food in the fridge necessitated forethought. Should she wait out her ordeal and hope to be released when the ransom was paid? It was probably the only sensible option, yet her instincts screamed at her to do something, to try to escape.

Overpowering Sean was an improbable option; he was a tall, well-built man, and at five-foot-two, Julie was no match for him, especially with her hands tied. If, by a miracle, she did manage to escape from the cottage, could she outrun him? Not with the pain in her knee; putting weight on her leg was excruciating. And where would she run to? From her hazy recollections of being driven here, the cottage was isolated and well away from any main roads.

Julie considered talking to Sean and reasoning with him, but this was another unlikely scenario. She remembered his eyes, which she'd once found attractive but now betrayed a chilling lack of empathy. Her assessment of him was so different from the Sean she'd met in the café, and Julie blushed with shame as she recalled her feelings towards him then. No, he was not a man to be reasoned with, not the man she'd thought him to be.

Pulling the duvet over her aching body and hoping for a temporary respite of sleep was tempting, but Julie was a natural fighter. Scanning the room, her eyes rested on the window, and she hobbled over to examine it, hoping to learn more about her surroundings. The world outside was cloaked in darkness, the moon obscured by a thick curtain of clouds. Only the silhouettes of trees hinted at a garden beyond. As expected, the old window frame was firmly shut, and the catch secured tightly. Sean was thorough and cunning. The fleeting idea of smashing the glass flickered briefly through her mind but was quickly extinguished. Even if she possessed the strength, the shattering noise would serve as an unwelcome alarm. Frustration welled in her stomach, and hot tears stung her eyes as she drew the curtains closed. With a sniff and a determined lift of her chin, she continued to scrutinise every inch of the room.

The wall adjacent to the window sloped to three or four feet from the floor. An ottoman fitted snugly under the eaves and Julie limped towards it, sitting on the upholstered top with a thump. Viewing the room from a different angle offered no new insight into a means of escape. A faint draught and a sliver of light came from under the door. Julie strained to hear any sounds but heard only her erratic breathing and the thumping of her heartbeat.

Assuming it was late and Sean had retired to bed, Julie finally crawled between the clean sheets and switched off the lamp, thankful for small mercies. She'd read stories of people being kidnapped and held in filthy, appalling conditions; it was hard to accept that the situation could be worse, but she persuaded herself it could be. The absolute silence enveloped Julie, and with the frightening events of the day looping through her mind, it took a long time for her to fall asleep, her pillow wet with tears.

CHAPTER THIRTY-EIGHT

It was 6am and Malcolm had been awake for most of the night. He and Danny talked into the small hours, covering the same ground without fresh ideas or insights on how to proceed.

Kate had phoned several times, and her husband, Geoff, spoke to both Malcolm and Danny, adding his opinion, which was to involve the police. Father and son were set against that course of action, and Danny struggled to keep his temper with his brother-in-law.

Malcolm dressed carefully, wearing one of the new shirts Julie had bought for him, in an attempt to make a good impression at the bank. There was no sound from the spare bedroom as he crept downstairs to put the kettle on, so he hoped Danny was still sleeping. The kitchen, Julie's domain, seemed empty and hollow without her presence. The whole house had a different feel, and thinking about it brought a lump to his throat. *Don't cry again, Mal. Pull yourself together.* Julie was the homemaker; without her, the atmosphere was cold and unwelcoming, and he longed to have her back with him, to hug her close and tell her how much she meant to him.

'Morning, Dad. Did you get any sleep?'

Mal hadn't heard his son enter the kitchen. 'Not much. And you?'

'The same. Are you making coffee?'

'Yes, want some?'

'Please. We need to eat something too. I'll get some bread from the freezer to toast; we can't be flaking out with hunger today.' Danny smiled at his father and Malcolm nodded, watching his son shuffle about while he made the coffee.

'Any new ideas overnight?' he asked. Danny shook his head. It was as Malcolm expected.

'I wonder how Mum is?' Danny voiced what they were both thinking and Mal groaned.

'Best not to go there, son.' He sniffed, passed Danny a mug of coffee and changed the subject. 'Do you think we should ring the banks or just turn up and ask to see the manager?'

'If we ring, they'll want to fob us off with an appointment some other time or ask too many questions. I think it's better to go and try to see someone in person.'

'Okay. The trouble is it's all these fancy machines they have these days and hardly any staff to speak to.'

'You'll have to insist, Dad. If necessary, threaten to move your account to another bank, which is what I'll be doing.'

Malcolm nodded and took a bite of his toast.

'I'll just ring Kate and then we'd better get going.' Before he could do so, the doorbell chimed and when Malcolm answered the door, Kate, Geoff, and Daisy were waiting to enter.

'Hi, Dad.' Kate kissed her father as Daisy reached out to be taken by him. 'Anything new?' The four adults settled in the lounge, and Daisy wriggled free to crawl on the floor.

'We've heard nothing else. The plan is still to go to the bank this morning and try to raise the money.'

Geoff seemed keen to voice his opinion which hadn't changed overnight. 'Are you sure this is the best way forward,

Malcolm? Let's call the police. They're the professionals and will get Julie back without paying a ransom.'

'Can you guarantee that?' Danny jumped into the conversation, clearly annoyed with his brother-in-law. 'If he knows the police are involved when he's specifically forbidden it, it's a huge risk. But if we give him the money, they can be involved after we have Mum back safely.'

'I disagree...' Geoff lifted his chin, staring at Danny.

'But she's not your mother!' Danny interrupted angrily. 'What is it with you? Do you not want to part with any of your share of the win now it's safely in your clutches?'

'Danny!' Mal grabbed his son's shoulder to keep him in his seat. 'We can do without you two arguing like schoolboys. Geoff, we're doing it this way. If you don't want to go to your bank for the money, I'll ask for more from mine.'

'No, honestly, Malcolm, it's not about the money. I disagree with paying blackmailers on principle.' Geoff's face reddened.

'Yeah, so do I, but this is Julie we're talking about, and I'll do anything to get her back. I believe doing what we're told is the safest way to achieve this. Now, will you try to get your third from the bank?' Malcolm replied. 'Or shall we count you out?'

'Of course we will,' Geoff looked at his feet, all bluster gone. Kate was crying softly, trapped between her husband's and her dad's opinions. She picked Daisy up from the floor and held her close.

'Good.' Malcolm stood to go. 'I'll be outside my bank as soon as it opens, and I'll not leave until I get the money. I suggest you do the same. And remember, don't mention this is to pay a ransom demand – they'll probably have to report it to the police.'

After agreeing to meet again after securing the funds, they trooped sadly to their respective cars.

CHAPTER THIRTY-NINE

Malcolm was the first customer through the bank's doors at 9.30am. One or two others followed him in and headed for the machines lining the walls, while Malcolm went to the only attended desk. Being a gentle, polite man, he greeted the clerk and asked if there was any way he could withdraw more than their £500 a day cash limit.

'Sorry, sir but not without seven days' notice.'

'Then could I please see the manager?'

'Do you have an appointment?' The bank clerk, who looked about sixteen, asked.

'No, but I have a situation which needs immediate attention.'

'I'm sorry, but if you don't have an appointment, there's no way the manager can see you today. Can I offer you a slot a week on Tuesday?' The child clerk blinked and stifled a yawn.

The sting of refusal set a vein pulsing angrily in Malcolm's temple. 'Look,' he said, leaning forward until his nose almost touched the plexiglass screen. 'I understand there are rules, limits, blah blah blah. But as I said, I've got a situation. A delicate, time-sensitive situation. And frankly, your daily withdrawal limit is an insult. I don't like to be pushy, but unless you ask the manager if he'll see me, I will insist on closing my considerable account and I'll not be leaving your premises until I have what I want.'

The clerk's nostrils flared. 'What name is it, please?' He swivelled his computer towards him and typed into the keyboard as Malcolm recited his name. 'Oh!' his face flushed. 'You're *that* Mr Grainger! Could you wait here a moment while I have a word with the manager?'

Malcolm nodded. The amount of money in his account was clearly more persuasive than anything he could say.

It took less than three minutes for the young man to return with the manager, who held out his hand towards Malcolm. 'Mr Grainger! Good to see you again. What can I do for you today?' The bank manager, a mousy man with a receding hairline, fidgeted with his collar.

'Could we talk in private?'

'Certainly. Please follow me.'

When they were seated at opposite sides of a large desk holding nothing except a computer, Malcolm inhaled deeply and attempted to phrase his request. 'I find myself in a somewhat delicate situation, Mr Billington, and need to make a cash withdrawal which exceeds your daily limit.'

'I see. Our limit is £500 but in your case I'm sure we can stretch it to, say, £1,000.' He smiled, the great benefactor.

'I had £350,000 in mind.' Malcolm watched the manager's chin drop as he leaned back in his chair.

'Er, may I ask why such a large amount?'

'You can ask but it's rather sensitive and I'm afraid I can't divulge my reasons. I assumed, as I was holding several millions with you, that this could be accommodated?'

'But these limits are in place for all our clients. Security protocols, you understand.'

'Security? I'm in a position where I need to move mountains, not worry about molehills.' Malcolm's voice was tight, barely controlled. He clenched his teeth, determined to get what he wanted in order to have Julie safely back home. This had to be fixed and quickly. He watched as the little man behind the big desk considered his position. In an effort to persuade him he reminded the manager, 'You're currently holding nearly twenty million pounds of my money – surely what I'm asking is just a small percentage of the whole?'

'We don't carry such large amounts of cash in this branch...' Mr Billington seemed to be considering the logistics of saying yes. Mal wanted to encourage him, to get him on-side.

'If it could be arranged, I'd be very grateful, and naturally, I expect to pay a fee for your inconvenience. I could come back later, but it's imperative I have the money today.'

'Can you give me a minute, Mr Grainger?'

'Yes, of course.'

Billington left the room, presumably, Malcolm thought, to make a call or two in private. The pulse in his neck throbbed again – he didn't dare consider what would happen if the answer was no – and how were Danny and Kate faring? Rubbing his temples, Mal concentrated on breathing regularly; he couldn't go to pieces now when Julie needed him more than ever.

Twenty minutes later, Mr Billington returned to his office with a folder in his hands. 'I've made a few calls and my superiors need to know why you're requesting such a large amount, so I have some forms...'

'No!' Mal's voice sounded angrier than he intended. 'I'm sorry but I told you I can't divulge why I need this money. It's a personal matter.' His leg started shaking and he pressed his hand to his thigh to control it. His heart pounded as he stared at the bank manager, willing him just to hand over the money.

'This puts us in a rather difficult situation.' He stroked his chin, thinking. Malcolm was feeling desperate. What could he do to persuade the man?

'I'm not money laundering or anything like that – it's money I need for a particular reason and, honestly, if you can't help me this once, I *will* move my account to another bank.'

With a raised eyebrow, Billington again excused himself and left the room. Malcolm rested his arms on the desk, letting his head drop onto them. Tears pricked the back of his eyes; he couldn't fail. Julie's life depended on it.

The door opening made Malcolm jump. Mr Billington entered the room and took his seat behind the desk. 'Good news, Mr Grainger. We can accommodate you this time, but we request that you provide us with more notice in the future. There will be an administrative fee, as we need to order a special delivery, which may not arrive until mid-afternoon.'

'Thank you, this means a lot to me. I appreciate you making this exception, and I'll certainly never ask again.' Malcolm spoke too quickly, his overwhelming relief coming out in garbled words as he shook the bank manager's hand. He couldn't wait to leave the bank and ring his children to see if they had been successful. Arrangements were made for Mr Billington to ring Malcolm when the money was available to be collected, and Mal left feeling one step closer to being reunited with Julie.

Once outside the bank, Malcolm grabbed his phone and scrolled to find Danny's number. When his son answered, the news was good; he'd also been firm and threatened to move his funds elsewhere, a tactic he disliked as much as his dad, but it had been effective. When Kate reported her and Geoff's success at their bank, everything appeared to be going to plan, and Malcolm hurried home to meet with his family.

CHAPTER FORTY

Pulling into the driveway of his home, Malcolm was dismayed to hear raised voices from inside. Opening the door, he was confronted by Danny and Geoff squaring up to each other with Danny about to punch his brother-in-law.

'What the hell's going on here?' His voice rose over those of the others and silenced them. Clearly they'd not heard him enter. The two stepped apart; Geoff turned to sit beside Kate, who was sobbing on the sofa, while Danny paced angrily around the room.

'Has something happened?' Malcolm feared the worst for a moment.

'Only that this idiot intends to go to the police!' Danny spat the words out, pointing at Geoff. Malcolm glared at his son-in-law.

'No police, Geoff. We agreed, and it's not your decision to make; it's mine, and we'll do it as the kidnapper says.'

'But there's no guarantee he'll release Julie...' Geoff stuttered.

'And there's no guarantee the police will find her either.' Malcolm's expression warned of the futility of dragging up this argument again. Geoff studied his shoes, silenced and outnumbered.

Kate blew her nose and stood. 'Shall I make some tea?'

'Yes, love, thank you. And if anyone wants to eat, there's bread and cheese but not much more.' Food shopping had been the last thing on Malcolm's mind.

Geoff followed his wife into the kitchen and Mal turned to Danny. 'Thumping him won't help. He has a right to have his opinion but I think he understands now that the decision is ours.'

'Bloody arrogant sod. He always thinks he knows better than anyone else – I don't know what Kate ever saw in him.'

'Enough, Danny. He's family and we'll treat him with the respect he deserves.'

'Only by marriage...'

'I said enough. We have other things to discuss.'

'Sorry, Dad. When do you think the kidnapper will ring?'

'He said forty-eight hours, and that was yesterday evening. I shouldn't think we'll hear from him until tomorrow.'

'So what do we do until then, twiddle our thumbs?' Danny was antsy, needing something to occupy his mind. 'Any ideas?'

Geoff and Kate returned to the lounge. 'Ideas about what?' Kate asked as she placed a tray of tea and cheese sandwiches on the coffee table.

'What to do. We can't sit around all afternoon and night until the kidnapper decides to ring.'

Malcolm spoke his thoughts. 'I was thinking about tracing Julie's last movements – see if anyone saw this man take her. I'm pretty sure she wouldn't have got in a car without a fight.'

'Not a bad idea, Dad. Where was she going when she left home?'

'To town. She wanted to stock up on fresh fruit and

vegetables at the market, but she'll probably have gone to other places too, maybe even for coffee somewhere.'

'It's somewhere to start and better than doing nothing. Kate, do you want to come? If we take photographs, we can ask some of the market traders if they saw her.' Danny had left Geoff out of the invitation.

Kate looked from her brother to her husband. 'If you think it will do any good, I'll come. Geoff, can you pick Daisy up from your mum's and look after her?' The answer was a curt nod as Geoff stood and left the room. Kate sighed. 'He'll sulk for a few hours and then come round. So, what's the plan?'

'I'll find some recent photos, and then I think we should eat those sandwiches and set off as soon as possible.' Malcolm left his children and climbed the stairs.

As soon as he was out of hearing, Kate turned to Danny. 'Do you think it will do any good?'

'Not sure. If anyone saw Mum being taken, surely they'd have called the police? But I can't sit and do nothing and it'll be better for Dad to be active rather than sitting around worrying.'

Twenty minutes later, the three headed for the town in Danny's car, each armed with a photograph. 'Did Mum take the bus?' Kate asked.

'Yes. We'll park on Tower Street. It's close to where she'd have got off the bus. Shall we split up?' Malcolm wasn't sure he wanted to do this alone.

'Maybe you and Kate should stick together and I'll go alone,' Danny suggested. 'I'll start at the market and visit all the fruit and vegetable stalls. You could try the coffee shops. Does she have a favourite, Dad?'

'She's mentioned Costa Coffee a few times recently; we'll try there first and then the one in Debenhams.'

Splitting up as they exited the car park, Danny promised to ring if he discovered a sighting of Julie, and Malcolm agreed to do the same. It was early afternoon and the town centre was buzzing with shoppers. As Kate and Malcolm entered Costa, the queue at the counter almost reached the door. 'Perhaps we should go on to Debenhams first; it might be quieter,' Kate suggested. Malcolm, who disliked Costa due to the noise of the coffee machines and the length of time it took to make a coffee, nodded in agreement and they left the shop.

On his way to Debenhams, Malcolm stopped at the butcher's shop Julie liked to patronise. After waiting in a queue for several minutes, he asked the young man behind the counter to look at the photo and tell him if Julie had been in the shop the previous day. The butcher looked suspiciously at Malcolm and then at the photograph.

'It's my mother; she's gone missing,' Kate explained.

'Oh, I'm sorry. Yes, I do know this lady. She's a regular, but she wasn't here yesterday. Hey, Paul!' he shouted to his colleague, who came over and looked at the photo. 'Did this customer come in yesterday?'

'Nah. It's been two or three weeks since she's been in.' Paul moved away to serve a customer, and Kate thanked the man and took Malcolm's arm to steer him out of the shop.

'Are you okay doing this, Dad?'

Malcolm felt sick and dizzy. This whole situation was surreal – they were just an ordinary couple, yet here he was, showing photos of Julie and asking if anyone had seen her. He was glad his daughter was with him.

'I'll be okay, love. It's just a bit odd. Thanks for stepping in there – I'd never thought about what to say if anyone asked why we were looking for her. We can hardly say she's been kidnapped, can we?'

'No, saying she's missing should be enough. That's all anyone needs to know.' They'd reached the entrance to Debenhams and Kate opened the door for Malcolm to enter.

The café was on the second floor and much quieter than Costa. Kate showed the photograph this time and did the talking but none of the staff remembered Julie being there the previous day.

On the way back to Costa, they called in at a bakery that Julie particularly liked and at the post office. No one had seen her recently.

The queue at Costa was much shorter than before, and they stood in line waiting their turn. While Malcolm checked his phone for any missed calls from Danny, Kate impatiently drummed her fingers on the counter. Finally, a girl looked at her and offered a 'Yeah?' Kate showed her the photo, explained it was her mother and asked if she had been in.

'Yeah.' Kate and Malcolm stared at the girl. 'She's the one who fell over and hurt her leg.'

'And this was yesterday?' Malcolm asked.

'Yeah.'

'What happened after she fell?' Mal was growing frustrated.

'Dunno. I went on my break, but I think the manager spoke to her.'

'And is the manager here? Can I speak to him?'

The girl shrugged.

'It's important!' Malcolm emphasised. She nodded and then disappeared through a door at the side of the counter. Kate took the opportunity to call Danny and tell him the news.

'I'm on my way!' Danny panted, already running.

CHAPTER FORTY-ONE

'Are you the couple asking about the woman who fell yesterday?' The manager hurried towards them and spoke rapidly, a frown creasing his brow. 'Because she admitted she tripped over her friend's foot – it wasn't our fault.'

'We're not here to apportion blame. My wife is missing and we're trying to discover where she is.'

'Oh, right. Look, why don't you come through to my office?' The man's face relaxed and as Malcolm and Kate followed on, Danny came dashing through the door and tagged on behind them.

With only one available seat besides the manager's in his cramped office, Malcolm gratefully sat down while Danny and Kate stood behind him. Kate passed over the photograph of Julie. 'Is this the lady who fell?'

'It is. And you say she's missing?'

'That's right. She didn't come home yesterday evening; as far as we know, this was the last place she was seen. Do you remember anything else about her?'

'Can't her friend tell you where she is? He went to get his car to drive her home, or I presume it was to drive her home...'

'Are you sure she was with a friend?' Danny asked.

'Oh yes. They occasionally meet here for coffee and always sit at the same table in the corner.'

Malcolm felt his heart pounding in his chest. Julie wouldn't have met a man here without his knowing. 'Please, look at the photo again. Are you sure it's her?'

'Yes. Gina recognised her too.'

Danny put his hand on his dad's shoulder. 'And what about her friend? Can you describe him?'

'Fairly tall and average looking. About the same age as the lady, I suppose. Look, if she's missing, shouldn't you go to the police?'

Danny chose to ignore the question. 'Do you have CCTV we could look at, please?'

'We have it, but I can't just let anyone see it – data protection, you know.'

'My mother is missing and we need to know who this man is!' Danny's voice sounded intimidating and the manager stood up.

'If you want to see the CCTV footage, you must return with the police. It's more than my job's worth to allow just anyone to see it.' He opened the door to allow the Grainger family to leave, saying no more.

No one spoke until they were back in the car. 'Maybe he's mistaken and it wasn't Mum.' Kate broke the silence.

'But the girl, Gina, recognised her too.' Danny chipped in, earning a dark look from his sister.

'Let's go home.' Malcolm sighed.

The journey was silent, but the car's three occupants were thoughtful. Malcolm searched his mind to rationalise why Julie would be with another man. Could it be someone she'd recently met and bumped into again? An old friend she'd forgotten to mention, or was the glaringly obvious answer the real reason – Julie was seeing another man behind his back.

The house felt cold, the silence oppressive. 'I'll put the kettle on.' Kate headed straight for the kitchen while Danny ran upstairs to the bathroom.

Malcolm removed his coat and shoes, pulled on his slippers and made his way to the lounge. He suddenly felt old and sad. The only bright spot was the welcome he received from Trixie, who bounded towards him with her three-legged gait. As he sat, she jumped up on his knee.

'Oh, Trixie! I don't know what to think now…' The little dog licked Malcom's cheek as a tear rolled down.

Kate brought in coffee and the leftover sandwiches from dinner time. 'Try to eat something, Dad. You need to stay strong.' She pushed a plate into his hand and a mug on the coffee table beside him.

Danny joined them and took a mug. 'It might not be what you're thinking.'

'And what am I thinking?'

'Come on, Dad. I saw your reaction when the manager told us Mum had been meeting with another man. All I'm saying is don't jump to conclusions. There could be a simple explanation for her seeing him, and we should give Mum the benefit of the doubt.'

The conversation was interrupted by the telephone. Malcolm answered and was distracted from other thoughts by the bank manager, who told him the money had arrived and would be ready to collect by 4pm.

'He suggested I take a large holdall or a suitcase,' Malcolm told his children.

Kate looked worried. 'My bank won't have the money until tomorrow at 10am,' she said. 'I thought that would give us enough time.'

'It will, love. I don't think we'll hear anything until the afternoon. How about you, Danny? When can you collect your money?'

'I have to be at the bank before 4.30pm. I'm going there as soon as I leave here.'

The discussion regarding Julie's relationship with the man they now assumed to be her kidnapper was pushed to the back of their minds as they made plans to meet later.

'I'm going now,' Malcolm said. 'I'd rather be early and wait, and I suggest you do the same, Danny. Kate, perhaps you should get off home to see Daisy and Geoff. I'll ring you when I'm back and you can come round tomorrow when you have your money. We can wait for the call together.'

Malcolm saw his children out and mechanically prepared to leave for the bank. His emotions felt shredded as the suggestion of the afternoon's discovery swirled in his mind. Surely Julie didn't know this man? Not his Julie…

CHAPTER FORTY-TWO

'A hundred notes in each bundle, a mix of twenties and fifties as you didn't specify...' Mr Billington's voice faded into the background as Malcolm's mind wandered. He wasn't entirely present, lost in thought as the bank manager filled the holdall with bundles of cash.

Mr Billington paused, staring expectantly at Malcolm, who finally registered the silence.

'Sorry, what did you say?' Malcolm was jolted back to the present.

'Just checking if you were all right, Mr Grainger. You seem a little preoccupied.'

'My apologies. I was miles away.' Malcolm forced a smile and held open the holdall he'd brought with him as Mr Billington lifted bundles of notes into it. Thankfully, no more questions were asked, and Mal was grateful to be out in the fresh air and on his way home.

Trixie greeted Malcolm with her usual enthusiasm and affection, and he fed her before taking her for a long walk, as much to clear his mind as to exercise his dog. The money was nestling in the back of the understairs cupboard where he'd thrown it on his arrival home. Barely keeping up with his dog, when they reached the park, Malcolm was happy to sit on a bench and allow Trixie to sniff around the trees; she never ventured far, always keeping him in her sight. Tiredness lay heavily on his body, the numbing cold adding to his misery.

As daylight faded, Malcolm's thoughts grew maudlin. He closed his eyes and imagined he was watching his wife and this man through the steamed windows of the Costa Coffee shop. His mind spun with unpalatable thoughts, as if he was an outsider, watching... curious, concerned. Well, terrified was probably the more accurate term. In his mind, he saw Julie talking to this man in the corner of the coffee shop, their heads close together in an intimate conversation. Who was he? Had she been seeing him romantically, or was there an explanation for her not mentioning him? More pertinently, was this stranger involved in his wife's disappearance?

Malcolm had never felt so alone in his life. Usually, Julie was there to talk to when something troubled him, her down-to-earth logic shrinking any problem as she offered solutions or even made him laugh at his concerns over trivial matters. Or he could talk to his dad, but he couldn't trouble Bill with this; he, Danny and Kate had decided not to tell him of Julie's kidnapping in the hope it would be resolved quickly.

Trixie barking interrupted Malcolm's reverie. Opening his eyes, he saw the little dog sitting before him, tongue lolling and head on one side as if curious about what troubled her master. Mal fished a tennis ball from his pocket and threw it for Trixie, her favourite game. She ran after it, tail wagging with such enthusiasm it seemed to propel her forward, making up for her missing limb, her ears flapping like wings in the breeze. Trixie skidded to a stop, her one front paw digging into the soft earth as she targeted the ball. With a joyous bark, she pounced, tumbling head over paws in a flurry of playful abandon. The ball, captured beneath her chest, became a prize which she picked up and carried proudly back to Malcolm, who rose from the bench and clipped Trixie's lead on her collar. 'Enough for now, girl. Let's go home.' The dog trotted alongside him, obedient and loving as if understanding his anguish.

The evening dragged, broken only by two phone calls, one from Kate and one from Danny, neither of which lightened Malcolm's mood. He forced himself to make and eat a fried egg sandwich, turned on the television and channel-hopped for half an hour before turning it off and climbing the stairs to bed.

The hours dragged as Mal tossed and turned, longing for sleep. Each time he drifted off, he'd reach out his arm and jolt at the realisation that Julie was not beside him. His eyes felt gritty, his body like lead, but he heard the church clock strike three before he finally fell into a restless sleep.

Malcolm was adrift, weightless, in a black expanse dotted with pinpricks of silver light. Each pinprick pulsed faintly and echoed in the silence. He reached out, fingers brushing against nothingness, and the light erupted around him. Faces he knew were suddenly before him – his mother, her smile strained; his father, eyes filled with sadness; his grandmother, who was trying to tell him something. Then Malcolm was at school again, the bullies taunting him, telling him his mother was going to hang. Phillip Rapier laughed in his face as he pushed him to the ground. Other faces appeared, strangers judging him, whispering, mocking.

His stomach lurched as the familiar weight of despair pulled him down into suffocating darkness. Malcolm clawed at the faces, their features blurring, their voices echoing in his skull as he plummeted into the void, the light fading, leaving him alone in the chilling emptiness.

CHAPTER FORTY-THREE

Malcolm woke to the sound of the doorbell. Reaching for the clock, he was horrified that it was almost 9am. He'd slept far later than intended. Danny's voice called up the stairs and Malcolm responded by pulling on his dressing gown and going downstairs. 'Sorry, son. I must have slept in. It took me ages to get over.'

'That's okay, Dad. I don't think any of us managed to sleep. Kate's just pulling up, looks like she's alone.'

'I'll have a quick shower and join you soon. Put the kettle on and make yourselves some coffee.' Malcolm climbed the stairs and headed for the bathroom. He heard his daughter's voice as he closed the door. It was good to have their support. He didn't think he'd get through this ordeal without them.

The jets of hot water were welcome as Malcolm rolled his shoulders to ease the tension in his neck and arms. He dried off and dressed quickly, anxious to talk to his children and get their thoughts on the day ahead.

Kate and Danny were in the kitchen and didn't hear their father approaching. Malcolm stopped outside the door and sighed. They were arguing again.

'What do you mean, Geoff has an important meeting? What's more important than getting Mum back? He's a selfish bastard. I don't know why you married him.'

'Because I love him? And don't call him that. It's awful! His mum's minding Daisy, and if Geoff was here, you'd probably only argue, so maybe it's better he's not.'

'Yeah, you're right there. He'd only want to involve the police and put Mum at more risk. Anyway, have you had any more thoughts on this man Mum was with in Costa? Do you think she's been cheating on Dad?'

'Oh, Danny, don't say that. She wouldn't. Mum's not like that, and she loves Dad.'

'They say that no one really knows what goes on in a marriage. Parents don't tell their children everything; look at the secret past Dad's been keeping from us all these years. We hadn't a clue about it, did we?'

'No, but this is our Mum we're talking about. And if she was having an affair with this man, why would he kidnap her?' Kate poured milk into her coffee and sat at the table, her face creased with worry.

'Maybe she hasn't been kidnapped and they're attempting to get the money to run off together?'

'Now that's just plain ridiculous. Half the money is Mum's anyway – why would she fake her kidnapping?'

'Yeah, I suppose you're right. It could be that he has nothing to do with her disappearance. She may have been taken after she left him.'

'But no one else appears to have seen her. It seems she didn't get any further than Costa.'

Malcolm couldn't listen to any more. He entered the kitchen and sat beside his daughter. 'Thinking up wild theories isn't getting us anywhere.'

Kate blushed while Danny looked away. 'Sorry, Dad.' Kate

reached over to take his hand. 'You know what it's like when you can't sleep and your mind goes to some pretty dark places?'

'Yes, I know, love.' Malcolm had also considered most of these scenarios yet couldn't admit it to his children.

'Sorry, Dad, but I must go to the bank now; it's nearly time to get the money.' Kate stood and kissed her father, leaving the two men drinking coffee and trying to think of something to say. When the door closed behind her, Malcolm chastised his son.

'You shouldn't be so hard on Geoff. He is entitled to his opinions, as we all are, and he's good to Kate and Daisy. He might not be your choice for your sister but she loves him.'

'Yeah, I'm sorry. I know he's good for Kate; it's just that sometimes he's so smug – he knows everything about any subject we're discussing, and it's irritating, to say the least.'

'We all have our faults, son. So, do you have the money?'

'It's in a bag in the lounge. And yours?'

'Under the stairs. I kicked it there when I got home and haven't touched it since. I'd gladly give him the whole twenty-two million to get Julie back.' Malcolm's face crumpled. He covered his eyes with his right hand. 'Do you think she was having an affair?' He looked up at Danny, tears in his eyes.

'No, I don't. If you heard my stupid conjecture, that's all it is, conjecture. Mum loves you. She wouldn't do anything to hurt you. Whatever's happened to her has nothing to do with her actions; it's that bloody man who's taken her. Look, Dad. I need to go out for an hour, will you be okay alone for a while? Kate shouldn't be long, and when I get back, we'll wait with you until we hear from the kidnapper. Goodness knows what he'll expect us to do, but we'll go along with him; anything else is too risky.'

'I'll be fine, Danny. You get off and do what you need to do. I've got Trixie for company. She'll be wondering where her breakfast is.' Malcolm scratched the little dog's ears and stood to prepare her breakfast while Danny quietly exited the front door.

While alone, Malcolm took the opportunity to make a phone call to the home where his father lived. Knowing Bill would be expecting him to visit, Mal was torn between going and telling his dad everything or making an excuse to protect him from the horrors of what his family were enduring. He decided on the latter.

As much as Mal hated lying, he dialled the number he knew by heart and spoke to the care home manager. Asking her to give a message to Bill, Mal told her that he and Julie had flu and were too ill to visit. The manager agreed they should stay away until clear of infection; she didn't need to elaborate on the effect of taking infections into a residence full of vulnerable people.

CHAPTER FORTY-FOUR

Gina Robinson hated her job at Costa. The manager was a bully whose overbearing presence greeted her each morning and he had a knack for belittling her in front of her colleagues. The pay was hardly worth getting out of bed for, and she didn't even like coffee. Give her a strong mug of tea any day.

The title of *barista* was meant to instil pride and accomplishment but a title couldn't pay the bills and Gina found herself dreaming of cash that could actually make a difference in her life. Even the customers could be demanding. They complained about everything from the prolonged waiting times and cramped seating to the draught every time the door swung open.

School holidays were torture when bored mothers brought screaming children to meet with their friends – anyone would think they were running a creche. The constant noise of the espresso machines and whingeing babies gave her a headache – what she wouldn't give for an easier way to make a living.

Occasionally, something happened to break the monotony. Gina had enjoyed watching her boss grovel when a lady tripped over, and he feared she might sue. The woman looked familiar, but Gina assumed it was because she was a regular customer. It wasn't until the following day that she recognised her family when they arrived asking questions. The son and daughter looked familiar, too, and Gina remembered seeing a picture of the lottery winners in the newspaper. They lived on the same street as her Auntie Babs; she was sure it was them but could hardly ask.

The boss was as snooty as ever and refused to help the family even when they said the woman was missing. When they left, Gina dreamed of what it would be like to win serious money. She took her dinner break shortly after they went and googled the family. Wow! Twenty-two million pounds! Gina whistled through her teeth.

What she'd give for that kind of money – she could give up her poxy job, travel to exotic places, buy a smart flat in a good area of town. She thought of the designer handbag she'd coveted in that posh department store, a win like that and she could get a dozen bags, and clothes and shoes! Gina was almost dizzy thinking of all the goodies she could buy.

When she'd finished her sandwich and can of Coke, Gina went outside and lit up a cigarette, still fantasising of what she could do with the money. Heading towards the coffee shop was the same man from the morning, the good-looking son, striding out with a purpose. Gina stubbed out the cigarette and put it back in the packet for later, then dashed back inside, her mind processing too many thoughts to be rational.

The young man bought a latte and took it to the corner table, the one where his mother usually sat. He seemed antsy, checking his watch and looking around all the time. Gina wondered if he was meeting someone. After a respectable time, she sauntered over to collect cups from the next table. He noticed her and she smiled – it wouldn't hurt to be pleasant to a good-looking young rich guy, would it?

'Hello again,' she said. 'Did you find the lady you were looking for?'

'No. Your boss wasn't very helpful.' He took a sip of his latte.

'That doesn't surprise me.' Gina smiled. 'Maybe I can help?'

He looked a little more animated. 'Is your boss not here?'

'Nah. It's his half day off; he left half an hour ago.'

'The lady we're looking for is my mother. She didn't come home last night and we're worried something may have happened to her. Is there any chance you could let me have a look at the CCTV footage for yesterday? Or perhaps you could copy it for me?' Danny held up a memory stick he'd brought for the purpose.

Gina moved closer so as not to be overheard. 'You're the guy who won the lottery, aren't you?'

'Well, my parents are; what's that got to do with anything?'

'Nothing – except one good turn deserves another. If I help you, I'd risk losing my job; maybe you could make it worthwhile?'

'How does a hundred pounds sound?' Danny sighed.

'Five hundred sounds better.' Gina countered without a breath.

'Five?'

'Shh. I'm taking a big risk. If you give me twenty minutes and come back with the cash, I'll see what I can do.'

Danny handed over the memory stick and drained his latte. 'Fine. I'll have to go to the bank, so twenty minutes?'

Gina nodded and moved away. The office wasn't locked as it doubled as a store room so she shouldn't have much of a problem. She told her colleague she had a headache and was taking five minutes to grab some paracetamol in the office. It was getting busy, so she shouldn't be disturbed. The system was basic, and it didn't take long for her to find what she needed.

While waiting for the footage to download, Gina wondered if she should give the man her phone number. The thought of all that money was seductive; she could be really nice to a man who was rich. Another thought crossed her mind – why had his mother done a runner? Maybe the bloke she was with was her secret lover and they'd run off together. Even now, they could be on a tropical island somewhere, enjoying the sun and sipping cocktails. Why didn't people like her win the lottery? Life wasn't fair!

Twenty minutes later, Gina watched the door anxiously. Had she asked for too much? But she was risking her job, and for a man with millions, five hundred wouldn't be missed. Still, seeing him enter only a few minutes late was a relief.

Gina walked over to look for empties away from prying eyes, and Danny moved alongside her. 'Well?' he asked.

Grinning, she took the memory stick from her pocket and slid it into his hand, pressing her boobs into his arm. Danny stepped back, and pulling an envelope from his pocket handed it to her and turned to leave.

'What's the hurry?' Gina placed a hand on his shoulder. 'I can let you have my phone number if you fancy meeting up sometime?' She tilted her head to the side, a playful smile on her lips.

'I'm choosy who I mix with.' Danny shrugged her hand from his shoulder and marched from the shop, leaving a red-faced Gina feeling angry and humiliated.

CHAPTER FORTY-FIVE

Sean Henderson was furious. He'd been enjoying his first cup of coffee of the day and dreaming about the money coming his way when the doorbell chimed, making him jump. Who the hell was calling at this time in the morning? He dashed to the door, determined to intercept whoever it was before Julie woke. A middle-aged woman stood on the step, a bicycle at her side and a beaming smile across her plump face.

'Good morning! I'm Maisie,' she chirped. 'I clean and look after the cottage for the owners and I wondered how you're settling in and if you need anything?'

The urge to snarl at the woman and chase her off was overwhelming but might raise suspicions. He forced a smile and pressed a finger to his lips. 'Shh, my wife's still asleep.'

'Oh, I'm so sorry...' Her giggle suggested she wasn't.

'We don't need anything, but thanks. Please don't bother to call again. Must dash!' Sean shut the door in her face and watched through the frosted glass as she mounted her bike and cycled away. He hadn't expected a nosy cleaner to come by – he'd explicitly told the owner he wanted solitude.

A loud rapping on the upstairs window startled him. Julie.

He sighed, a wave of relief washing over him – that was a close one. It was time to face his captive.

Julie's sleep had been punctuated by the pain in her knee and fear of the following day's outcome. She had no way of knowing the time, but it was daylight when the sound of a doorbell woke her. Pulling herself together, she took a few moments to remember where she was before hearing voices from below the window. Unable to make out the words, she struggled to climb from the bed and hobbled over to the window in time to see a woman peddling away from the cottage on a bicycle.

Her heart pounded. *No, no, no!* Julie banged on the window, tears streaming down her face as she shouted and slammed the glass as hard as possible. The woman didn't look back and soon disappeared through the trees and into the distance.

Julie was furious with herself for missing the chance to attract attention. She hobbled back to the bed and lay down, but the sound of a key in the door terrified her.

'What the hell do you think you were doing? If that woman had seen or heard you, I'd have had to kill her and maybe you as well!' Sean spat the words out, causing Julie to tremble. She clutched the duvet to her chest as if it could protect her from his anger. 'You can bloody well stay locked in here now – no more concessions!'

He turned, slammed the door and Julie heard the key turn in the lock. It was one of the saddest sounds she'd ever heard and profoundly affected her. Was Sean a killer? She didn't know him, and it was a chilling thought. Julie sat still, frozen in both body and mind. Any bravery or tactics she might have considered the previous night deserted her as she stared into the pretty cottage bedroom, her chintzy jail.

Julie was hungry but, more urgently, needed to pee. Should she bang on the door and beg Sean to allow her to use the bathroom? No. Some pride remained in her, but might not if she didn't pee soon.

Recalling her search of the room the night before, Julie remembered a bucket and some cleaning materials in the back of the wardrobe. Needs must, she thought and used the bucket to relieve herself.

Staggering back to the bed, Julie glimpsed her image in the dressing table mirror – she looked awful. Her face was swollen, with a crust of dried blood on her lip where Sean had struck her. He was clearly an angry man, but was he violent enough to kill her as he'd suggested? Her knee, too, was swollen and more painful than the previous day. All thoughts were negative – not surprising. Julie had never been in a situation like this. Danger and violence happened to other people, not ordinary middle-aged women like her.

Feeling sorry for herself wouldn't get results; she needed to be proactive. Did Sean have a weakness she could exploit? Julie didn't know the man, so this was a dead-end. Could she somehow overpower him? Gazing around the room for a potential weapon, the lamp seemed the most likely tool. She unplugged it and removed the shade. Yes, it was a heavy base. When Sean next came into the room she could hit him over the head and make a run for it.

But what if the blow didn't render him unconscious? She'd be afraid to hit him too hard in case she killed him – Julie couldn't live with someone's death on her conscience, even someone as despicable as Sean. If he was unconscious, would she be able to escape? Wouldn't Sean have all the doors locked and maybe even the keys hidden? And if she did get outside, how would she reach safety? They appeared to be in the middle of nowhere, and her leg was virtually useless.

Think, Julie! You're not a quitter – you have so much to live for.

Julie's head ached. She couldn't think straight. Thirst gnawed at her and her stomach growled. Curling into a ball on the bed, she was inclined to do nothing, to wait it out and hope and pray that her family would pay the ransom, or if the police were involved, they would find her. Pulling the duvet over her head, Julie pressed her eyes tightly closed to hold in the tears she was ashamed to let go.

CHAPTER FORTY-SIX

Kate arrived back at her parents' home before her brother. Malcolm was relieved to see her; being alone was excruciating and his thoughts ran riot without the distraction of company. 'Did you get the money?' he asked, knowing it was a stupid question as his daughter was lugging a large holdall through the door. Kate nodded.

'Where's Dan?' She looked past her father to the kitchen, but everything was quiet.

'He had to go out and didn't say where.'

'Typical. He shouldn't have left you alone, Dad.'

'No worries, I'm fine.' The look on Kate's face told him she didn't believe him. He changed the subject. 'Is Geoff coming round later?'

'If he can get away from work, he'll be here, but we haven't any idea when we'll get the call, have we?'

'No. I shouldn't think it'll be late. The kidnapper will be almost as anxious to get this over with as we are.'

'To get hold of the money, you mean!'

'I'll willingly give it to him if only he lets your mum go...'

'I know, Dad.' Kate hugged her father, led him into the kitchen and turned on the kettle.

'You're just like Julie. A cup of tea and a chat solves everything, but this time it doesn't!' The door slamming saved Kate from having to reply. Danny shouted hello and joined them in the kitchen.

'Where've you been? You shouldn't have left Dad on his own.' Kate frowned at her brother.

'I had something to do – something I hope will be helpful.' He pulled a memory stick from his pocket. 'This should tell us exactly what happened to Mum. Where's your laptop, Dad?'

Malcolm hurried off to find it while Kate asked what was on the memory stick. As Malcolm returned with the laptop, Danny took it from him and fired it up. 'This is a copy of the CCTV from Costa!' If his words had been written, they would have been in a cursive script, ending in a flourish.

'But how did you get it? The manager was adamant he wouldn't let us see it.' Kate was stunned.

'I didn't ask the manager. I approached that dozy girl, Gina or something, and she was interested in earning a few quid on the side. Serving coffee all day doesn't exactly pay well.'

'How much?' Kate asked.

'A hundred,' Danny lied, reluctant to reveal the true figure. 'And I hope it's money well spent. You see, money does talk.'

The three leaned over the kitchen table to watch the memory stick load onto the laptop and reveal its secrets. 'There might be nothing on it, of course. The manager did say they usually sat in a corner, didn't he?' Danny's insensitive words earned him a kick under the table from Kate.

The footage, with a time stamp in the corner, started at 8am. 'Fast forward,' Malcolm urged. 'I don't want to watch hours of people getting coffee. Try around 10am. Your mum was still home when I left at 9.30, so she wouldn't have been in town much before ten.'

Danny scrolled through the footage, pausing occasionally to check the time. Slowing back down to real-time, the three watched silently as people flickered across the screen – grabbing coffees, greeting friends, carrying out cardboard trays of steaming drinks. At precisely 10.25am Malcolm drew in a sharp breath. 'There she is!'

He pointed to the screen but didn't have to. Julie was unmistakable as she approached a table at the far end of the café. A man sat with his back to the camera. Julie's gentle touch on his arm sent an unwelcome jolt through Malcolm's body. Watching the scene unfold was both painful and surreal. He swallowed, grateful for the comforting squeeze of Kate's hand on his.

Julie spoke briefly to the man and then went to the counter to order.

Malcolm's eyes bored into the back of the man's head, willing him to turn around to allow them to see his face.

Julie returned to the table, slid into the seat opposite the man, and placed two cups on the table. She smiled warmly at him.

'She certainly knows him then,' Danny observed. The others remained silent, eyes glued to the screen.

Malcolm's heart raced, each beat thumping loudly in his chest until he was sure his children would hear it. It came as something of a relief when he noticed Julie shake her head at something the man said. She looked away as if saddened by how their conversation had turned, and Mal's hope sprung again to life. They continued their conversation until Julie stood again, and Malcolm sat forward in his chair. His eyes followed his wife intently as she almost immediately tripped over and fell to the floor. Her companion was on his feet, helping her, as other customers offered assistance. When the man turned towards Julie, his face became visible, and Mal almost choked. 'No, damn it, no! It can't be…'

Kate grabbed his arm. 'Dad, what is it? Do you know him?'

'Yes, it's Phillip Rapier!'

'Rapier? But it can't be.' Danny tapped the keyboard to enlarge the image. 'Are you sure?'

Malcolm put his head in his hands as Rapier's face expanded on the screen. 'Yes, it's him, there's no doubt.'

'But I thought he'd returned to Liverpool – the police scared him off, didn't they?' Kate shuddered as she stared at the man's face. Danny had paused the footage as the three discussed this staggering development.

'He was released with only a caution, partly because Dad wouldn't press charges!' Danny looked scathingly at his father, whose face reflected the horror and fear he was feeling.

'Enough, Dan!' Kate stopped him from saying more. 'What's done is done. We have to get through this now. Does knowing it's Rapier make a difference? I mean, when he gets the money, the police will be able to find him, won't they?'

'Don't bank on it!' Danny hissed. 'He appears to have more guile than we gave him credit for.'

'Danny's right. He must have sobered himself up and applied thought to this plan. He's more astute than I gave him credit for. Play the rest of it.' Malcolm stiffened as he turned back to the screen.

The incident played out before them. Julie was clearly in pain as she struggled to rise and rested back on the chair. Rapier was attentive, and Malcolm wanted to smash the phoney, concerned look off his face. They watched Rapier leave, and the manager approached Julie with more fake concern. Malcolm almost broke down as he watched his wife grimace with pain and, a few minutes later, let Rapier lead her from the shop, supporting her on his arm.

The atmosphere in the kitchen was grim as the family processed this new information and tried to assess if it made any difference to their plan. Malcolm was the one to make the decision. 'I think we should go along with what Rapier says and not let him know we've discovered his identity. If he thinks he's been rumbled, he might harm Julie, and we can't risk that happening. Hopefully, now we know it's Rapier, it will give the police something to work with when we have your mum safely at home.' His children nodded. It was the most sensible thing to do. Neither of them had an alternative suggestion.

'Bloody Rapier!' Danny banged the table with his fist.

Malcolm placed his hand on Dan's arm and, with his other hand, took hold of Kate's hand. 'We have to play his game, son, and it's a waiting game until we hear from him.'

CHAPTER FORTY-SEVEN

While the Grainger family enjoyed their Florida holiday, Phillip Rapier skulked back to Liverpool. His anger at Malcolm Grainger had barely diminished, and the man figured largely in his frequent daydreams of revenge. Phillip hadn't been in the house for ten minutes before the nosy hag from next door rang the doorbell, unable to wait to tell him the police had been around looking for him.

'I know,' he lied. 'I witnessed an accident, and they wanted a statement. Nothing to concern yourself with, Mabel.' Closing the door in her face, Rapier swore under his breath. Perhaps he shouldn't have approached Grainger personally. He should have done it anonymously so he wouldn't be on the police radar. But he smiled to himself as he pondered plan B, which he'd had the forethought to implement alongside his direct approach when he learned of the Graingers' lottery win.

In the kitchen, he opened the fridge. Nothing but a stale lump of cheese and a couple of cans of beer. Grabbing a beer, he slumped on the sofa and pulled the ring tab. Gulping nearly half the contents, Rapier reminded himself that he must keep control this time; he had kidded himself that the alcohol helped him think straight, knowing he'd messed up and would have to be more circumspect.

He'd enjoyed playing with Julie, pretending to be an admirer and spinning his sob story – he even quite liked the woman – Grainger was a lucky man. But Julie was a commodity, the way to his fortune, which meant he'd have to tread carefully.

Since his old school friend had struck lucky, Rapier's thoughts had travelled down some strange rabbit holes. Why should he give up his quest to squeeze money from the Graingers? They owed him now, especially after involving the police. Tipping the remaining contents of the can down his throat, he vowed to try again. This time, he'd make sure his plans were foolproof – he'd already devised a strategy and put in hours of work gaining Julie's trust. It was time to reap the rewards of his efforts and make his second attempt, which would command a higher reward, and he'd have to disappear afterwards.

As his anger fizzled out, Phillip focused on his plan. First, he turned on the heating; the house was freezing. Next, he unpacked and threw all his clothes in the washing machine. Then, he searched for his passport to check if it was still in date. It was. With a smile, he turned on his laptop and commenced his research with a notebook at his side.

An hour later, Phillip Rapier's face held an even broader smile. He'd always fancied visiting the Caribbean and was delighted that the Dominican Republic was ready to welcome him with open arms. A visa to travel there for less than thirty days was unnecessary, and only a nominal tourist card fee was incorporated into airline charges. Further research encouraged him to believe the cost of living was almost forty per cent cheaper than in the UK, and best of all, no extradition treaty existed. Foreign nationals could purchase houses if they had money and could apply for citizenship after five years. Gorgeous beaches and sunny weather topped his celebration cake with icing.

On his first night home, Rapier dreamed of hot sand between his toes, cheap alcohol, blue skies and beautiful girls. Awaking in a good mood was a novelty for him, and after showering and dressing, Phillip, keen to set the cogs in motion, left the house in search of breakfast and a visit to the supermarket.

Returning home, he put away his groceries and then spent half an hour deciding what to do with his possessions. He owned little of value – a thrill passed through him as he thought how this was about to change – and resolved to pawn or sell what he could. The house was rented. He was in arrears for several months, which no longer worried him. He planned to go soon without leaving a forwarding address. Phillip chuckled, remembering how, as a child, he dreamed of being the invisible man. His dream was about to come true.

The following part of his plan was to rent an out-of-the-way place reasonably near Burnbridge. It was out of season, so hopefully he could pick up a bargain; no one wanted a country cottage in early October. The internet came to his rescue again, and he found the perfect holiday cottage, two miles from the nearest village and only seven miles from Burnbridge. There was a direct number for the owners, and it took only twenty minutes to secure the cottage for three weeks, starting in the second week of October. He paid in full on his credit card, a card he wouldn't be paying off – he'd be out of the country before the bank discovered his abuse of their system. Having spun a tale of being a writer needing quiet to complete his latest novel, renting the cottage didn't appear suspicious.

Shopping for his trip commenced with a fancy new luggage set, purchased with his credit card, naturally. Summer clothes were next on the list. Over the following days and two lengthy trips to Liverpool centre, Phillip decided he had enough – he could buy whatever he wished for in the Dominican Republic.

With his preparations complete, Rapier's final task was to write a letter to his landlord. He slipped it into an envelope, sealed it, and sought out his relentlessly nosy neighbour, Mabel. Casually, he asked her to pass the rent cheque on to the landlord, telling her he was off on another trip. Naturally, Mabel bombarded him with questions, which Rapier skilfully deflected and made his escape. If Mabel could read the contents of that envelope, it would turn her face a dozen shades of crimson.

CHAPTER FORTY-EIGHT

The day stretched on, each minute an eternity. Malcolm watched the clock hands crawl, his children mirroring his anxiety. No one felt much like eating, but Kate, stepping into her mother's shoes, coaxed them into sharing a sandwich, a small act to maintain their strength.

Angie rang Danny several times, asking for updates and each time, the answer was the same: there were none. Although she wanted to help, it had been decided it would be better for her to remain with Tom and Becky; the less the children knew of the situation, the better for all.

Geoff kept in constant touch with Kate, who informed him when they discovered the abductor's identity. Through his wife, Geoff made another attempt to persuade the family to go to the police, arguing that this new information significantly increased their chances of apprehending Rapier and bringing Julie home.

'No.' Was Malcolm's final say on the matter. 'I know Geoff means well, but we'll continue with Rapier's instructions. Once Julie's safely home, we'll go to the police, not before.' The subject was finally closed.

The atmosphere grew incredibly tense as time dragged on.

Fear was perhaps the dominant emotion – fear for Julie and that they were doing the right thing. Malcolm remained quiet, only speaking when asked a direct question or when he needed to correct or comfort his children, yet he could barely hold himself together. When would Rapier ring?

Danny hovered by the phone, although it was decided that Malcolm should answer when the call came. His eyes oscillated from the phone to his father and then his sister. Malcolm sensed the anger rising within him. Waiting was an agonising limbo that the three felt to varying degrees.

Kate wavered between bouts of silence and talking too much, too quickly. Mal could tell his daughter was nervous as she attempted to mother them all, making endless unwanted cups of coffee and repeatedly saying their ordeal would soon be over.

Malcolm knew she was right, yet couldn't control his fearful thoughts about how it would end. Would Julie be safely returned to them? His fear was compounded by pre-emptive guilt. Would he mess up Rapier's instructions? Should they have involved the police? Had he somehow put Julie in the position of seeking comfort with another man?

Periods of talking lapsed into deafening silences. Malcolm didn't know which was preferable; he longed for the telephone to ring so he could do something to bring Julie home. He paced the floor, looking out the window, hoping to see Julie coming down the garden path, laughing and saying it had all been a colossal mistake. It wasn't going to happen. Fanciful thoughts brought more pain, which could only be eased by knowing his wife was safely home. The sight of Julie's knitting bag, tucked away behind a chair, brought a lump to Malcolm's throat. How he longed to see her doing something as mundane as knitting while he watched the football on the telly.

The clock on the mantelpiece chimed the hour – 3pm – and

the phone finally rang. Malcolm scrambled for it, his palms sweaty, his heart hammering against his ribs. 'Yes?' his voice was hoarse.

'Drive south of Burnbridge to the old quarry,' the distorted voice instructed, flat and devoid of warmth. 'You'll find a row of recycling bins at the gatehouse. Stash the money behind them. Then, go to the far end of the quarry and take the first right, leading back onto Burnbridge Road. You'll find a lay-by about a hundred yards down; park there and wait. Once I've confirmed everything is in order and that you're alone, Julie will be released to meet you there.'

'Let me speak to Julie!' Malcolm was terrified Rapier would end the call, leaving him unsure if his wife was okay. 'Then I'll bring the money.'

'I'm the one giving the orders.' Rapier almost barked the words before laughing humourlessly.

'Mal?' Julie's voice sounded weak, fearful.

'Julie! Are you all right, has he hurt you?'

'I'm okay... please come and get me...'

'Right, Grainger, you've heard your wife, now get in the car and drive to the quarry – alone – or perhaps your precious Julie won't be so okay!' The phone went dead.

'Dad, let me come with you,' Danny pleaded.

'No, Dan. You heard him, we'd be risking your mum's life. I'm going to do as he says, then he's no reason to hurt her, and he doesn't know we know his identity.' Malcolm was shuffling his feet into his shoes as he spoke. 'You stay here with Kate and I'll ring as soon as I have your mum back.'

'And what if you don't?' Danny snapped, earning a reproachful look from Malcolm.

Holding back her tears, Kate hugged her father as he set off, and Danny clasped his arm, his expression showing remorse for his comment.

Immediately after Malcolm left, Danny called Angie to update her, and Kate moved into the kitchen to call Geoff. They knew the old quarry wasn't far, only about five miles out of town, but it was anybody's guess how long Malcolm's mission would take or if it would be successful.

CHAPTER FORTY-NINE

Malcolm reversed his car out of the driveway, suddenly panicking about whether he had enough petrol for the journey. The petrol gauge showed the tank to be half full, and he whispered a prayer to thank God, whom he hoped was on his side.

At the end of the road, he waited to turn right, aware of his heart pounding and his hands trembling. Inhaling deeply to calm himself, Malcolm knew he'd be no good to Julie in a state of panic. He must be strong and concentrate on Rapier's instructions – it was a matter of life and death.

Malcolm kept to the speed limit. This wasn't a time to be pulled over for speeding or to have an accident. Most of the traffic was heading north, early commuters returning to Burnbridge from Leeds and Harrogate. The quarry was well known to locals, even though it had been disused for many years. It wasn't a place Malcolm had visited before.

He turned into what would have been the work entrance and drove two hundred yards down a rough track, peering ahead to see the row of bins Rapier had mentioned. A small hut, presumably the gatehouse, came into view, and as he'd been told, a row of dusty bins was lined up adjacent to the hut. Malcolm pulled up alongside them and exited the car. Taking in his surroundings, he thought he saw movement beside an abandoned portacabin. Could Rapier be watching him? Was Julie with him?

Opening the boot, Mal hauled the bags from inside and placed them behind the bins as instructed. He glanced again at the portacabin, not wanting to stare in case he spooked Rapier – if he was there.

Adhering to the instructions, Malcolm climbed back into the car and drove slowly to the far end of the quarry, where he turned right. As Rapier had said, there was a lay-by about a hundred yards along the road where he pulled in and switched off the engine. It was a long lay-by, the sort lorry drivers used for rest breaks. There were no lorries, but another car was parked about sixty yards from his, and he could make out two figures inside. He hoped the presence of another vehicle wouldn't deter Rapier from releasing Julie.

Malcolm sighed, wondering how long he would have to wait. He attempted to put himself in Rapier's shoes. He'd probably wait to ensure Malcolm was alone and no one was following him, so it could have been him near the portacabin. Presumably, after a reasonable time, he'd collect the money, check it and then release Julie. Maybe he'd let her out of his car near the lay-by and make his escape before Malcolm could see him or his vehicle. It was all speculation. He needed fresh air and stepped out of the car, taking in huge gulps of the cold, damp air.

Glancing towards the couple in the car at the other end of the lay-by, he thought were looking at him. He hoped they didn't think he was a Peeping Tom and wished they would leave before Rapier saw them. Should he go over and ask them to go? He'd be risking an argument, or worse, but they could ruin his chances of getting Julie back. He walked towards the car, unsure what to say but terrified their presence would scare Rapier away.

Before Mal reached the car, a man climbed out and strode towards him. Was he in for a thump?

'Mr Grainger!' The man knew his name – what was going on? 'Please go back to your car. We're here to help you get your wife back.' He briefly waved what Mal thought was a warrant card. Malcolm was stunned. Police. How did they know where he was? The answer was clear: it had to have been Danny or Kate who were the only ones who knew the meeting place – Mal's money was on Kate, or more likely Geoff if she'd told him.

'Get away!' Malcolm shouted, waving his hands frantically. 'He said no police!'

The officer jogged closer. 'Please return to your car and wait inside, Mr Grainger, and I'll do the same. We'll not move until we know your wife is safe.' He turned and walked back to his colleague. Malcolm hurried back to his car, angry tears streaming down his face. As he closed the door, his phone rang.

'Mr Grainger, this is the police. We're here to help apprehend Phillip Rapier and return your wife to you. Please stay in the car. We have other officers in the area.'

'No! Rapier said no police, you're putting Julie in danger!'

'Not if you stay calm and wait for Rapier to come. We'll take it from there...'

Malcolm ended the call before the officer could finish. He then found Kate's number and rang her. 'What the hell have you done?' he shouted.

'Dad, listen – Geoff said it was better to get the police involved. They'll follow Rapier and get the money back.'

'No! I don't want the damn money; I want your mum! He had no right to involve the police – they're sitting in the lay-by for all to see! Rapier won't be fooled by them pretending to be a courting couple!'

Kate's response was to sob, repeating *sorry* to her dad.

Malcolm ended the call and allowed his thoughts to wander to dark places. All seemed lost. Was it Rapier he'd seen near the portacabin or more police? All he could do was wait and hope Rapier wouldn't see the police and stick to the plan.

CHAPTER FIFTY

An hour crawled by, the sky darkening as rain gathered, heavy clouds promising a downpour. Malcolm remained in his car, unmoving, oblivious to the cold seeping into his bones and the tremor running through him. His mind held only one thought: he'd blown it. Rapier wouldn't leave it this long to get his money and release Julie – unless perhaps he was waiting for the cover of darkness; that would make sense, or was Mal fooling himself?

As heavy drops of rain pounded on the car roof, Malcolm's phone rang. It was the police. 'Are you sure you have the right place, Mr Grainger? Could you have misunderstood Rapier's instructions?'

'I'm sure. And I'm sure I want you to leave – the man won't come when he sees another car!'

'We are about to move off now. We have colleagues hidden at the quarry. Rapier hasn't shown up yet, but they'll see him when he does.'

'Don't underestimate him. I made that mistake the first time, so I want to play it his way. Tell your colleagues to go too, please!' Malcolm begged, close to tears.

'Try to stay calm, sir. We're here to help but will be leaving the lay-by now.' The call ended. Mal watched as the car started up and drove slowly out of the other exit at the far end of the lay-by. So much for a covert operation. How could they think Rapier wouldn't be suspicious of another car in the lay-by? Suddenly aware of the cold, Malcolm turned the engine on and nudged the heater on high. He was beginning to feel his fingers again when his phone rang.

'I said no police!' Rapier's voice dripped with anger.

'I didn't know they would be here; my son-in-law must have told them. Please, I'll go back and get the money and meet you somewhere else, please...' Malcolm would have grovelled on his hands and knees if he thought it would help.

'Too late, Grainger – it appears you don't want your wife back, so I'll have to decide what to do with her.' The connection died. Malcolm almost screamed into his phone, 'No, no, no!' but Phillip Rapier was gone.

With his head on the steering wheel, huge sobs wracked Malcolm's body. He banged his head several times, wanting to feel pain, deserving of feeling pain. Would he ever see Julie again?

Ten minutes later, Malcolm's trembling hands gripped the steering wheel as he turned the car back towards the quarry. If Rapier had spotted the police and fled, the money would still be there. He had to retrieve it, hoping for another chance to save Julie. Pulling up beside the bins, he stepped out into the pouring rain. As he heaved the heavy bags of money back into the boot, a sound cut through the downpour – running footsteps. Five or six police officers, two of them with guns drawn, surrounded him.

'You're too late!' Malcolm screamed, his voice raw with desperation. 'He saw you! He's gone! If he hurts Julie, it's your fault!'

The armed men lowered their weapons as the officer in

charge approached Malcolm. 'He didn't come, Mr Grainger. Why don't you head home and we'll meet you there to discuss what happens next?'

'He didn't come because he saw you! If you'd have kept away, Julie would be with me now...' Malcolm was close to breaking point. The officer nodded to his colleagues, who dispersed as a car pulled up beside Malcolm.

'You're in no state to drive. This officer will take you home, and I'll follow in your car.'

Mal hadn't the energy to argue. His hope of a reunion with his wife was crushed, and Rapier knew the police were involved – what would that mean for Julie? Allowing himself to be ushered into the car, Malcolm felt defeated. Anger with his son-in-law bubbled inside him – had he not made it clear to Geoff that the police were not to be involved? He was going home without his wife, without Danny and Kate's mother. What would they think? He had failed in the most important task of his life.

Malcolm leaned his head back on the seat and closed his eyes. He didn't want to talk, and he didn't want to face his family, but he knew he must. Remaining silent throughout the short journey home, he only opened his eyes when the car pulled up outside.

Kate stood in the open doorway, arms wrapped around her body, her face tear-streaked. Malcolm climbed wearily from the car and walked through the rain, not caring about the cold and wet. Kate reached out to hug her father but he flinched at her closeness. 'I'm so sorry, Dad! Geoff thought he was helping...'

Malcolm shook his head and pushed past her into the house where Danny waited, pale and anxious. 'What the hell happened, Dad?'

As the police officer followed them inside, the family's conversation was guarded. Mal braced himself for a barrage of questions when he only wanted to get the police out of his house to wait and hope Rapier would ring again.

The doorbell startled him. DS Tim Matthews entered the lounge and looked from Malcolm to Danny and Kate. Without preamble, he sat opposite Mal and asked, 'Mr Grainger. Why didn't you come to us when your wife was abducted?' The detective didn't wait for an answer but offered his sympathies for how things had turned out. 'If you'd come to us sooner, we'd have had more time to prepare – to work with you.'

'I decided to do as Rapier said, although I didn't know it was him who'd taken her then...'

'Perhaps you'd better tell me everything from the beginning?' DS Matthews knitted his fingers together and leaned forward to listen as Malcolm related the last few days' events.

CHAPTER FIFTY-ONE

Julie had lost all track of time and was unaware it was a significant day. When daylight arrived, she slept through much of it as sleep eluded her in the darkness. On waking the day after the visitor had been, she found a sandwich and a glass of water on the dressing table by the window. The temptation was to gulp the water and eat quickly, but Julie restrained herself, allowing only sips of water and small, measured bites, uncertain if more would come. Grateful for small mercies, she refused to think about Sean being in the room while she slept. At least she was no longer tied up.

In a surreal way, the room she was locked in became her solace. A warm bed brought comfort, and sleep was her escape. Her grand ideas and strategies to escape seemed no more than impossible fantasies. The reality was that she was in no state physically or emotionally to fight or take flight. Julie became resigned to her fate being in the hands of other people, mainly her family and the police.

While in a state of semi-sleep, she heard the key in the door and sat up quickly. Sean stood in the doorway, speaking on his phone. With four strides, he was close, too close and shoved the phone to her ear. Hope soared as Julie said her husband's name.

'Julie! Are you all right, has he hurt you?' Mal's voice crackled.

'I'm okay... please come and get me...'

The phone was snatched away, and Sean hurried from the room locking the door behind him. Julie was wide awake, her heart pounding as she realised what the phone call meant. If Sean had rung Mal and allowed her to speak, they must be going to meet. Sean would release her for however much money he'd demanded.

With little time to dwell on the possible outcomes, Julie heard the key turn again and dearly hoped it would be the last time she would hear it. Sean entered the room, this time in a hooded coat. He approached his captive, grabbed her roughly by the arm and dragged her towards the door. Julie screamed with pain as her knee twisted, aggravating the already painful joint. When they reached the hallway, Sean threw her coat at her and as she struggled to put it on, he took the opportunity to cover her face with a chloroform-soaked cloth, which had the instant effect of rendering Julie unconscious.

Julie slowly awoke, a singing noise in her ears and a tingling in her arms and legs. Thinking it was a dream, the sensation of moving was not unpleasant until reality dawned on her. Julie opened her eyes – she was on the back seat of a moving car, underneath a rough blanket with her wrists once more tied. It didn't take long for her to remember Sean dragging her downstairs from her room, and as she peeped from under the blanket, it was no surprise to see the back of his head in the driving seat. Julie remained quiet, not wishing to attract his attention, while she tried to think and reason what was happening. The memory of Malcolm's voice on the phone filled her with hope – they must be on their way to meet him – on their way to freedom. A seed of hope filled Julie's heart. Could her ordeal finally be coming to an end?

The car swerved suddenly onto a bumpy road, causing Julie to feel the pain in her knee, which was just one of her injuries. Briefly, she imagined a hot bath, a meal, and a large mug of tea, which made her stomach growl, but her daydream was interrupted as the car came to a halt. She closed her eyes tightly, waiting to see what Sean would do next – he turned in his seat to look at her but did nothing, so she pretended to be asleep.

Julie estimated their wait to be about an hour. As her body protested and her legs cramped, she bit down on her lip, struggling to maintain her silence. Just when she felt she could no longer remain still, Sean shouted an obscenity from the front seat, started the car engine, and reversed out of their parking spot.

This wasn't what Julie expected or hoped; she'd been longing for release, either to be handed over to Malcolm or dropped by the side of the road; she didn't care as long as she was free. Struggling to lift her head to see from the window, she broke her silence. 'What's happening?' Julie asked as the car gathered speed.

'Your idiot of a husband brought the police! Seems he doesn't want you back, eh?'

'No! Please, let me out!'

'And why would I do that? He was told what the consequences would be…'

Julie wriggled around on the back seat, unable to free her wrists or sit up as the car moved quickly. Hot tears stung her eyes as she wondered what would happen to her and why Malcolm had brought in the police.

When the fearful journey finally ended, Sean exited the car, opened the back door and dragged Julie out. Falling on her knees sent an excruciating pain through her leg, causing her to scream. Sean covered her mouth with his hand and dragged her towards the door, dropping her inside like a bag of shopping. He took great pains to lock the door before turning to Julie again.

'If your old man doesn't want you, and I certainly don't, whatever will become of poor little Julie?' The cold glint in Sean's eyes was terrifying, pure evil, and Julie turned her face away. Heaving her to her feet, he dragged her back upstairs. Taking a knife from his pocket, he sliced through the binding around her wrist and then pushed her into the room she had hoped never to see again. The door slammed closed, the key turned in the lock and Julie had never felt so alone and afraid. She gave way to huge sobs, which shook her body to the core.

CHAPTER FIFTY-TWO

Exhausted from sobbing, Julie perched on the edge of the bed and tried to think. It must have been late; it had been dark for several hours, but time was becoming her enemy rather than her friend. The hope it had previously afforded her shattered when the afternoon's events turned sour.

Why would Malcolm involve the police when Sean explicitly said he shouldn't? It wasn't like him, and she was pretty sure he'd gladly hand the money over in exchange for her return – if the tables were turned and Mal was abducted, she'd do anything to get him back. It was a depressing thought, but worse was wondering what would happen next.

Perhaps she should try to sleep. It was unlikely Sean would be making decisions tonight; he'd need time to consider his position. And what about Mal? What was he going through? She could imagine Danny and Kate being with him to support him, but they would be distraught, too.

With some dark thoughts running through her mind, Julie lay down and pulled the duvet over her. Trying to ignore the pain in her body, her hunger and raging thirst, she squeezed her eyes closed and fell into an exhausted and thankfully dreamless sleep.

———

Phillip Rapier was furious. He'd spent a restless night with very little sleep as he attempted to work out his next move. The plan had been so simple but that fool Grainger couldn't even do as he'd been told. Awake early and stomping about the kitchen, muttering under his breath, he vowed to make the Graingers pay – another million or two, perhaps?

He'd let them stew for a couple of days before making contact again; the only downside was that he'd have to take care of Julie. He'd need to buy more food for them both, and going out was risky. The extra time would also help the police in their search. At least they didn't know who he was and, as Sean Henderson didn't exist, they should be chasing their tails for a while.

Although angry, Rapier knew he should take some food and water upstairs to Julie; having her die of thirst would complicate matters. Shopping would have to wait until later, so they'd have to eat the dry sandwiches left in the fridge. He'd enjoy coffee and the one remaining doughnut while Julie would have to make do with a stale sandwich and water – a smile flickered across his lips at the triumph depriving her gave him.

As Rapier reached into the refrigerator to retrieve the milk, a sudden wave of exhaustion washed over him, causing him to fumble and spill the milk over his shoes. Feeling light-headed and unable to bend down to clean up the mess, a throbbing headache began to form behind his eyes – a likely result of the frustrating day. When the dizziness stopped, Sean filled a mug of water, grabbed one of the unappealing sandwiches from the kitchen counter, and turned towards the staircase. He would feed Julie and then concentrate on making decisions when he felt more like himself.

Rapier's foot caught on the edge of a step, causing him to stumble as he made his way up the stairs. Desperately clutching the handrail, he struggled to pull himself up to the top, his breaths coming in shallow gasps. A weird sensation washed over him, leaving his face strangely numb and his mouth drooping. The headache lingering in the background intensified, the dizziness became overwhelming, and his vision blurred as if peering through a foggy window. It felt as if he had consumed too much alcohol, though he knew that wasn't the case.

Suddenly, a crash shattered the stillness, and he looked down to see the mug he had been carrying in his left hand had bounced down the stairs and shattered on the newel post at the bottom. Panic surged through him as he attempted to move his left arm and found it unresponsive, the weakness and drooping sensation spreading down his entire left side, leaving him feeling utterly helpless. Terror gripped him as his left leg buckled beneath him, and he fell over, landing with a thud outside Julie's bedroom door. Rapier couldn't speak, and a series of grunts exited his mouth as he tried to shout for help. But who could help him? Only he and Julie were in the cottage, and he'd locked her in the room and hidden the key.

CHAPTER FIFTY-THREE

Malcolm remained stubborn. When asked, he refused to let the police tap his telephone line, nor would he assure them he'd liaise with them if Rapier contacted him again.

He could tell DS Matthews was frustrated at his lack of cooperation, yet he no longer cared. He'd convinced himself the police presence had led to the handover fiasco. If there was a next time, he vowed to stick to Rapier's rules. He wondered if it was safe to confide in anyone, even his children.

Kate remained quiet throughout the police interview; Danny chipped in where he thought necessary; and Malcolm was decidedly obstructive.

Danny tried to reason with his dad. 'Now they know about Mum's abduction, they have to be involved. I was all for going it alone until Geoff put his nose in, but things have changed. Everything's different.'

'No, Dan. The only difference is that the police turned up and we may have lost Rapier's trust. We don't know if we'll hear from him again; he might have been scared off for good. If he does get back in touch, I'll explain what happened and do as he says.'

'He won't believe you, Dad.'

'He's right, Malcolm, and you have lost his trust, which makes him dangerous,' DS Matthews interjected.

The doorbell interrupted the conversation. Kate answered it and returned to the lounge with Geoff behind her.

'You meddling bastard!' Danny flew at his brother-in-law and thumped him on the chin. Geoff fell to the floor, holding his jaw and moaning. As Danny scrambled to jump on top of him, Geoff rolled over, knocking a lamp from the nest of tables.

Danny grabbed his arm and twisted it behind his back until Geoff yelled in pain. Kate shouted at the two men to stop but to no avail. Before Danny could do further harm to his brother-in-law, DS Matthews and the uniformed PC intervened and dragged the two apart.

Kate knelt beside Geoff with angry tears as she shouted at her brother. 'This won't solve our problems, will it?' She helped Geoff to his feet and onto the chair. 'I'll get some ice.' Heading towards the kitchen, she glared at Danny, who was still trying to get to Geoff.

'Enough of this!' Malcolm pushed his son down onto the sofa, his disgust with his family turning to anger. He didn't care if the police were there as he continued. 'Geoff, you shouldn't have interfered – I expressly said there would be no police involvement. If they hadn't turned up, Julie might be with us now. You had no right to interfere! And, Danny, what good will it do to beat your brother-in-law up? What's done is done – we have to hope for another chance.'

Kate returned with a packet of frozen peas wrapped in a tea towel, which she pressed to Geoff's chin. 'I hope it's not broken.' She noticed the trickle of blood running from his mouth.

'I think a tooth's loose,' Geoff mumbled as Danny smirked.

'And I think it's time for you all to go home,' Malcolm

added. 'We'll achieve nothing tonight, so you may as well get some rest. I want to be alone tonight.'

'What if Rapier rings again? Shouldn't I stay?' Danny asked.

'I doubt he'll ring. He'll need to consider his next move just as we should. Go home, please.'

They observed Mal's request without further protest and promised to return the following morning. DS Matthews remained while his colleagues also left.

Malcolm retreated to the kitchen, where he put the kettle on. Tim Matthews followed.

'Rough day,' Matthews uttered.

Malcolm shrugged. His appearance was an adequate answer. Making two cups of strong tea, he passed one to the detective and sat opposite him at the kitchen table.

'I'm not changing my mind.' It was a statement rather than the opening of a conversation.

Tim Matthews raised an eyebrow. 'We don't want to take over, Malcolm, just work with you for the best possible outcome. Will you at least listen to a few ideas we could consider?'

Mal shrugged again and sipped his tea, craving the hot liquid.

Tim nodded and proceeded to outline what the police could do. 'We can try tracking Julie's phone but if it's switched off we'll only get the location of the last place she had it on.'

'It goes to answering service when I try to ring.'

Tim nodded. 'It's switched off. Rapier's probably taken it from her, or he may even have disposed of it. You also said you thought he was behind the nuisance calls before he took Julie. We may find his phone number if you permit us to access your phone records.'

'It was a withheld number.'

'There are ways to get around that. We can also dig into

Phillip Rapier's past – his financials and any contacts he may have in the area. It's possible he may not be working alone.'

'Do you think he'll hurt Julie?' Malcolm bit his bottom lip.

'The chances are good that he won't. There's no benefit to him in hurting her; she's still valuable, a commodity he'd be foolish to harm.'

Malcolm nodded. 'That's what I've been hoping. But if he gets in touch again, I want to meet him alone. Can you do all this other stuff and leave me to deal with Rapier?'

Tim nodded solemnly. This was probably the best deal he would achieve. The detective stood to leave, feeling it inappropriate to continue the discussion or to wish Malcolm Grainger a good night.

After closing the front door behind DS Matthews, Malcolm turned to Trixie. 'Just you and me now, Trix.' He sat down, sniffing away the tears he'd been holding back, and the little dog jumped up on his knee and licked his face.

Malcolm didn't make it to bed that night. He sat with his faithful dog keeping vigil with him. Perhaps he dozed intermittently, but his mind wouldn't allow him to rest. Could he have done things differently? Would Rapier ring again? So many questions without a single answer. He tried to convince himself that Rapier would give him another chance out of greed if nothing else. The man had invested time and effort in his get-rich plan and surely wouldn't give up at the first hurdle. And what about the police? Would they prove to be an obstacle – could they force Mal to cooperate? It was indisputably the longest night of Malcolm's life.

CHAPTER FIFTY-FOUR

Julie's heart raced and she jumped at the sudden loud thud outside the bedroom door. Her mind reeled with possibilities as she moved closer to the door, holding her breath as she strained to listen. The noise from outside was muffled and indistinct, a feral groan which sent shivers down her spine. Was it an animal? It couldn't be, yet it sounded undeniably like a living being. The noise stopped, and she momentarily relaxed until it came again, a distinct grunt or moan which could only come from something living.

Common sense told Julie the noise had to be Sean. Was he trying to scare her? He was certainly succeeding. Holding her breath again and pressing her ear to the door, she strained to hear the source of the sound. It was barely discernible, and Julie decided it must be Sean, and if so, he was either in pain or playing mind games with her. Had he suffered a heart attack? If he was incapacitated in some way, she felt very little sympathy for the man, yet panic set in as she wondered where it would leave her and what would become of her if anything happened to her captor.

After several tense minutes, the house fell silent again, the only sound being the rhythmic patter of rain against the window. Julie tried to convince herself that she was imagining things or that the relentless downpour outside was playing tricks on her senses. Every house had its unique character, complete with creaks and groans that often echoed in the stillness of the night, and this country cottage, nestled in an isolated spot, was no exception.

She took a deep breath, the weight of hunger and exhaustion tugging at her as she climbed onto the bed. The shadows in the corners of the room loomed larger than life, but Julie forced herself to block out the terrifying thoughts of what awaited her tomorrow. Staring up at the ceiling, she tried to focus on the sound of the rain, letting it drown out the unwelcome scenarios threatening to creep back into her mind.

With a heavy heart and a mind racing with worries, she turned on her side, pulling the duvet closer around her. Sleep eluded her, but she shut her eyes tightly, yearning for the sweet escape of slumber, which felt just out of reach. She told herself it was time to rest, even if the darkness seemed more fearsome than ever.

Julie fell asleep only to be woken by another noise. She was suddenly alert, unaware of the time or how long she'd slept. Another bang – as if someone was kicking the door! Then, the same feral moan as previously. With a pounding headache, probably from lack of water, pain in her knee and increasing dizziness, Julie doubted her ability to make a sound judgment. Was she hallucinating or still asleep? No, she was awake and felt compelled to investigate. Hobbling towards the door, she tapped tentatively on the wood. 'Hello?' After listening for a moment, the noise came again – undeniably human – it must be Sean!

The dark thoughts of earlier stung her again. There was no

way out of the room and if Sean was ill and unable to move, what would happen?

Don't go there, Julie – think – think!

Dragging herself from the door, she opened the curtains and judged it to be early morning. Birds sang in the semi-darkness, the dawn chorus and a carefree day for them. Julie was beyond anticipating anything carefree, and her thoughts strayed to the conclusion that she would never leave the cottage alive.

Sitting on the ottoman, Julie felt a slight draught on her legs. As she examined the wall where it dipped below the eaves, she was reminded of their attic at home. The walls there were similar, and Malcolm had used the space under the eaves for storage, cutting a small door into the plasterboard. Julie tapped the wall and discovered it was hollow. Moving as quickly as physically possible, she pulled the ottoman away from the wall where a wooden panel covered a small opening. A cut-out handhole invited her to explore, and she was amazed when the panel came easily from its nook, revealing a hole leading into the eaves.

Julie saw a small space, enough to crawl under the eaves. But could she do it? Even if she could, where would it lead? The thought of crawling on her knees was far from appealing, but if the space led into another bedroom, could it be a means of escape?

Standing and moving back to the door, Julie knocked on it. 'Sean! Are you there?' After a moment, she heard a moan and then a scuffle as if he was trying to move. 'Are you ill? Can you tap on the door if you are?' Another scuffle and, finally, a weak tapping answered her questions.

Julie sniffed away the tears threatening to engulf her. It was time to be strong, not dissolve into a quivering wreck. But how would she manage to crawl with the pain in her knee, and even if she got inside the eaves, would it lead to freedom? There was only one way to find out.

Whipping off the pillows from the bed, Julie removed the pillowcases and tied the first one around her knee, tucking the edges in to hold it in place. Wincing as pain shot through her leg, she gritted her teeth. Wrapping the second pillowcase over the first added extra padding, and she limped towards the crawlspace. Grateful for her slim figure, she clambered through the hole. The pain made her shout out, but she persevered – the situation required strength and determination; it was no time to be a wimp.

CHAPTER FIFTY-FIVE

At 8.30am the doorbell chimed, and Malcolm, expecting it to be one of his children, was surprised to see DS Tim Matthews standing with his hands in his pockets and his collar up against the wind and rain.

'You still on duty?' Malcolm asked as he stepped aside.

'I managed a few hours of sleep. And you?'

Malcolm shook his head as he led the way into the lounge, where Trixie danced in circles on her hind legs. Tim tickled her ears and made a friend for life.

'I haven't changed my mind, and if Rapier calls today, I'll go alone.'

'I understand. We've set in motion some of the things we talked about last night. Officers are searching his financial records and any social media history, and his telephone provider is sending his call history ASAP. Our colleagues in Merseyside will be visiting his property this morning, and although we don't expect him to be there, they'll have a search warrant, which may turn up something useful.'

'Thank you.' Malcolm was grateful; these were avenues not

open to him and Rapier wouldn't be aware of the investigations until it was too late. 'Do you think he'll ring?'

'I think it's a strong possibility. Julie's a valuable asset, and keeping her safe is in his best interests.'

The telephone interrupted the conversation, and Malcolm picked up the handset with trembling fingers. Could it be Rapier? Tim studied his face as he listened in silence for a few moments. Malcolm's face reddened.

'Where did you get your *information?*' he shouted. 'Well, you're wrong, and if you print any of this, I'll sue your paper for every penny you have!' Slamming the phone down, he turned to DS Matthews. 'That was the local paper. They've heard that Julie's been abducted and wanted a story.'

'Did they say how they heard?'

'The girl in the Costa Coffee shop contacted them. She knew we were looking for Julie and Danny paid her for their CCTV footage. She must have recognised us, put two and two together and now wants to milk it for more money. They won't print anything now I've denied it, will they?'

'Unfortunately, a blanket denial could increase their interest. I'll call our press office and get them to contact the paper with reporting restrictions. Despite what people think, the press is usually cooperative in sensitive cases.' Matthews pulled out his phone to make the call, and Malcolm used the opportunity to switch the kettle on. His mouth felt like sandpaper, and he was sure DS Matthews could use a coffee, too.

While he was in the kitchen, Danny arrived and found him making coffee.

'What's he doing here so early?' he frowned. Mal appeased him by quickly explaining what the police were doing to help. Taking three steaming mugs of coffee into the lounge, Danny acknowledged Tim Matthews with only a curt nod. Tim said good morning and updated him on the earlier conversation with his dad.

The atmosphere was heavy, and DS Matthews finished his coffee. He stood to leave, the mug clinking on the table as he set it down. 'If Rapier does get in touch and you'd like our help, please ring.'

Mal answered with a tight smile before showing the detective to the door and thanking him for his efforts.

'Are you working with the police now?' Danny scowled as his dad returned to the room.

'I will do whatever Rapier says and *not* tell the police. But they can do things we can't and I can't stop them investigating now they know a crime's been committed. They're not the enemy, Danny.'

Kate arrived carrying Daisy. Malcolm was pleased to see them, particularly Daisy, whose little face lit up as she reached for her granddad. Taking her in his arms, he talked nonsense to her, and she nodded understandingly.

Danny and Kate almost immediately began arguing.

'Stop it!' Mal ordered. 'It's going to be a long day. Can't we spend it amicably, at least for Daisy's sake?'

'Sorry, Dad. I had to bring her. Geoff must go to work, and I can't keep asking his mum to look after her.'

'I don't mind; it's good to see her, but we don't want our anxieties to pass on to her, and she shouldn't hear you fighting.'

His children looked suitably chastised, their expressions filled with regret. Malcolm placed Daisy on the floor and went to find the bag of toys they kept for her visits. The baby provided a welcome distraction. Unaware of her family's difficult situation, she smiled as she played, demanding attention and keeping them occupied during what would prove to be an extremely long day.

Malcolm told Danny and Kate that the press had been on

the phone fishing for a story. When he explained where they got their information, Danny was furious, but Kate calmed him down before they lapsed into an uneasy silence, their focus on Daisy, not daring to verbalise their fears for what was to come.

CHAPTER FIFTY-SIX

Once inside the gloomy crawlspace, Julie paused. The stale air was heavy with dust, tickling her nose and catching in her throat. Faced with a choice of direction, she tried to recall her limited knowledge of the house's layout. After a moment's hesitation, she chose to go to the right. Almost instantly, the choice was validated as a faint draught cooled her skin.

Each movement was agony. She couldn't lift her head too high as rafters loomed above, not always visible in the poor light. Inching along, Julie wondered at the sense of her actions, but the alternative was doing nothing, something not in her nature. At least attempting an escape occupied her mind. Problem-solving required concentration and left little room for panic or feeling sorry for herself.

Dragging her leg was painful, and progress was slow. Cobwebs caught in her hair and face, reminding her of one of those old ghost trains at fairgrounds that she loved as a teenager. But this was reality, and Julie knew she might not exit the dark safely this time.

It was possible the space would lead nowhere, a dead-end, and she'd have to crawl back into her chintzy prison. Her mind refused to dwell on what she might do if she didn't find a way out. One step at a time...

Although it felt more, Julie had probably only progressed three or four yards, yet it had taken an age. As she paused for breath, a chink of light in the wall just a few more yards ahead caught her attention. It must be an exit – possibly into another bedroom. Julie heaved herself forward again until level with what appeared to be a panel similar to the one she'd come through. Pushing hard, she felt the panel give way slightly. A deep breath and another harder push and the panel fell away from the wall with a crash onto a carpeted floor. Julie wanted to cry with relief but knew her ordeal was far from over.

Struggling through the gap, Julie was in another bedroom similar to the one she'd been locked in. The bed was unmade and clothes and towels were strewn on a chair and the floor; it must be the room Sean was sleeping in. Remaining on the floor to catch her breath, Julie looked down at herself. Her clothes were covered in dirt, her hands filthy, and her knee throbbed with pain, the pillowcase padding hanging off. Nothing mattered but getting out.

With a determined effort, Julie hauled herself up using a chest of drawers for support, then limped towards the door. After turning the handle on the door and discovering it was unlocked, her chest felt as if it would burst with fear or anticipation – Julie couldn't describe it. Before opening it fully, she listened. Only the constant thrumming of rain could be heard, so she ventured onto the landing where Sean lay sprawled on his back, eyes closed and unmoving. At first, Julie feared he was dead, but a slight rise and fall of his chest indicated he was still breathing. Bending down, with her fingers trembling, she gently shook his shoulder. The only reaction was a flicker of his eyelids. He was out, cold.

Julie reluctantly slid her hand into his trouser pocket,

hoping to find a key or a phone before deciding how she would escape. She found neither. Moving downstairs, she tried the door, which, as expected, was locked. Sean's jacket was on the back of a kitchen chair, but first, she needed a drink.

Grabbing a mug from beside the sink, she filled it with water and downed it in one go. Repeating this twice, Julie felt much better; the craving for water was assuaged, and her attention turned to the jacket, where, joy of joys, she pulled a phone from the pocket.

Her smile turned to a frown when she couldn't turn it on – Sean must have a security pin, or perhaps his fingerprint would open it. Climbing back upstairs, Julie approached Sean as if he was about to jump up and surprise her, but he didn't. She took his right hand and placed his forefinger on the phone, but nothing happened. *Maybe he's left-handed,* she thought. But that didn't work either.

Returning downstairs, Julie needed to rest. Still weak with hunger and in pain, her mind felt like cotton wool and it was impossible to focus. Opening the fridge, a single sandwich gave her little choice, and she pounced on it greedily then filled the mug with more water and sat on the sofa to eat and drink.

It was fully daylight and, although exhausted, Julie knew there was no time to waste. It was possible Sean could recover sufficiently to lock her up again, or worse if the mood took him, although if it was a heart attack or a stroke, as she suspected, he might not recover at all. It wasn't only her life she was fighting for; Sean needed medical attention, and only Julie could help him.

Working methodically, she searched the cottage. A key was the prize she sought, or perhaps her phone – Sean had used it to allow her to speak briefly to Malcolm, so it must be somewhere.

Julie stopped occasionally to gaze from the windows where the isolation of the cottage was apparent; her abductor had chosen well and she wondered how long he'd rented it for. If it were a holiday cottage, the owner would probably check up on it or have someone to clean it when it was vacated. The thought was a comfort – someone would come to rescue her at some point, but it could be too late for Sean. Strangely, Julie didn't want Sean to die. After all he'd done to her and her family, she despised the man but didn't want his death on her conscience. Moving away from the window, she continued her search, wondering where he could have hidden the key.

CHAPTER FIFTY-SEVEN

Kate passed Daisy to Malcolm while she took Geoff's call. Danny rolled his eyes and sarcastically said, 'He'll be protecting his interests!'

'That's unkind, Dan. Geoff may have gone against our wishes but he only has our best interests at heart.' Malcolm shook his head as his son raised an eyebrow in disbelief, then he turned his attention back to his granddaughter.

It wasn't even midday, yet the day felt endless. If only Rapier would ring again – give them another chance. Daisy was chuckling as Malcolm built up a tower of four bricks for her to knock down; at least she was too young to understand her family's anguish. To Daisy's delight, Trixie tried to get in on the action, rolling onto her back.

'I need some air. Shall I take Trix?' Danny asked.

'Please, and pick up some fresh milk at the corner shop, will you?'

Even though the weather was frightful, Danny left with an excited dog lolloping beside him. Malcolm was grateful for his children's support, but Dan was so volatile he felt like a referee between them, particularly when Geoff was there.

Kate was on the phone for over fifteen minutes and when she returned her eyes were red and puffy. Malcolm jumped up and put his arms around his daughter. 'It'll be okay, love, you'll see. I'm sure we'll get your mum back today.'

Kate shook her head. 'It's not that, Dad, it's Geoff. We've been rowing lately, and he's suggested a divorce...'

'No! Is it because of all this... bringing the police in and everything?' Mal was stunned.

'It hasn't helped but there's more to it. I'll make us some tea and tell you, shall I? Where's Dan?'

'He's taken the dog out. I'll make the tea; you play with Daisy.' A rather confused Malcolm went into the kitchen. This was a complete surprise. He had no idea his daughter and Geoff were having problems but to ask for a divorce now was cruel. He could hardly believe it of his son-in-law.

'Here you are, love. A cup of tea always makes things feel better.' Mal passed a steaming mug to Kate and sat beside her on the sofa.

Kate sniffed. 'I think it'll take more than a cup of tea, Dad.'

'This has rather knocked me for six, lass. I thought everything between you and Geoff was good. Do you want to talk about it?'

Kate nodded. 'It was good until recently, but I don't want you thinking it's all Geoff's fault. I haven't given him much attention since Daisy came along. You know what it's like, I'm permanently tired... But I thought when you won the lottery, things would change. Geoff's quite materialistic, and I think he was more delighted than I was. Maybe it was already too late – I think there's someone else – a girl at work.'

'No, he wouldn't do that to you!' Mal was saddened and angry. He'd like to give his son-in-law a piece of his mind.

'I don't honestly know. He mentions her name occasionally and she's started ringing him at home. He says it's about work, yet if I press him, he clams up. I kept hoping things would change, and when we were in Florida, I thought they had. But she rang him while we were away. Geoff said it was to clarify a point in a client's contract, but he left the room to talk to her and we argued about it afterwards. Then, the last couple of days, with Mum being abducted and the arguments about the police... I feel I don't know him anymore.'

'But a divorce? It's so final; can't you wait until things settle down and your mum's back home? Or maybe counselling would help?'

'I suggested therapy but he won't listen. I admit I was surprised when he proposed a divorce, but it was in the heat of the moment, he probably wasn't thinking straight. Geoff's embarrassed about what he did by going to the police and is furious with Danny. I think this was the last straw, and *apparently*, I didn't support him enough. Sometimes, I'm not allowed to have an opinion of my own.'

'That's ridiculous! You've always supported him.' Malcolm felt his daughter's pain. Kate's words were telling. Perhaps Geoff wasn't the man Malcolm had thought and didn't treat his daughter as well as she deserved. 'I can't believe he's chosen to ask for a divorce today with all that's going on.'

The sound of the front door halted the conversation. Trixie came running in for a fuss and Kate tried to dry her eyes. Danny followed the little dog, shrugged off his coat and shook the raindrops from it. 'It's blowing a gale out there... what's going on?' Danny asked as the room went quiet. Mal and Kate exchanged a look.

'You might as well tell him. I'll pour another cuppa.' Mal left the room so his children could talk. He took his time making another pot of tea before returning to find Kate in tears. She ran past her father, almost knocking the mug from his hand, dashed upstairs, and they heard her old bedroom door slam.

'What did you say?' Mal put the mug on the coffee table and stared at Dan.

'What do you expect? I told her she'd be better off without him. What the hell's he playing at doing this to her now when Mum's missing?' He had a point; it seemed like the worst possible timing. Danny was angry and protective of his sister but his next words stunned Malcolm.

'Do you think he's got anything to do with Mum's abduction?'

'What? Are you suggesting Geoff is working with Rapier?' Mal's nostrils flared. 'That's ridiculous. Kate said they'd been having problems lately and how could he know Rapier, let alone help him?'

'I don't know but I wouldn't put it past him. Maybe we should tell the police?'

'No way! If Geoff had been involved, he wouldn't have gone to the police himself. You're wrong, Dan, and you'd better not let Kate hear you say this.'

'Say what?' Kate stood in the doorway, resembling a little girl. Daisy reached her arms to her mother, and Kate picked her up, holding her close for comfort.

'Nothing,' Danny snapped. 'Has Geoff said anything about the *terms* of a divorce?'

Kate turned away and remained silent.

'He has, hasn't he? What does he want, Kate?'

'You don't have to tell us if you don't want to, love. This is hardly the time to discuss divorce settlements.'

'Kate?' Danny wasn't going to let it drop.

'He said it's only fair if he has half of everything,' Kate almost whispered.

'Including the million Mum and Dad gave you?' Danny was on his feet, pacing. Kate hung her head. 'It's no wonder he *needs* to go to work. If he were here, I'd–'

'Enough, Danny. We'll say no more about it. Haven't we plenty to worry about without you making matters worse?'

'How's he making it worse?' Kate looked from her dad to her brother. 'What were you talking about when I came downstairs?'

'I suggested Geoff might have something to do with Mum's abduction...'

'That is so out of order! He may not be perfect, but he'd never do anything so horrible!'

'Yes, you would say that, but think about it. His interference prevented us from getting Mum home – could it be part of the plan?'

'No, you're wrong – Geoff's Daisy's father. He's a good man and would never do such a thing!' Kate was sobbing, and Malcolm took Daisy from her arms as the little girl looked as if she might cry, too. His mind spun with the nauseating possibility that his son-in-law could have had something to do with Julie's abduction – no, surely not.

The doorbell rang. Mal jumped in surprise, and Daisy really did start crying. He opened the door to find DS Tim Matthews on the doorstep.

CHAPTER FIFTY-EIGHT

The wind howled, and rain lashed against the cottage windows. Julie wrapped her arms around herself, shivering as she continued her search for a key or a working phone, her heart racing with unease. Time no longer had meaning yet stretched endlessly, she didn't know what time of day it was, and the dark weather didn't help. A mental picture of Sean nagged in her brain – was he still alive?

With a deep breath, Julie ascended the stairs with dread. At the top, her eyes fell upon the man sprawled on the floor, his skin an unsettling shade of grey and his breathing shallow. Should she intervene? Panic gripped her at the thought of touching him, but she steeled herself; doing nothing would make her no better than Sean himself; she needed to act.

Using all her strength, Julie rolled him onto his side, recalling the recovery position from a long-forgotten first aid course. On her second attempt, she succeeded, and relief washed over her; at least he wouldn't choke if he vomited. Stepping into the small bedroom Sean had occupied, its disarray mirrored her frantic thoughts. Julie grabbed the duvet from the bed, took it onto the landing and carefully draped it over him.

He looked so helpless lying there. Simultaneously, she wanted to kick the man and save him. Julie had always believed all life was sacred, even someone as vile as Sean Henderson.

A sudden urge to use the bathroom compelled Julie to hobble away from her comatose captor and into the modern, sleek bathroom, where a wave of relief washed over her. Using a toilet felt wonderful compared to the repulsive bucket she'd been forced to use in the bedroom.

It was a simple luxury that she'd always taken for granted. The clean tiles underfoot, the flush of water, all these little comforts had been stripped away from her, making her acutely aware of how precious they were. Julie would never take the mundane things of life for granted again. After washing her hands and face in warm water, Julie investigated the bathroom. Sean appeared to have brought very little with him, probably expecting to have completed his nefarious task by now and be off spending his money. No key, no phone. Another fruitless search.

Returning to the bedroom, her attention turned to Sean's clothes, reaching into pockets and shaking them out to double-check. Nothing. She stripped the bed and, with great effort, lifted the mattress. The result was the same. Zilch. The furniture was next: drawers, wardrobe, bedside cabinet, all to no avail.

Leaving the room in an even greater mess than she'd found it, Julie returned downstairs glancing only briefly at Sean as she passed by, knowing there was nothing more she could do for him.

After searching the lounge for the second time, Julie turned to the kitchen. A peninsula separated the two spaces, and she pulled out the drawers and opened the cupboards. The kitchen was well-stocked with crockery and cooking equipment, making her task more challenging as she tipped over every mug, pan, and pot she found. A rather dry-looking cactus plant sat on the kitchen windowsill, and she carefully lifted it down to check behind it. As she moved the plant, her phone fell from its hiding spot and into the sink. Julie grabbed it, hardly believing she'd finally found her lost phone. Pressing the button, she willed it to light up, but nothing happened – the battery was dead.

In a moment of anger, Julie threw the phone across the room, then flopped down on the sofa and allowed her hot tears to flow. Would this nightmare never end?

CHAPTER FIFTY-NINE

DS Matthews brushed the rain from his coat with his hand and wiped his feet before following Malcolm into the lounge. His presence was clearly interrupting something; Kate's face was damp, her eyes red, and Danny scowled at the inspector. 'Anything to report?' Dan came straight to the point.

'Yes, we have.' Their eyes swivelled to Tim Matthews, and Daisy stopped crying as if listening. 'But first, will you tell me if you've heard from Rapier?'

'No, nothing at all,' Mal answered. The detective nodded before continuing.

'Your wife's phone provider has confirmed her last phone usage. We can narrow its location to between two masts, an area estimated to be within eight miles of Burnbridge.'

'Eight miles! So, what are you doing to find her?' Danny snapped. 'Is her phone switched on?' Malcolm stared at his son, marvelling at his sudden change of heart and expectation.

'No, the phone isn't active. The last time it was switched on was when Rapier rang to let you speak to Julie. As to what we're doing, we have units combing the area looking for likely premises where she might be held. It's rural and heavily wooded in places so I've requested a police helicopter search, but until my boss is sure you're not negotiating with Rapier, he won't authorise it, so I need you to be honest with me.'

'It's the truth – we haven't heard from him. If your men find a likely hideout, won't it put Julie at risk?' Malcolm's hopes were tempered with caution.

'It's not our intention to go barging in. If we find somewhere likely, we'll wait and watch before deciding what move to make. We have a hostage negotiator standing by, and hopefully, we can open a dialogue with Rapier.'

'But if he knows you've found him, he might hurt her!' Kate, wide-eyed, clung to her daughter.

'To be blunt, we have no guarantee he hasn't already hurt your mother. I'm sorry but there are several possibilities, one being that he's abandoned her; therefore a search is prudent. As for approaching him, we'll decide when we have more information.'

'And we don't get a say?' Danny took a step towards DS Matthews, who replied calmly.

'Danny, I know this is a difficult time for you and the family, but we will only move in when we know it's safe. If you haven't heard from Rapier, what's your next move?' The question silenced Danny. They were at Rapier's mercy and could do nothing until they heard from him. At least the police had a lead.

'Can you get the helicopter out?' Mal asked. 'And if we hear from him, we'll let you know immediately.'

'Good. Our plans are fluid and depend on the situation as it unfolds.'

Malcolm saw the DS to the door and secured his promise to keep him updated. He then returned to his children, both of whom looked anxious. 'We need their help.' He explained, glancing from Kate to Danny. 'We've got nothing left.' His look dared them to disagree, but they hadn't the heart to take up the argument.

It was early afternoon. The day dragged on. 'I think you should have mentioned the situation with Geoff to the sergeant,' Danny said, reopening their previous conversation.

'Geoff's got nothing to do with this!' Kate countered.

Mal rolled his eyes and held up a warning hand. 'That subject is closed. We have no proof, Danny, it's all supposition, so I suggest we drop it and concentrate on facts. The police are out actively looking for Julie with a specific area to focus on, which is more than we've had to hope for since your mum went missing.'

CHAPTER SIXTY

Julie must have fallen asleep and woke with a pain in her neck. Outside was dark – late afternoon or early evening – she couldn't decide. Limping to the sink, she ran another glass of water and drank it in one go. Although trying not to think about Sean, he was on her mind and her conscience led her upstairs to check on him.

He hadn't moved and remained in the recovery position. A closer inspection revealed he was breathing, and Julie sighed with relief. Supposing she should continue to search for a means of escape she trailed back downstairs, switching the light on as the darkness deepened.

After so much time spent searching, Julie believed she knew every inch of the cottage, each nook and cranny, but there must be somewhere she had missed. Sean had chosen his hiding place well. Searching places for the second time to ensure she'd missed nothing was disheartening. Julie pushed herself through the exhaustion, longing to sit down and rest, yet she knew that if she did, she might never continue the hunt for a means of escape. It would be so easy to give up – to resign herself to her fate...

A noise caught Julie's attention, a faint whirring sound which made her stop to listen. It couldn't be traffic; they were well away from any road. Yes, it was getting louder, coming closer. She'd heard a similar noise on occasions at home when Malcolm told her it was a police helicopter searching for a suspect. Could this be the police searching for her? Dashing to the window, ignoring her knee pain, Julie squinted into the darkness but saw nothing. The noise faded and she shouted out and banged on the window. *No, no, no!*

Within minutes it grew louder again, the helicopter must be coming back. Julie banged harder on the window and shouted, knowing it was futile. How would something as noisy and as far away as a helicopter hear someone banging from inside a cottage?

Think, Julie, think!

There was only the downstairs light on in the cottage. Maybe they would notice if she could switch on all the lights. Struggling from one room to another, Julie moved as quickly as possible until every light in the cottage was blazing. Fuelled by adrenaline, she picked up a kitchen chair and smashed it against the window with all her strength but it wasn't enough to break the double-glazed windows.

The helicopter hovered nearby, and Julie could see a pinprick of light flashing in the sky – they must be looking for her. The flashing light gave her an idea. If she could make the cottage lights flash, maybe they would notice and come to investigate. Julie had seen the electricity metre in a kitchen cupboard, and dragging herself to it, she opened it and reached for the switch. Suddenly plunged into darkness, her heart leapt. Counting to three, she flicked the switch again, and the cottage flooded with light. One, two, three and she flicked the switch off again. One, two, three – on. Blinded by the sudden light and then dark, Julie kept up the rhythm for several minutes.

The noise above continued, although it was impossible to judge how near the helicopter was.

As exhaustion threatened to overcome her, the whirring noise which had brought her so much comfort and much-needed hope grew fainter.

'No! Please come back...' Her voice bounced off the walls into the empty room. Silence again became her companion as her hope of rescue dissolved. Perhaps she'd been kidding herself. It may not have been a helicopter, and if the police were looking for her, how would they know where to search? Julie shuffled to the sofa and lay down. Too exhausted to scream and shout about the unfairness of her situation, she lay staring at the ceiling, warm tears silently sliding down her face.

CHAPTER SIXTY-ONE

The tension was almost palpable in the Graingers' house. Danny and Kate remained with their dad, waiting and hoping for news. They jumped at the sound of every passing car, but it was two hours until DS Matthews arrived again, looking tired but with a slight smile. Once inside, all eyes turned to him as he updated them.

'The helicopter crew spotted a possible location. It fits with the last phone signal, and it's possible someone was trying to attract their attention from an isolated cottage. They passed the coordinates to personnel on the ground and left the scene. We'll be the first to know as soon as there's any news.'

'An isolated cottage? I don't understand – was Julie outside attracting attention?' Malcolm was trying to process this development.

'No. The lights were flashing on and off. We're looking into who owns the cottage and hope to gather as much information as possible before our men approach.'

'If they approach and Rapier's holding Mum there, won't it be dangerous?' Danny asked.

'We're leaning towards the theory that your mother is locked in alone. Rapier would hardly allow her to signal the helicopter crew if he was guarding her. But we do have an armed response unit on standby. Every move will be carefully considered.'

Danny nodded and noticed his sister shivering, although the room was warm. He sat beside her and slid an arm around her shoulder. Daisy lay asleep in her mother's arms, oblivious to the drama playing out around her.

'Why don't you take her up to bed?' Malcolm asked. 'The cot's made up in the spare room.' Kate nodded and took the baby upstairs. When she'd left the room, Malcolm asked, 'Do you think an armed response unit is necessary? Is there reason to believe Rapier is armed?'

'We have no evidence to think he's armed, but we're not taking any chances. The unit will only be called in as a last resort, and their presence will hopefully persuade Rapier to give himself up.'

Malcolm nodded. 'I'll make some tea.' He needed something to do. Never had he felt so helpless when he knew his wife needed him more than ever.

Kate returned to the lounge just as Malcolm brought in tea and biscuits, more to give them something to occupy themselves with than out of a desire to drink tea. DS Matthews' phone rang and he left the room to take the call, the others feeling on edge. Danny stood by the door, listening intently. 'Sit down, son. He'll tell us soon enough,' Malcolm urged.

When the detective returned, he brought news which wasn't as good as they'd hoped. 'We've discovered the cottage is a holiday rental,' he said. 'And the owners have confirmed that a Mr Sean Henderson currently occupies it. Does that name ring a bell?'

'No, I've never heard of him,' Malcolm answered, and his children shook their heads in agreement.

'That's not surprising. If it is Rapier, he'd hardly have given his real name. This man claims to be a writer needing solitude to work on a project, which is all the owners can tell us. The booking was made on the phone and they didn't meet the man, the key was left in a key safe at the property for him. The update from the team on the ground is that they're cautiously approaching the cottage, and everything seems quiet.'

'What will they do next – get Julie out?' Malcolm's voice was anxious.

'Only when they're certain it's safe. They'll ring me again before making a decision.' Tim Matthews picked up his drink and sipped the welcome liquid.

The room fell silent, its occupants each nursing their fears and dreading the evening's outcome. Kate hugged a cushion on the sofa, tears trickling down her cheeks. Danny crossed and uncrossed his legs, sighing loudly every couple of minutes. Malcolm's thoughts were of Julie. His fear was bad enough, but he hardly dared imagine what she was going through – the terror she must be feeling – that is, if she was still alive...

CHAPTER SIXTY-TWO

Julie lay still for what felt like hours, not knowing what to think. Had she really heard and seen the helicopter, or was her imagination playing tricks on her? If the police were involved, as Sean had told her, it could have been them searching for her. The silence dragged on – the doors were still locked – she was still hungry and in pain – would she ever get out of this wretched place? Perhaps she should check on Sean, but she could do nothing for him. He needed medical attention if it wasn't already too late.

Every light in the cottage still blazed, casting shadows against the walls. Julie had consciously decided to keep each light on, a beacon for anyone searching for her. Yet, despite her intentions to remain strong, despair settled into her heart. The outside world was silent again and shrouded in darkness, leaving her with the sinking suspicion that no one would embark on a search until the first light of dawn.

Julie remained unmoving, in a trance-like state. Thinking she heard a noise from outside, she lifted her head and listened intently, but there was nothing; it was her imagination. The only sounds were the leaves rustling in the breeze and the odd hoot of an owl. Julie stood and walked over to the window at the front of the cottage. There it was again, a sound like someone walking through the dry leaves. She thought it was probably a fox but pressed her face against the window and banged on the glass, hoping she was wrong.

Julie jumped as a figure staggered out of the darkness towards the cottage. Screwing up her eyes to see more clearly, and cupping her hands on the glass, she recognised the shape as a policeman in full combat gear. Her reaction was to scream and bang even louder on the window, but she'd already attracted his attention. A tremendous crash at the cottage's front door was followed by several police officers entering the room, alert and looking in all directions. Julie fell back against the table, stunned and trying to process what was happening.

'Are you alone?' the first officer shouted to her.

'Yes! No – he's upstairs but unconscious...' Julie sobbed with relief, gulping in huge breaths of air. The officer was swiftly beside her, his arm around her shoulders as he guided her outside.

'Ouch, I can't hurry,' she sobbed. 'My knee.' The officer slowed his pace.

As soon as they stepped outside, the scene was chaotic. Officers bustled around the cottage like a swarm of agitated bees.

Blue and red lights flashed as a police car pulled up to the gravel driveway, its engine idling. Julie was ushered toward the vehicle without hesitation, her heart racing, and was carefully guided inside. A female officer appeared from nowhere and climbed into the back of the car beside her. The door closed with a decisive thud. There was so much Julie wanted to tell them, to explain, and she babbled incoherently.

'You don't have to talk now. We'll get you to the hospital, and you can tell us all about it when you're feeling better.'

'But, Sean! He needs an ambulance. I think he's had a heart attack or a stroke...'

'Our officers are with him and an ambulance is on its way.' She nodded to the driver, who put the car into gear, and they moved away into the night.

'My husband? Has anyone told him I'm okay?' Julie gripped the young officer's arm tightly, still tense and trembling with shock.

'Yes, he'll know by now. He's been kept informed throughout the operation.' She smiled at Julie, who rested her head on the window, lulled to silence by the motion of the car, hardly daring to believe her ordeal was finally over. Muddled thoughts raced through her brain. She longed to see Malcolm and her family but dreaded admitting how foolish she'd been to be taken in by Sean Henderson. Would Malcolm ever forgive her?

Julie closed her eyes as the heat from the car seeped into her body, yet couldn't sleep; her mind was too active. The journey took about half an hour before she was being helped from the car into a wheelchair.

Julie surrendered to the nurse's and doctor's ministrations. She hadn't the energy to protest and was grateful when they offered her pain relief as they examined her and asked questions. After taking the medication she was wheeled away for an X-ray on her knee. On her return, Julie watched as a nurse attached a drip to her arm. Just as she drifted off into sleep, the swish of the curtains around her bed heralded Malcolm's arrival.

Malcolm held her tightly, whispering his relief at having her back. Julie felt his tears mixing with her own on her face. At that moment, nothing else mattered – any recriminations could wait. They were together, something she had feared might never happen again.

Finally pulling away from his wife's arms, Malcolm smiled. 'The children are outside, and the nurse said they can see you for a minute, then we must leave you to sleep.'

Julie nodded. Malcolm left the room, returning almost immediately with Danny and Kate. Hugs and tears expressed their relief at being reunited, but it was clear to her family that Julie needed rest. The mounting questions and explanations could wait until later. They left with promises to return early the following morning – they, too, would welcome a good night's sleep.

CHAPTER SIXTY-THREE

Julie slept well, dreamless hours free of the pain and worry of the last few days. Waking early, the room was still semi-dark, light coming from the corridor outside. A nurse walked past, and Julie called out to her to ask the time.

'It's not yet six. You could go back to sleep if you like?'

'Any chance of a bath? I really need one,' Julie asked. Having caught sight of herself in the bathroom mirror the evening before, she'd been horrified to see the state she was in. The nurse had helped her to wash, little more than what her mother would have called a cat-lick, but her hair was lank and dirty and dirt was ingrained in her skin. She looked hopefully at the nurse.

'Okay. If we're quick, we'll beat the morning rush.' The young woman grinned before hurrying away to fetch a wheelchair. The patient had been instructed to keep off her leg as much as possible.

Ten minutes later, Julie was relaxing in a huge bath with warm water up to her neck. It was a struggle to get in and the nurse had suggested using the hoist, but independent as ever, Julie climbed in with some assistance.

'I'll leave you to enjoy your soak,' the nurse said. 'When you're ready or need help pull the string behind the bath.' Leaving the room, she winked conspiratorially at her patient.

The hot water felt heavenly. Julie slid completely beneath the surface and washed her hair with the shampoo the nurse had left. After rinsing it out, she used a soap with a somewhat clinical scent to thoroughly clean her entire body, gently bathing her swollen knee. The tender bruising on her face from when Sean hit her reminded her that there would be much explaining to do when Malcolm arrived. He hadn't mentioned the bruises but she was sure he would have noticed.

Julie lay in the bath until the water began to cool. Pulling on the string brought the same nurse rushing in to help. 'Feeling better?' she asked.

'Much. Thank you.'

'Breakfast will be another hour so would you like a cup of tea in the meantime?'

'Sounds perfect.' Julie smiled. When she left the hospital, she would buy the nurses the biggest box of chocolates she could find; they deserved it.

The smell of breakfast was welcome. Although her mouth was sore, Julie was hungry, and chose orange juice, scrambled eggs, toast, and marmalade. Having managed to eat it all and drink another cup of tea, Julie felt strengthened and clean for the first time in days and considered herself ready to see Malcolm. Resting her head on the pillows and closing her eyes, she soon became aware of someone watching her and opened her eyes to see her husband smiling down at her. As he bent to kiss her cheek, Julie's emotions surprised her, and she cried.

Conversation was delayed while she sobbed in her husband's arms. 'Do you want me to call the nurse?' Mal frowned, but she shook her head. 'Probably delayed shock.' He nodded almost knowledgeably, which made Julie smile.

'You're right, I'm sorry, love.' Julie blew her nose on a tissue and pulled herself into a more comfortable position. 'When are the children coming?'

'Well, the doctor said you may be able to be discharged later today so they could come to see you at home.'

'That would be wonderful! It seems like an age since I was at home. Pull up that chair and we'll have a chat. I think I owe you an explanation.'

Malcolm did as she asked and took Julie's hand in his. 'You've been through quite an ordeal, love, and if talking about it will upset you, you don't need to say anything.'

His concern made her feel worse. Yes, she'd been through an awful experience which she wouldn't wish on anyone but part of her felt culpable. If she hadn't met Sean...

'I need to explain. The man who abducted me, Sean Henderson...'

'No, Julie. He wasn't called Sean, it was Phillip Rapier.'

'What! No, I can't believe it. How do you know?'

'I know it's Rapier because I saw him lead you from Costa after you fell. It was all on the CCTV camera.'

Malcolm's words shamed Julie. What an absolute fool she'd been, whatever would her family think of her? 'It's not what it seems... I met him a few weeks ago and we struck up a conversation, nothing more. When I knew he wanted to take it further, I agreed to meet him one last time after we returned from Florida to tell him I couldn't see him again. We only ever met in the coffee shop. Nothing ever happened!' Julie gripped his hand, desperately wanting her husband to believe her.

'I know, love. He tricked you. When his plan to blackmail me fell through he had a backup plan – you. You were a victim of his twisted mind, and I don't blame you at all.'

His words were such a relief. She'd never forgive herself for being so gullible but was so grateful she hadn't lost Malcolm.

'Do the children know?'

'Yes. It was Danny who got the CCTV footage from Costa, but they don't think any less of you. There's nothing to berate yourself for.'

'Is he still alive, Rapier, I mean? The nurses don't know anything, or they're not telling me anyway.'

'As far as I know, he's alive but in ICU in a pretty bad way.'

The conversation was interrupted by the doctor, who entered the room smiling. 'It's good to see you looking so much better, Julie.'

Malcolm moved away so the doctor could examine her. He looked at the chart on the end of the bed, shone a light into her eyes and asked if she felt any dizziness. After a negative answer, the doctor looked from his patient to Malcolm. 'If you think you can keep your wife off her feet for a few days, we can discharge her later today. The X-ray shows no broken bones but it appears you've torn your medial collateral ligament. It could have been worse. Tearing the anterior cruciate ligament would have required surgery and a longer recovery time. If you keep off your knee for the rest of the week you should see reduced swelling. We'll give you some painkillers and see you in a week when I'll refer you to a physiotherapist. You may need crutches afterwards, but we'll monitor the healing.'

'Thank you, doctor. Can I leave now?'

'No. The physiotherapist is coming to see you after lunch. We'll take a second X-ray to confirm the diagnosis and then you can go. Any other questions?'

Julie looked towards Malcolm who asked what they were both wondering. 'How's Mr Rapier – the man brought in with Julie?'

'Ah, yes. I'm sorry to tell you that he died early this morning. He'd suffered a stroke. As medical attention wasn't immediately on hand, if he had survived, he would have been severely brain damaged. I've been informed of a little of the circumstances, but there was nothing you could have done to save him; he needed specialist treatment, which he received too late.' The doctor patted Julie's hand and left them alone.

'It was his fault.' Malcolm turned Julie's face to his. 'In keeping you a prisoner, he'd imprisoned himself and was unable to receive the help he needed.'

'Yes,' Julie whispered. 'He brought it on himself.'

CHAPTER SIXTY-FOUR

Julie left the hospital in the afternoon, promising to be good and obey the doctor's instructions – the family would keep her to it. Danny and Kate were at home waiting for her but didn't stay long, feeling it prudent to allow their parents to spend time together. They would come for a longer visit the following day with the children. Trixie was beside herself with excitement. The little dog jumped up and down, and Malcolm had to put her in the kitchen until Julie was settled on the sofa. When released, Trixie jumped beside her mistress and settled down for the evening.

True to their word, Julie's children arrived mid-morning the following day. As practical as her mum, Kate had been to the supermarket and was weighed down with several bags of groceries. 'Your fridge has never been so empty, so I thought I'd stock up with fresh food. I daren't tell you how badly Dad's been eating while you were away.' She placed Daisy on the floor to entertain her grandma while she busied herself in the kitchen.

'Is she okay?' Julie asked Malcolm when Kate had left the room. 'She doesn't seem herself.'

'Just leave her be. She'll tell you in her own good time.' Malcolm's words worried Julie but as far as she could see Kate looked physically well and Daisy was her usual lively self.

When the four were all together with morning coffee in their hands, Julie felt an explanation was in order. She briefly told them of her shock at learning the man she thought of as Sean Henderson was Phillip Rapier. Without going into details, she related how she'd met him 'by chance' and the tale he spun her about his ill mother. They accepted that letting this acquaintance bring her home after her fall in the coffee shop was only natural.

Julie was reluctant to go into details of her time locked in the cottage, although she did make sure they knew he'd not raped her, and she played down the physical abuse, knowing they'd seen the bruises and would put two and two together.

Tired of talking, Julie turned her attention to Daisy, who happily sat on the carpet, chewing the ears off her teddy. 'And how's my lovely girl?' she asked. Daisy smiled up at her grandma, oblivious to the drama the family had suffered. When Julie raised her eyes, she noticed the tears in her daughter's eyes. 'What's wrong, love?'

Kate looked at her dad who stood and turned to Danny. 'I think we should take the dog out for a walk.' They all understood his reasoning.

Once alone with her mother, Kate poured out her problems with Geoff. Julie was as stunned as Mal had been; there had been no signs of a rift. 'And do you think the marriage is over?'

'I honestly don't know. Geoff and I will have to get together to discuss practicalities. He's staying at his mother's house, but that can't be a permanent arrangement.'

'Let me put it another way.' Julie paused and turned her daughter's face to hers. 'Do you want the marriage to be over?'

'No, Mum! I still love him, and I want to believe he's not

been having an affair, but I can't think of any other reason for his sudden closeness to this woman and his secretiveness. We always shared everything. And he's a great daddy to Daisy. He did ring to ask how you were as well...' Tears rolled down her face. Julie felt helpless. Kate needed advice but she could hardly offer it.

'Why not leave it a few days and then arrange to meet him? You need to talk but maybe he needs to be honest with you first so you know where you stand.'

'You're right, Mum. I can't face a confrontation at the moment, anyway. More coffee?'

The doorbell interrupted them, and Malcolm, who'd returned from his walk, shouted that he'd answer it. Julie and Kate recognised DS Tim Matthews' voice as he entered their home.

Julie rolled her eyes. She'd been expecting him to call and knew there were questions to answer. Malcolm showed him into the lounge, where he smiled at the women and accepted Kate's offer of coffee.

'Do you want me to leave you alone?' Malcolm hesitated and looked at the detective.

'No, it's okay with me if you want to stay. Julie?'

Julie wasn't sure she wanted Malcolm to hear the reality of her last couple of days, but excluding him seemed hurtful, so she nodded. Malcolm sat beside her and took hold of her hand.

'How are you feeling?' Tim Matthews began with a genuine smile on his face.

'Much better for being home.' She squeezed Malcolm's hand. 'And thank you for all your efforts to help me.'

'My pleasure. I'm delighted it worked out well in the end. Are you feeling up to answering some questions?'

'Yes, I suppose so, although I did think now that Sean... sorry, Phillip Rapier is dead, we could put it all behind us.'

'In a way, yes, but to tie up loose ends, I'd like to take a statement.' Julie looked puzzled as he continued. 'Our main concern is ensuring Rapier was acting alone. We don't want to relax the investigation only for another incident to occur.' Julie rolled her eyes and groaned at the prospect as Matthews continued. 'We also need a full statement to complete our paperwork on the case – there's always paperwork.'

For the next half hour, Julie related everything that had happened, starting with meeting the man she now knew was Phillip Rapier and continuing through to his collapse and her eventual rescue. At times, she faltered, thinking carefully about how to express herself as Malcolm listened intently.

Kate brought in coffee, a welcome distraction for Julie, who was tired and quite emotional at having to re-live her experience. Finally, Tim Matthews put away his pen. 'So, as far as you know, Rapier was working alone? There were no furtive phone calls to or from anyone else?'

'No. Nothing. I think I'd have known if he had an accomplice,' Julie answered honestly. She would never know how relieved Malcolm was to hear her words. He'd not seriously considered that Geoff could have been involved, but he knew Danny had given credence to the idea.

DS Matthews left the Graingers, promising the investigation would be wrapped up swiftly and he would not need to trouble them much more. As Malcolm showed him to the door, he apologised for not always being cooperative. Matthews stopped him, completely understanding of the circumstances, and the men shook hands as they parted.

CHAPTER SIXTY-FIVE

Three days later, Malcolm parked by the kerb in front of a bungalow, stepped out of his car and stretched. He wasn't expected and felt unsure how his visit would be received. The day was bright and sunny but chilly, with the pavement covered in swirling golden, red, and brown leaves, reminding Malcolm of how quickly the year was passing. It was early November, and Julie was already planning for Christmas. He didn't mind; it gave her something good to focus on and helped to take her mind off recent events.

The gate creaked as he opened it, and Mal was sure he saw the lounge curtain twitching. Would he be sent away with a flea in his ear? He'd soon find out. The doorbell echoed throughout the house, and a woman opened the door. The two looked at each other momentarily until Malcolm broke the silence. 'Hello, Lynn. It's been a while.'

'It has. I was hoping you'd come. I suppose it's Geoff you want to see?'

Malcolm nodded and sidestepped through the semi-open door. Lynn caught his arm. 'Do you know what's going on? He hasn't said a word to me. If he's done something to hurt your Kate, I'll clip him round the ear no matter how old he is.'

'Kate hasn't said much either, but she's not happy. Is he here?'

'He's in the bathroom getting ready to take Daisy out this afternoon.'

'Yes, I hoped to catch him before he goes.'

'Come into the lounge and sit down; I'll tell him you're here, then make you a coffee while you wait.'

Malcolm obeyed, perching on the sofa's edge and chewing at his thumbnail. He didn't enjoy interfering in other people's problems but couldn't bear to see Kate so miserable. It was affecting Daisy too, who was becoming fractious, crying at the slightest thing, totally incongruent with her usual sunny personality.

Lynn returned with coffee. 'He'll be out in a minute. I hope you're going to lay the law down. Whatever's happened can be put right – Geoff and Kate are made for each other.'

'Agreed, but it won't be sorted out unless Geoff tells someone, preferably Kate, what's happening. They seem to have gone straight to considering divorce without any real effort to make things right.'

Lynn nodded as her son entered the room. 'I'm going to leave you men to talk. I'll be in the kitchen if you want me.' She closed the door behind her. Geoff looked pale and drawn as if he hadn't been sleeping as he sat in the armchair opposite his father-in-law.

'What's going on with you and Kate, son?' Malcolm spoke calmly with empathy. He wanted to give Geoff a fair chance to explain.

'Don't you think that's between us?' Geoff lifted his chin but couldn't meet Mal's eyes.

'Yes, I agree, but when I see my daughter looking so

miserable and confused, I can't help but get involved. Kate deserves an explanation – the truth about what's going on. She's blaming herself, not eating properly and making herself ill.'

'That's the last thing I want!' Geoff looked at Malcolm then, concern in his eyes. 'I can't tell her – it would ruin her opinion of me – I couldn't bear to have her think badly of me.'

'She doesn't know what to think except that you must be having an affair, and it's breaking her heart.'

'No! I told her there was no one else.'

'Then what's she supposed to believe? This woman from work keeps ringing you, and you won't tell her why. Hell, she even called you when we were on holiday.'

'I told Kate it was about work...' Geoff ran his fingers through his hair, tears welling in his eyes.

'Then why suggest a divorce? Is it what you want?'

'No. I love Kate. She and Daisy are my life. Look, I've had problems at work – my fault entirely. I've done something stupid and I don't want everyone to know about it. I've let Kate down when she deserves better. I only mentioned a divorce in the heat of an argument; it's not what I want, but maybe she'll be better off without me.' Geoff put his head in his hands and sighed deeply.

'This thing at work – it isn't an affair then?'

Geoff looked up. 'No. Laura's been ringing me because I helped her out of a spot of trouble, but in doing so I've got myself in hot water.'

'Geoff, lad. You're talking in riddles. Start at the beginning and tell me what it's all about. Maybe we can work something out.'

Geoff was silent for a moment, his brow furrowed with worry. It was clear he was deeply concerned about the situation. Eventually he decided to talk and, as Mal suggested, started at the beginning.

'Laura is my secretary and has been for six years – a very good one, but we're not having an affair. She's a widow with a teenage son. Laura came to me several weeks ago in a state of distress. Her son, Mike, was involved with some drug dealers who were turning on him. He's not a bad lad, but has become hooked on drugs and is in debt to the dealers. These people don't play fair. They offered him a way out of debt by doing a few jobs for them – deliveries and the like. Mike had an idea he was delivering drugs, but as he didn't have the money to pay them off, he felt there was no alternative. He expected to do a few "jobs" and then his debt would be cleared but once these men get a hold, they don't let go. As he was still using, his debt mounted up again and they demanded money. Mike went to his mother, who was naturally horrified but wanted to help. Laura offered to pay off the debt but when Mike told her how much she was stunned. It had run into thousands, and they couldn't go to the police as Mike's involvement would be considered dealing.' Geoff sighed and rubbed his eyes with the heels of his hands.

'So you offered to help?' Malcolm asked.

'Not exactly. Laura asked if she could get an advance on her wages and a loan from the firm, which she'd repay as quickly as possible. I told her I didn't have the authority and would have to go to the partners but she wouldn't let me. Laura was afraid she'd lose her job if they knew about Mike's activities, which was a possibility. They like all employees to be squeaky clean. If I'd had the money, I'd have given it to her, but we'd used all our savings on the new kitchen we'd put in, and it was before your win. I didn't know what to do.

'Laura came in one morning with a proposition. These drug dealers had beaten Mike up pretty badly and given him an ultimatum – a time to pay the debt. She was distraught but said her elderly father was selling his home and moving into sheltered accommodation. He'd agreed to give her the money, but the sale hadn't been completed and would take another three weeks. Laura suggested that I authorise a "loan" from the clients' account, which I have access to, and she would pay it back in three weeks when the sale went through.' Geoff was quite emotional and breathing rapidly.

'And you agreed to help her?' Malcolm finished the story for him.

'Yes.' Geoff's eyes brimmed with tears. 'It was stupid and unprofessional, and I regret it. The house sale fell through and she can't repay the money. I'll lose my job if the partners find out... I feel so ashamed, I can't tell Kate, I've let her and everyone else down!' Geoff broke down and allowed the tears to fall. Malcolm's heart ached for him. His intentions had been worthy, but his actions were ill-advised to the point of stupidity.

CHAPTER SIXTY-SIX

Malcolm watched his son-in-law's distress with a heavy heart. He took no pleasure in seeing his daughter's husband in such turmoil when he had the power to help him. Mal decided to do so, especially as Geoff hadn't asked. Mal looked at the troubled man before him, the weight of his worries etched on his face. 'Why didn't you come to me or at least use the money I gave you and Kate?'

Geoff shifted uncomfortably, looking at his feet as he spoke. 'The money is in Kate's account, and I was too ashamed to ask her. And honestly, I didn't want to approach you either. If the family found out what I'd done, I'd feel humiliated.' The admission was barely a whisper. Malcolm raised an eyebrow, sensing Geoff's underlying fear.

'By family, I assume you're referring to Danny?'

'Yes,' Geoff acknowledges quietly. 'I know I'd never hear the end of it from him. He doesn't have much regard for me and I can't bear the thought of giving him more fuel to belittle me. But then Julie went missing, and you all had bigger things to worry about than my problems. I couldn't come to you then.'

'So, you'd rather jeopardise your marriage and risk losing

your daughter and perhaps even your job to avoid the humiliation and embarrassment of admitting your mistake?'

Geoff shook his head. 'It's not as simple as that. I misappropriated funds that belonged to my clients; that's a serious crime, Malcolm. If this gets out... I could go to prison!'

Malcolm dropped his voice to almost a whisper. 'Is it possible for you access the account from home?'

'Well, yes, technically, but why?'

'Danny's been teaching me how to do internet banking. If you think you could rectify the situation, I could transfer the funds directly into your clients' account right now.'

'I can't let you do that. It's my mess!'

'I'm not doing it for you; I'm doing it for my daughter and granddaughter and because I believe you're genuinely sorry.'

Geoff left the room only to return moments later with his laptop. The tension in the room eased somewhat as, with Malcolm's phone, they completed transferring the necessary files. Within minutes it was done and Geoff breathed a sigh of relief. 'Thank you, Mal.' His voice was filled with gratitude. 'Once Laura sends me the money, I promise I'll repay you. This means so much, you'll never know what a weight off my mind it is.'

'What about your conscience? Can you live knowing what you've done, even if no one ever finds out?' Malcolm's gentle challenge hit home for Geoff. He winced, feeling the truth of the words resonate within him. Deep down, he understood that simply replacing the borrowed money wasn't enough. It wouldn't absolve him of the guilt gnawing at his insides.

'You're right.' Geoff's voice steadied as he resolved. 'I'll talk to Kate this afternoon and confess everything to her. I owe her that much. And I can't keep this from the senior partner any longer. What I did was wrong. You've helped me make recompense, but I won't be able to forgive myself unless I come clean.' The thought of facing possible repercussions was daunting but for the first time in a long while, Geoff felt a flicker of hope that his actions might be forgivable.

As he left to go home, Malcolm smiled. He had no idea if Geoff's boss would be sympathetic, but it was the right thing to do, whatever the outcome. Hopefully, his marriage would soon get back on track. There was little doubt that Kate would forgive him and face any consequences with him. His daughter was like her mother, and he was confident things would work out well.

CHAPTER SIXTY-SEVEN

Over the following days, Malcolm and Julie remained mostly at home. Julie rested her leg and felt the benefit of doing so, and the couple also took the chance to talk. Malcolm told his wife of his conversation with Geoff and his intervention. Julie was surprised at him taking the initiative.

'You're a wise man, Malcolm Grainger, and I've not always given you credit for it.' Perhaps there were still facets of each other's personalities they had yet to discover.

As they opened up about recent traumas, their conversations turned toward the future, especially concerning their relocation plans. The discussion centred around the search for a home to accommodate Bill and their needs. With a tingle of excitement and anticipation, Julie took to the internet, exploring a wide array of stunning properties. She revelled in the virtual tours, which allowed her to see the potential of each one.

After a thorough online search, they created a shortlist of promising properties to visit when Julie felt ready. This process provided a much-needed distraction and ignited optimism in both of them. The idea of moving and a new beginning allowed them to dream about their future together.

Kate and Geoff had resolved their differences. Honesty was all Kate wanted; she was ready to forgive and support him in making amends. Telling the senior partner at work was the hardest part for Geoff, but he found his boss to be remarkably understanding. The man decided not to disclose the events to the other partners as the situation had been rectified and he could see no value in taking things further. He was sure Geoff had learned his lesson and would be a better manager. Kate also asked her parents not to go into detail about Geoff's troubles with Danny. She hoped her brother would accept the explanation of a misunderstanding and assume it was a storm in a teacup. Indeed, Danny appeared to be trying to get along with his brother-in-law, or perhaps he was simply busy with his new role as director of the Grainger charitable trust, which was in its infancy.

During the weeks of Julie's recovery, the family met several times to add flesh to the bones of the plans conceived in Florida. Julie expected the discussions to cause friction with conflicts of ideas, yet this didn't happen. Geoff remained relatively quiet when he attended these meetings, although if he made any suggestions, Danny received them well and considered them along with everyone else's. Julie and Mal exchanged many a knowing look and smile during these discussions, delighted at the maturity of their often feisty son. Maybe the lack of friction was because there was plenty of money to utilise – it was a new experience for the family not to consider the cost of what they wished to do.

Malcolm continued visiting his dad regularly, and once Julie was more mobile, she joined him. 'We've been looking at several houses, Dad,' Mal said, watching his father attempt a smile. Ever since they'd agreed that he would live with them, Bill

Grainger had been eager for the move. 'We've narrowed it down to three. One stands out as our favourite, it's still in Burnbridge, but we're visiting all of them this week to get a proper feel for each.' Mal paused, excitement building at the thought of their next steps as a family. Julie could barely contain her enthusiasm.

'We've already lined up a builder to start the renovations as soon as we choose the house. Since we're cash buyers, everything should move quickly and it'll be all systems go!'

Bill offered another crooked smile, clearly sharing in their excitement.

'Danny's doing a fantastic job managing the trust,' Mal continued. 'He's really enjoying it. He said he'll stop by tomorrow. He's been researching special equipment for when we move and wants your input on what suits you best. It's great seeing him so engaged, and even the kids are getting involved. They're still hoping for their donkey sanctuary, but maybe Angie's cat shelter will keep them happy for now.'

The visit ended on a high note, leaving Mal and Julie energised for the tasks ahead. With so much to do to improve not just Bill's life but their own, they hardly needed encouragement to throw themselves into house-hunting.

EPILOGUE

Malcolm and Julie Grainger took great care in considering the additions to their new home, meticulously outlining their vision and specific requirements to an architect. The house they selected was a stunning property perched on the edge of Burnbridge, offering breathtaking panoramic views of the valley that stretched out below.

Julie was particularly enthusiastic about the prospect of having ample space. She imagined an environment where she could finally bring to life all the luxurious features she had only previously admired in the property shows she loved to binge-watch on television. From airy open-concept living spaces to stylishly appointed rooms, she dreamed of creating a home combining comfort with elegance. They enjoyed watching their dreams become reality, appreciating every detail and remaining grateful for their good fortune.

Malcolm worked closely with the architect to provide an area to meet his father's needs, and Danny sourced some fantastic equipment to improve Bill's life considerably. There was a new computer that could be operated by blowing into a tube, which was great for those days when his hands failed him.

They purchased a custom-made wheelchair, which could be angled in a way to support the whole body and was operated by a simple knob on the arm.

Bill's room would be an annexe at the side of the house, with bi-fold doors to the front elevation, allowing him to appreciate the glorious views. A fully equipped bathroom, with an air bath and a hoist, would be for his sole use. The whole family were thrilled when it was finally ready, and Bill's face spoke volumes as he saw it for the first time.

Considering they'd both retired, Malcolm and Julie were busier than ever in administrating the various projects they'd become involved in, although the bulk of it fell on Danny's shoulders. This was what having money was about – making it work for themselves, their family, and the wider community.

Malcolm and Julie had experienced a whirlwind of emotions over the past eighteen months, which included exhilarating highs and challenging lows. As the sun set, casting a warm glow over their plush new living room, Julie turned to her husband. 'What would you say we've learned from our lottery win?'

Mal leaned back, his brow furrowed in concentration. 'Too much!' he exclaimed, a hint of laughter in his voice. 'We've discovered our true friends and who we can trust. Some people's reactions have been astonishing, far from what I imagined.' He paused, memories flooding his mind. 'I suppose we've also come to appreciate the immense value of family – and the bond we share.' A warm smile spread across his lips as his gaze reflected his deep love for Julie.

She returned his smile. 'People assume money equals happiness, but that's not always true. Sure, it can buy amazing experiences, but not happiness itself. We had that long before we had money.' She reached for his hand, squeezing it. 'You know, Malcolm Grainger, you're a wonderful man, and as usual, you're right. This money has brought good and bad into our lives, but aside from the worst moments, I have no regrets.' She hesitated, then added with a playful smirk, 'Just promise me one thing?'

'Anything.'

'Don't buy another lottery ticket.'

THE END

AUTHOR NOTES

This book was written prior to the UK government's debate on assisted dying. During the editing process, Members of Parliament agreed on the first stage of the bill, which remains an ongoing discussion.

I did not intend to write a novel about assisted suicide; I was actually searching for a historic family secret that some might consider shameful and open to blackmail, while others might see it as heroic. However, as the characters developed and began to take on their own personalities, their perspectives on the topic became divisive – completely understandable given the emotive nature of the subject.

My intended theme was to *be careful what you wish for; you may get it,* and I'm sure you'll agree that not everything we desire is good for us. I hope you enjoyed the Graingers' struggles with their life-changing win, and may your good times not be blighted by such dramatic events!

ALSO BY GILLIAN JACKSON

The Pharmacist

The Victim

The Deception

Abduction

Snatched

The Accident

The Shape of Truth

The Charcoal House

The Dead Husband

Little Black Lies

———

Remembering Ellie

Ask Laura

A Measure of Time

ACKNOWLEDGEMENTS

As always, I am grateful to my husband and family for their unwavering love and support during the countless hours I spend writing. And to the exceptional team at Bloodhound Books, your invaluable help in bringing this book to life is truly appreciated. Each book is a collaboration. I have the privilege of crafting characters and spinning plots, while you diligently work on refining and presenting. Your dedication, professionalism, and guidance have been invaluable throughout this process.